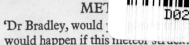

'Dr Bradley, would you would happen if this meteor struck?

Bradley hesitated. 'Well,' he said, 'let me start this way. A mass of rock a mile in diameter, travelling at 30,000 miles an hour, would blast a crater fifty miles across and approximately five miles deep.'

The other men stared at him blankly, trying to visualize this appalling prospect.

'This meteor is *five* miles in diameter. Its striking force is equal to two million five hundred thousand megatons of TNT.'

Bradley paused to let the figures sink in. 'That's ten orders of magnitude larger than the largest earthquake ever recorded. It would hurl into the atmosphere five billion tons of earth and reduce solar radiation for decades to come. It could be the start of another ice age.'

METEOR

EDMUND H. NORTH
AND FRANKLIN COEN

Hamlyn Paperbacks

METEOR

ISBN 0 600 20016 7

First published in Great Britain 1979
by Hamlyn Paperbacks

This edition published by arrangement
with Warner Books, Inc.

Copyright © Edmund H. North and
Franklin Coen 1979

Hamlyn Paperbacks are published by
The Hamlyn Publishing Group Ltd,
Astronaut House,
Feltham,
Middlesex, England

Made and printed in Great Britain
by Hazell Watson & Viney Ltd, Aylesbury, Bucks

The
Beginning

Before man climbed down out of the trees – before he learned to use tools or build a fire – the heavens looked very much as they do today, an infinite vastness punctuated by a myriad of stars.

In our own galaxy, the Milky Way, are perhaps a billion of them, including the one we call the Sun.

Around this single star – our source of light and food and life itself – the other bodies of the solar system wheel majestically in their timeless orbits. Nine planets, thirty-one moons, thousands of asteroids – all moving in a miraculous clockwork of order and precision.

Occasionally the tranquillity of this delicate mechanism is threatened by a fiery intruder from beyond. A comet, millions of miles long from its flaming nucleus to the end of its fiery tail, blazes across the infinite vastness of outer space, an awesome object given birth by one of the monstrous collisions that attended the creation of the solar system.

Sometimes, arcing past Earth in a spectacular display, comets are watched by men with awe and wonder.

Other times, one will flash unseen by man, through the Asteroid Belt, a vast junkyard of metal and rock orbiting the Sun between Jupiter and Mars. Within the Belt are thousands of asteroids, some as small as a fist, some as large as a city.

If the orbit of the comet fails to intersect that of an asteroid or any other heavenly body, it will pass harmlessly by and all will be well.

If, on the other hand, the comet should collide with another object, the impact can produce results that are beyond imagination.

I

The observatory was tucked into the side of the famous mountain, so that, while not completely concealed from the climbers, it drew no special attention. It might well have been a Japanese government forestry station, its observatory tower sited behind a rise in the terrain.

Dr Fakuda, whose tour of duty it was that night, was not particularly concerned with visitors. What bothered him most as he looked through the telescope was the cold. It cut into his flesh like a thousand knives; his clothing could have been the thinnest of paper. He cursed the undeniable fact that heat could not be supplied; it played tricks with the infinitely valuable telescope lens.

Suddenly the state of his body was of little consequence. What he was seeing through that lens drove all else from his mind. He had to force himself to turn his head, blinking rapidly, before concentrating on the eyepiece again, and on the event – or more accurately, approaching event – he was witnessing millions of miles away.

Yes, it was so.

Undeniably.

Dr Fakuda rose slowly. He was not a man to acknowledge fear, but he was aware of it now. He had completely forgotten the near-zero temperature permeating the starkness of the observatory.

He made the telephone call.

In Canberra, Australia, the observer at the Mount Stromlo Observatory had just come to work after a fine dinner with wife and friends to celebrate a fifth wedding anniversary. He loved his wife, he loved his work, he counted himself a lucky man. He had drunk too much wine, not a usual occurrence, and was aware of a slight headache as he positioned himself in the steel-backed chair that rotated with the telescope.

The telephone was ringing.

With a mild curse, he raised himself out of his catbird's seat, walked carefully down the steel steps to the wall phone and listened to the voice of the director of the Institute in Canberra.

Seeming only mildly concerned, the director went on for several minutes with the information he had to impart. 'But you know the Japanese, Farkman. Not nearly as inscrutable as they should be.' He chuckled dryly, enjoying his own small joke. 'Still, Tokyo called me, so I'm passing it on to you.'

Farkman nodded back into the receiver. 'Right. I'll check it out.'

Farkman climbed back up the steps, his heavy aviator's boots giving out a clanging sound.

He made the adjustments necessary and was now in another quadrant of the heavens.

He looked a long while before pulling back and carefully removing his glasses.

'Jesus Christ,' he murmured, unaware he had spoken aloud.

It was 2:00 A.M. in Southern California when the call reached Dr. Samuel Pendleton, who was manning the 28-inch telescope on Mount Palomar. In point of fact, he was taking a coffee break and yakking with his colleague Art Moore, who was fine-combing a new batch of photos.

Pendleton was on the phone a long time, answering in monosyllables, and when finally he hung up, Art Moore was openly curious.

'What's up. Your wife leave you?'

'Fun-unn-y!' replied Pendleton.

The last thing he had been told on the phone was to keep his mouth shut until the report could be verified. If it could be, then he was to keep his lip buttoned for sure!

Pendleton didn't like the idea of playing games with Art Moore, who was, after all, a respected astronomer. On the other hand . . . well, on the other hand, what? Hell, he told himself, it was nothing but a ridiculous piece of hocus-pocus brought to you by those people in the Far East who as everybody knew, smoked opium for breakfast.

'So what was it?'

'The hot water heater,' said Pendleton. 'Ellie was taking a bath and the damn heater conked out. She wanted to know what to do about it.'

'At this hour?'

'She realized how silly it was to call. Just thought if I wanted a warm shower, I'd better take it up here.'

Art grunted, then went down to his film tanks. Pendleton went upstairs to the telescope.

He worked there a long time, plotting the precise location in the Asteroid Belt that had been indicated in the phone call. He was a careful man and would not hurry himself. He zeroed in on the phenomenon-in-the-making, although he would not call it that yet. Perhaps it would never be called that. Perhaps it was simply a rare, extremely rare, accident of nature.

But four hours later, when he was absolutely certain, he plodded back down to the phone and dialled.

God, how he wished it was the hot water heater!

2

'*Challenger 2*,' Sam Mason, the Capsule Communicator, asked, 'how do you feel about making a slight detour?'

Mason could have sworn that behind him the entire control centre at Houston had suddenly fallen silent. Actually, he was right. At every console, on each bank, an operator had paused, then glanced up at the spacecraft on the master screen, at the men in *Challenger 2*. Mason, who would be thirty-four in a week, felt older by fifty years. Why in hell was this his job?

They all could see Tom Easton coming into view on the master screen; apparently he'd been doing a routine check on the guidance system, whose guts were hidden behind a partition.

Tom responded with a cheerful grin. 'What do you call slight?'

Bill Frager and Elliot McKendrick appeared behind Tom, shadowy at first, like sharks in a dark-green tank. Now all three astronauts were in plain view, all wanting to be a part of whatever was going on.

Frager, the baby of the team, stuck his face into the camera. 'Lay it on us, sweetheart,' he said.

Frager would hear about that breach of communications protocol, Mason decided – for all the good it would do; the boy had no fear of man or beast.

'A hop, skip and a jump, two days at the most.'

That didn't seem to bother Frager or McKendrick, who obviously welcomed any relief from routine. It did cause Tom Easton, the Commander, to frown. Across the hundreds of thousands of miles that separated them, Mason could sense Tom tightening. It wasn't that Tom resented a break from routine; he disliked anything that disrupted order. And *Challenger 2* did have its priorities, which Houston, at this point, was arbitrarily setting aside.

'What happens to our schedule?' Tom Easton asked, as Mason had known he would.

'Don't worry about it, Tom. We'll take care of everything from here. Your primary mission will have to wait.'

Tom Easton's voice was heard next as if filtered; the result, perhaps, of a temporary solar disturbance. 'Whatever you say. Where are we going?'

Mason was aware that Harold Sherwood, chief of the Centre, a tall man with tousled silver-grey hair, had come in through a side door with General Easton, Tom Easton's father. The General wore a slightly preoccupied look – how would I feel if it were my son up there? thought Mason – as he took a stance behind Mason. I will not interfere, his position said. The General could have posed for a recruiting poster: How you will look in thirty years if you enlist now!

Tom Easton's voice came over again, under control but with some hesitation. It wasn't often a carefully plotted flight plan was radically altered in mid-course. 'Where are we going, did you say?'

'The Asteroid Belt,' Mason said.

His eyes caught Sherwood's; then General Easton's. No comment in either face, only the blank masks of command.

'What for?'

'There's a comet about to go through it.'

Mason could feel the tension building in the communications centre behind him. The news had spread all right, and the full implications had been included. The men at the consoles were not simply highly trained robots, wizards at manipulating dials and analyzing readouts; these men were sophisticated in the science of the heavens, in the heavenly changes, in the heavenly dangers. Up there, they knew – interpret it your own way – were the gods!

Tom Easton had been thinking. 'Comets go through the Asteroid Belt all the time,' he said from *Challenger 2*.

Harold Sherwood took a step to Mason's side. 'Sherwood speaking, Tom. This one's a little different. We figure it was wrenched out of orbit by Jupiter's gravitational pull.'

For Tom, for Frager, for McKendrick, this piece of information was neither complete or altogether satisfactory.

'How big is this comet?' McKendrick asked.

The set of the heads of the three astronauts – close together, looking into the tube – made it clear that a lot of knowledgeable questions were being tossed back and forth in the spacecraft, but out of range of the mike.

Sherwood nodded to Mason, who answered. 'Four hundred and eighty kilometres in diameter, which makes its nucleus big enough to do real damage if it hits anything.'

Frager had spun a few more words at Tom Easton, words they couldn't hear in Houston.

Sherwood took over again, feeling that Mason had shouldered enough of the load. Sherwood always sounded as if he had gravel in his throat, but there was a softness there too, that characterized the man. He had been one of the first in this game. He had been up there himself, so he could talk with the brass in Washington and make sense. More important, he had the charisma of an early astronaut and could pull in the appropriations.

'Attention *Challenger*,' he said. 'It's heading towards Orpheus – that's the big one in the Apollo group.'

Behind Sherwood, every eye in the room shifted to the big screen. No secrets anymore, not among them. Every man present could give a dozen variables on what *Challenger* would find and have to cope with, and damn few of those variables would please an insurance actuary.

'Right. Back with you in a minute,' Tom Easton said.

Inside *Challenger*, they were taking things in stride. Always better to be in the cockpit than downstairs. McKendrick had got out the 'Red Book' – navigation was his sport. While he pored over the charts, the other two men tucked current work sheets away in the slots provided. A meal had just been finished; the detritus was stowed in an aft compactor.

McKendrick, satisfied with his preliminary study, said something to Easton, who spoke to Houston. 'Change of course acknowledge. Where do you want us to park?'

From far below, from Earth, came Mason's answer, filtered into a sepulchral bass. 'Put a dime in the meter near Triton, about twenty-five thousand kilometres this side.'

McKendrick, nodding, made some hieroglyphics on a pad clipped to the chart book.

After a brief pause, Mason continued his briefing. 'You'll be there three hours before the comet shows. We want all the information you can give us about the size and composition of the nucleus.'

'Maybe a few pictures . . .' Tom Easton suggested.

'A lot of pictures. We've started things going down here. You'll be changing course in five minutes. Acknowledge, please.'

'We read you, Houston. Five minutes to course change.'

Easton gave the interior of the craft a swift eyecheck. Everything looked shipshape, including Frager's African luck piece, a naked babe sculptured in ivory on a long gold chain from which it snaked aimlessly in the weightlessness of outer space. It was good that they couldn't see it in Houston; its presence was strictly counter to NASA regulations.

Tom pivoted back to the camera. 'My old man with you?'

In Houston, watching the screen, General Easton wore the tiniest of smiles. Tom was his eldest. But the General kept silent.

'He's here,' Mason said.

'Tell him hello,' Tom Easton said.

'Will do,' Mason replied.

Sherwood, standing next to the General, couldn't help being amused. So typical of the stiff-necked bastard! Principles first. Other men were up there along with his son. No cosy family chats for them, right? So Tom and I continue to observe strict professional silence.

Deep in outer space, McKendrick, who was working out a complicated equation, looked up suddenly. 'This comet got a name yet?'

Mason's deep voice came through promptly. 'Not yet, just a number.'

McKendrick shot a wicked grin at Tom Easton and Bill Frager. 'We could call it Farrah Fawcett . . .'

A chuckle rumbled through the Houston centre. Smiling, Mason said, 'We read you, McKendrick.'

Challenger 2, responding to a quick burn of her rockets, turned lazily like a great fish in a limitless, azure sea, and began to move off on the new plotting.

A half-million-mile journey, McKendrick informed Easton, who wrote it down in his log.

In the beginning, outside of monitoring the computer, making visual checks to be certain McKendrick had made no error in his computations, the crew had little to do but watch the skyscape on the screen or change lenses, according to whim or preference, on the big outboard telescope.

Although the speed of the craft was tremendous, they had no feeling of speed. Only the slowly receding size of the earth and the moon gave them a sense of how fast they were indeed travelling into the endless, jewelled belly of the universe.

They were a new breed of soldier-scientist, these men. They were not poets, but they sat in awe of the beauty and vastness around them, each man alone with his thoughts, excited, fascinated by the challenge of exploring a part of the heavens man had seen before only through telescopes.

Hours had passed; they seemed days.

The men looked and ate and slept; they carried out the necessary duties, their discipline superb. Houston was in constant communication, unceasingly demanding what seemed unimportant readouts on position, on the condition of onboard equipment – even, at one point, on the disassembling and reassembling of an auxiliary stabilizer, on the grounds that the computers at Houston were signalling a possible malfunction. Phony, of course – the stabilizer was one hundred percent.

Tom Easton went along with it all without complaint. He could read Mason and the others like a book: 'Keep 'em occupied up there,' the word had gone out, he knew. 'Don't give 'em a chance to think.'

So they worked their asses off as they watched the universe open up before them, a wide-screen display that was superior to any movie extravaganza.

McKendrick kept close to his charts and the directional computer. McKendrick knew his business. It was late Saturday – course had been altered just two days ago – when he informed Tom Easton that they were approaching the target area.

No need, really, for McKendrick to so indicate. Easton and Frager could see for themselves.

Although inside the craft it seemed as if they were proceeding in slow motion, actually Easton knew it was at unimaginable speed. He wondered if he should cut the computer and assume manual control, then realized that at this particular moment his judgment was not as good as the machine's.

'Jesus!' whispered Frager. No need for the periscope now; the awesome panorama of the Asteroid Belt could be seen with the naked eye.

Then the call came from Houston. *Switch us in, please.*

Having completely forgotten Houston, Tom Easton switched them in at once, keeping himself still riveted to the view ahead.

In Houston, the moment the outboard periscope on the *Challenger* brought the Asteroid Belt into focus, it was as though the room had been hit with a giant fist. There was three-dimensional fidelity, and it was a sight no one in the famous room had ever seen before. Not a voice could be heard, not so much as a murmur. Sherwood, Mason, General Easton, the lot of them, stared like children at the large screen. It was the notorious junkyard they saw up there, filled with all kinds of stuff. Some of the jagged pieces, Mason thought, looked as big as icebergs.

'Have you got it?' *Challenger* was asking.

'We've got it,' Mason said, hoping he sounded calm. 'Can you pull Orpheus out for us?'

'Can do,' *Challenger 2* replied.

Challenger switched instantly to its most powerful lens.

And there she was, a twenty-mile-wide chunk, a great whale of an asteroid, rough and black as an island of pure coal, slowly being pulled towards them as the lens zoomed in.

They had seen her before as a tiny dot on a film. The sight of her now was another thing altogether.

'Let's have some information,' Mason said.

From the spacecraft Tom Easton replied, 'We'll get you a reading.'

In space and in Houston, people pulled themselves away from the screens and went to work. Estimated size, weight, speed, orbit, probable composition – they marked up a sheet on her as if she were a newborn baby.

Time passed. Hot, black coffee was consumed in gallons down below; a new pick-me-up brew recently perfected for astronauts was drunk up in the spacecraft.

Several hours had passed before McKendrick, constantly charting orbits, caught sight of the newcomer. A bright white pencil point, it was growing steadily larger as it approached the Asteroid Belt from the northern quadrant.

'That's it,' Tom Easton said.

McKendrick, his beloved charts in front of him, nodded. 'Right on schedule.'

They watched it from below in Houston, of course, all other work suspended.

On the far right of the screen, it was no longer a pencil point; it was perhaps the size of a small orange. Even at that distance it had an awesome, eerie quality – a flaming nucleus riding in front of an enormous, slashing river of light.

Easton spoke to McKendrick without turning his head. 'How would you estimate its speed?'

McKendrick's concentration was still on the inboard screen. He was uncharacteristically subdued. 'Hundred thousand miles an hour. Maybe a hundred and ten.'

They were also making computations below, in Houston.

'She'll go straight through like a dose of salts!' Houston could hear Frager exclaim exultantly.

But at several of the Houston consoles, where prior information on positions and orbits had been fed, the readouts said differently. The information was transmitted at once to Mason at Control. Mason scanned the strips, passed them wordlessly to Sherwood. Sherwood, after a quick glance, hesitated, then held them out to General Easton.

The General had to fish for his glasses. What he read caused his lips to compress. Without knowing it he made a fist, crumpling the readout.

On the spacecraft, they were spectators at a vast cosmic ball game. Only it wasn't a ball game. The comet had shot up in size. It was suddenly a great, frightening, blazing mass travelling at incredible speed, headed on a certain collision course for Orpheus.

'Jesus, get away from there!' Mason shouted.

But it was too late. In Houston, they knew it. The comet was already upon Orpheus. They remained glued to the screen, not speaking, not even breathing, as the comet plunged into the huge bulk of the asteroid.

The interior of *Challenger 2* lighted up as if from a lightning bolt. The fearful explosion spewed forth a gigantic eruption of fire and debris as Orpheus was struck and broken into a thousand flying pieces.

There was shouting from aboard *Challenger*; Houston could not distinguish who was shouting what. McKendrick, it was thought later, had cried out, 'My God, My God!'

Challenger's jets were functioning; that could be seen as she tried to manoeuvre away from the scarlet cloud filled with fire and smoke and flying fragments.

In the Communications Centre, it was absolutely still. Every face was taut, every eye focused on the screen.

Then, suddenly, there it was – a huge hunk of debris, heading like a locomotive for *Challenger*'s throat. It was longer than a locomotive, they estimated later, and twice as wide.

It struck *Challenger 2* amidships, bursting it apart.

At Houston, the screen went sickeningly black.

No one said a word, no one consciously looked at General Easton, who had stood through it all without moving. Then, his face chalk-white and expressionless, keeping himself still somehow erect, the General made his way to the door.

3

On Long Island Sound, the sleek 52-foot yawl *Blithe Spirit* had
just completed the upwind leg of the course. Her skipper, Paul
Bradley, kept close watch on the black-hulled sloop *Capricious*
off his starboard bow. *Capricious* was three boat-lengths behind, having lost precious seconds on the windward leg by taking four tacks to Bradley's two.

'Nice going, skipper,' Snowden said, beaming at Paul. *Blithe
Spirit* was his boat, but today he was crewing. Snowden knew
his limitations, and this was a race he wanted to win. Admiral's
Cup, last race of the season.

'Not over yet, Charlie,' Bradley said softly.

Snowden was a nice man for a multimillionaire, and Bradley
liked him. Bradley liked to be sure before counting his marbles.
Not that he had any real doubts. The Sound was being kind
today – a steady wind and cobalt-blue water with just a slight
chop.

On a broad reach now and moving smartly, *Blithe Spirit* was
on her best point of sailing. A beautiful, spirited boat, but
Bradley felt she could do even better.

'Harden up on the jib.'

The crewman tending the jib sheet took a couple of turns
on the handle of the heavy winch.

Bradley nodded, feeling the slight surge of added power.
'Cleat her off right there.'

The distance between *Blithe Spirit* and *Capricious* was
slowly but perceptibly widening. Charles Snowden could already picture the big silver cup in a glass case in the den of his

Larchmont mansion. But suddenly a frown clouded his face. The imposing white hull of a Coast Guard cutter loomed off the port beam.

'What the hell, Paul?' he asked.

Bradley had seen her too. And what the hell was right! The cutter was continuing its run towards them, ignoring the frantic signalling of *Blithe Spirit*'s crew. What did that cutter captain think he was doing? For chrissake, he was no stranger to these waters! He couldn't help knowing about the race!

The cutter swung around, paralleling *Blithe Spirit*, and the voice of a uniformed officer on the bridge bellowed from a bullhorn.

'Dr Paul Bradley aboard?'

Bradley gave the wheel to Snowden and crossed the slanting deck to the rail. He looked like the rugged schoolmaster of a spartan English boarding school, the kind where the kids have to get up before dawn to take cold showers. And he was damn angry now.

'Who the hell wants him?'

'Orders from NASA to pick up Dr Paul Bradley,' the bullhorn shouted. 'Is he aboard?'

The bullhorn was shouting something more, but Bradley couldn't hear it. Snowden had already managed to lose a bit of headway; the mains'l was starting to luff over Bradley's head. Snowden corrected rapidly, and the sail filled again.

'What?' yelled Bradley, playing for time.

'This is an emergency!' the bullhorn called, clear as a bell.

'So is this!' Bradley yelled back, doubting they could hear him. 'We're trying to win a race, and you're screwing up our reach!'

This seemed to be of little importance to the Coast Guard vessel. 'We'll have to cut across your bow,' the bullhorn shouted implacably.

Bradley was a fighter but he wasn't a fool, and knew there were times when you simply have to give in.

'All right, goddamn it, get out of our way! We'll heave to.'

And to Snowden: 'Sorry, Charlie. Bring her up into the wind.'

The Coast Guard officer was a young chap named Lockly and, having proven his case, he was exceedingly polite. Waiting at *Blithe Spirit*'s slip, ignoring the openly disgruntled reaction of her crew, he moved at once with Bradley towards a government car on the yacht club driveway. An Air Force driver stood by the car smoking a cigarette.

Bradley was not one to hold grudges, particularly against uniformed men; he had been one himself long enough. But there were questions to be asked.

Lockly shrugged them off.

'All Mr Sherwood told me was to get you off that boat and on your way to Houston. There's a NASA jet laid on.'

The driver tossed his cigarette stub onto the yacht club's manicured lawn, nodded to the approaching men, and got behind the wheel.

Bradley hesitated at the car door. 'You'd really have cut across my bow, Lieutenant?'

Lockly answered promptly. 'Yes, sir.'

Bradley slid in the car's front seat alongside the driver. 'I'd have rammed you!' he said, and slammed the door shut.

Lockly didn't flinch. 'And gone right to the bottom, sir!' he said to the open window.

Bradley grinned, and the Air Force driver took off as if he were piloting a jet.

They had the plane ready at the naval station just up the Sound. There had been no time for Bradley to collect even an overnight bag.

Bradley, who had long since quit being mad, was merely curious now, but the pilot offered no information. He had his hands full anyway, as there were a couple of early season storms to bypass.

Soon they were over the Appalachian chain, the Blue Ridge mountains a carpet of rich browns and reds below them, and then they were above the cloud cover into the intense blue, headed straight as an arrow for their destination.

Bradley thought of things he would have to take care of as soon as possible after reaching Houston – the switchboard at Columbia, number one. As occupant of the Rockefeller Chair of Space and Technology at the university, he was responsible to no one, but courtesy required that his chairman be advised he'd be out of circulation for a few days. Then the speech he was to deliver at the Hudson Institute; they'd have to replace him. Bradley also remembered with just a touch of pain that he was to have lunch Wednesday with Helen to discuss a new doctor for Jamie. Jamie!

But the sun and sea and wind had taken its toll, and he slept. He figured he needed it; whatever they wanted him for in Houston, it would be nice to be wide awake. In order, he decided with wicked anticipation before dozing off, to ream them for barging back into his life this way. Or had they forgotten Paul Bradley didn't work for them anymore!

Then, suddenly, wheels had touched down, and the plane was taxiing towards a jeep where another chauffeur waited. A smooth transfer, and without dropping the baton, so to speak.

Bradley was on home ground here, and alert as a retriever with a bird fluttering to earth. At the Houston Space Centre Administration Building entrance, he got slowly out of the jeep, took a deep breath, then started up the steps. He had climbed only a few of them before he stopped and yelled back to the jeep driver, 'Don't go away. I might be right back!'

Mac, at Reception, recognized him at once. 'Mr Bradley! Great seeing you! Glad you're with us again!'

And before Bradley could give a proper response, Mac added. 'Mr Sherwood is expecting you. Don't have to tell you where his office is, sir.'

*

Harold Sherwood was indeed expecting Bradley, had been given the signal that he was now in the building. Sherwood had wanted this warning – from here on in it could be delicate.

'Well, he's here,' he told the men with him, Mason and General Easton and Peter Watson, one of Sherwood's bright new young ones.

Sherwood lit a cigar, a long, dark brown number like a twisted rope. It smelled horrible but seemed to do something for Sherwood's black moods, so the cigars were put up with.

'He's got a short fuse,' Sherwood said, as if he were imparting a state secret to the three men. 'Let me handle it.'

'Surely when he hears what's happened, he'll co-operate,' Easton said.

'Eventually, General, yes. He was before your time, wasn't he, Mason? By a year, if I'm right?'

'Yes.'

'And of course before yours, Peter. But I know the man, I've worked with him.'

'We'll let you handle it, Harold,' General Easton said.

Sherwood thought it wonderful the way Easton was holding up after the loss of his son. He wished he had time to talk to the poor bastard. There wasn't time to console him properly. There was just too much for all of them to do.

Paul Bradley was deliberately taking his time saying hello to Edith, Harold Sherwood's secretary. It hadn't hurt that Edith had sprung from behind her desk to welcome him properly. It was just a pity that Edith was somebody's darn good wife. She was a handsome woman.

'Paul, it's good to see you again!'

'Good to see you, Edie. How's the husband, kids, golf?'

'In that order, fair, fine, great,' Edie said. 'You owe me ten dollars.'

'I do?'

'My handicap's gone down to twelve.'

'No wonder it's good to see me,' Bradley said, with a grimace. 'I'll pay you on the way out.'

But Edith had something else on her mind. 'Paul,' she said in a different kind of voice, 'I'm sorry about you and Helen. I mean it.'

'It's all right.'

'She wrote me just last month.'

'We're still friends, you know. And Helen's fine. So am I. The kids, too.'

'Jamie?' she asked. 'How's he?'

'Jamie is okay. He'll be okay, I'm sure,' Bradley said firmly, and Edie could tell by the way his lips were set that this was all the information she was going to get. Bradley was a man who could slam the door on a subject when he wanted to.

'Now what the hell is this?' he asked, the old bantering tone suddenly back. His glance had fallen on a suitcase with the initials P.B. in one corner. The suitcase was new, genuine leather, very expensive.

'Yes, it's yours. Mr Sherwood thought of it. He —'

Bradley had picked up the bag and was sailing through the door to Sherwood's office, where he stood like an accusing ghost on the threshold.

'Wonderful to see you, Paul. And I'm terribly sorry to do this to you,' Sherwood said.

The three other men were staring at him, but Bradley ignored them. Sherwood obviously wasn't sorry at all about screwing up a yacht race, not to mention a couple of days in his life, and Bradley wished the guy would stop pretending.

Sherwood closed the door and went back to his huge rosewood desk, clean except for a model of his first spacecraft. Bradley held the new suitcase up in the air as if it were something with a bad smell, just a few feet from Sherwood's eyes.

'Ah, yes . . . Knew you hadn't time to bring anything.' Sherwood shrugged lightly. 'Just pyjamas, some socks, underwear, things you'll need . . .'

Bradley gave him a hard smile of disbelief and annoyance.

'Paul, this is damned important!' Sherwood said.

The tone stopped Bradley in his tracks. His glance locked with Sherwood's. The two men knew each other extremely well. No fun and games, Sherwood's look said. Bradley's flare-up – partly felt, partly dramatized – began to recede.

Sherwood took immediate advantage. 'You've met General Easton?'

'Once, in Washington. Hello, General,' Bradley said.

'Good of you to come,' the General said.

For whatever reason, Bradley thought, the General was sleepwalking.

'Sam Mason, our Capsule Communicator. Peter Watson, Flight Director.'

Bradley shook hands all around.

'Put that bag down, Paul! Small Scotch?'

'Large.'

Bradley placed the bag on the desk. He had taken a good look at Sherwood, and he knew this was not one of the man's well-known ploys. He seemed haggard, and, most unusual for the impeccable director of NASA, was badly in need of a shave.

'We could all use a drink, I think,' Sherwood said. And to Watson: 'Peter, would you mind tending bar?'

As Watson went to an adjoining room, Sherwood indicated the conference table. At the end of it, fitted into the wall panelling, was what appeared to be an oversized television screen. Bradley knew it could give Sherwood an instant overview of any part of the vast NASA complex. How many hours the two men had sat before that screen, sometimes boozing, endlessly debating policy, tactics, the future of space travel.

Sherwood sat behind the small operating console at the head of the table, General Easton to his right, Bradley to his left.

Mason, who was somewhat in awe of Bradley's reputation, gave him what looked like a sympathetic smile and parked himself alongside.

'How big's your boat?'

'Fifty-two feet,' Bradley said. He rather liked Mason on sight.

'I do a bit of sailing when I can find the time,' Mason said. 'Where do you . . .?'

Impatient, Sherwood rapped hard on the table. Stopped in mid-sentence, Mason gave Bradley a conspiratorial half-grin.

'A lot's happened here, Paul. None of it good,' Sherwood said in his gravelly bass.

Bradley looked him straight in the eyes. 'I left NASA five years ago,' he said bluntly. 'What am I doing back here?'

'Let me tell you.' Sherwood paused, as if to exorcise a debilitating apparition, and leaned back in the leather chair. Then, by some surge of will he was himself again, composed, confident, in command. 'Seven days ago Japan and Australia reported the discovery of a comet. Confirmed at Palomar.'

Watson came in with a tray of drinks. The men helped themselves, except for Sherwood. He went on talking to Bradley. 'Nothing spectacular about the discovery of a comet. It was where this one seemed to be going.'

Now Sherwood did pick up a glass.

'The Asteroid Belt,' Mason filled in.

'So?' Bradley said.

Sherwood sipped his whisky. 'When they called me, it was a couple of hundred thousand kilometres from the Apollo Asteroids, give or take a few. We had a space probe in the vicinity, with General Easton's son Tom in command.'

The General, Bradley saw, was downing his Scotch-on-the-rocks as if it were water.

Sherwood had touched a button on the console. On the screen, a still photograph of *Challenger 2* jumped out at them in perfect colour.

'Mason,' said Sherwood, 'give Paul a copy of my report to the White House and the National Security Council.'

While Bradley studied the slide projected on the screen,

Challenger up there in the middle of the Asteroid Belt, Mason dropped the report in front of him. My God, Bradley thought, it's a tome!

Mason said, 'Synopsis of vital information pages one to five.'

Nodding, Bradley tore himself away from the picture on the viewer. He began to peruse the pages and suddenly, without willing it, he was back with NASA, all the special argot comfortable in his brain, as if he had put on an old favourite hat.

As he read on, the import of the deliberately low-key language began to penetrate. When he looked up, he saw that the General was into his second drink.

After what seemed to the other men an extraordinarily slow read – it was actually quite fast – Bradley put the pages down.

His face told them nothing.

Sherwood hit a button on his console again. The screen showed the final still picture of *Challenger*, caught as she was disintegrating, the killing splinter literally cutting her in half.

The sharpness of the colour and the background clarity lent a special impact, a breath-stopping vitality, to the picture. The destructive force captured on film seemed to Bradley to symbolize man's helplessness against the outrageous tantrums of nature.

'I don't think I'll ever forgive myself,' Sherwood was saying. 'I should have figured . . .'

'No guilt, Hal. We'd all have given the same order.'

It was General Easton. He can hold his liquor, Bradley thought. His voice was steady; you'd never know he'd taken a drop.

Bradley rose and walked to the window. The Space Centre was functioning as usual. In the brilliant Texas sunlight he could spot all the familiar activity in the airfield beyond. He could see a large cargo ship gently touching to a landing. Near it, on an adjoining runway, a jet-powered chopper was ascending like a startled bird, almost vertically.

He turned to the men in the room, but his question was

spoken primarily to Sherwood. 'Who knows about this?'

'Outside of the NSC and the President?'

'Yes.'

'At the moment, nobody.'

Bradley nodded. He walked back to the table. Sherwood had removed the *Challenger* slide. Bradley picked up the report for a moment as if weighing it, then dropped it. He turned to Sherwood.

'Hal,' he asked quietly, 'what is it you want me for?'

'You should be able to figure that out.' Sherwood's eyes were levelled on his. 'After all, you're the man who developed Hercules.'

'What's that got to do with it?' There was a harsh edge to Bradley's tone, a clear resentment at the mention of the Hercules Project.

Sherwood spoke softly, ignoring the hostility in the other's voice.

'Listen to me, Paul – listen real good. There's a chunk of Orpheus headed towards Earth. A big chunk.'

Bradley's face didn't change expression, but his hand tightened on the glass he was holding. 'You have a confirmed orbit?'

'We're still running a series of checks,' Sherwood said, 'but the odds don't look good.' His lips were drawn tight. 'There are smaller fragments out ahead, but our main concern is the big one.'

Trying to relax his grip on his glass, Bradley raised and drained it.

'What's the time factor?'

Mason stepped in. 'The data's not completely collated, but the estimate is six days till impact.'

Sherwood was watching Bradley closely. 'We thought you might have some ideas about diverting it.'

'Ideas like Hercules, you mean?' The sharp edge was back in Bradley's voice.

'Why not? That was the intended function of the damn

24

thing, wasn't it? For precisely such a situation as this.'

'That's what I thought. But you people decided to use it for something else!'

It had suddenly become war between Bradley and Sherwood. The others sensed at once the renewal of a long-buried conflict. Mason guessed its area – at least thought he had. Peter Watson, assuming a hoary quarrel having to do with a power struggle, was way off base.

General Easton was not an insensitive man and so he picked up the signals, but he was too fuzzy by now to give them any kind of proper reading.

Sherwood moved away from the conference table. His smile at Bradley was one of frank concession.

'You were right, Paul. You said this would happen someday, and here it is. This is a chance to prove how right you were.'

Bradley faced him without answering.

Sherwood accepted that silence as some sort of acquiescence.

'I've convened a meeting at NASA headquarters in Washington tomorrow morning. I want you to come.'

They all waited for Bradley's reply, having sensed, in the brief time they had known him, his independence and unpredictability.

But Sherwood knew better, knew he had given Bradley no choice.

'We appreciate it, Paul. We've delayed a commercial flight for you. Leaves in an hour. I'll clean things up here with Mason and take a later plane.'

Sherwood removed a document from a desk drawer, slid it across at Bradley's suitcase. 'Up-to-date material on Hercules. You'll be met at the other end. Your hotel room's booked.'

Bradley picked up the material and jammed it into the suitcase.

'You sure you haven't forgotten anything?' he growled.

The two men were suddenly back on the track again, Bradley's heavily sarcastic tone having punctured the tension.

Sherwood smiled. 'One more thing, Paul. You remember the Icarus Project?'

He reached into the desk again, then sailed another thick set of pages at Bradley. 'You might refresh yourself on that, too.'

The Houston-Washington plane was full, but Sherwood had reserved a first-class seat for Bradley, not typical of a man who prided himself on keeping to as lean a budget as possible. Sherwood himself, when going commercial, travelled tourist.

Bradley's thoughts, as the plane took off, were considerably muddled. His meeting with Harold Sherwood (Sherwood was his ex-wife's uncle, and had introduced them . . . how many years ago? Nine?) had inevitably brought back painful memories of his failed marriage. Beyond that, the return to Houston, where he had spent so many good years before the crisis that had brought about his departure, reawakened in him a dismaying sense of loss. Missing from his life, he now realized, was the camaraderie he had experienced in NASA. There was not only the satisfaction of serving his country; there was also the real enjoyment of the work itself – the immediate thrust and importance of it.

He was being foolish, he supposed.

At Columbia they were properly impressed with him. A new department, which he would head, was in the making. One of the country's largest foundations was considering a grant in the millions to fund a laboratory and buildings on land the university owned across the Hudson.

He would have carte blanche, his own 'shop,' as they so neatly put it.

And yet . . .

The 'No Smoking' signs above his seat were off, and people around him were beginning to rid themselves of their seat belts. A little old lady in a window seat, wearing a straw hat with plastic flowers on it, had hauled out a package of cigarettes and was puffing away, giving him a tiny smile. He returned it, preoccupied. No, he was saying fiercely to himself, Sherwood could go screw! The man was a manoeuvrer, a political animal who was probably using this Orpheus business to pull Paul Bradley back into NASA's orbit . . . you could bet he'd check their figures! They were worrywarts; they were probably off in their calculations by thousands of miles!

He was in the washroom, splashing water on himself, trying to bring back a little freshness before tackling those reports, when there came a *ping*, followed by the Captain's voice on the overhead speaker: 'We're heading into a little turbulence. Take your seats, please. Should be through it in a minute or two.'

Bradley, a nonconformist in such matters (when he was not in command) took his own good time, absorbing the errant up-and-down plunges the turbulence was causing and finishing his ablutions at his own pace.

Moving back to his seat, he encountered hostile glances from the stewardesses and from the worried, strapped-in passengers. The plane was still jitterbugging across the sky, and nobody was liking it.

As he sat down, he noticed that the little old lady was no longer smoking. She was just clutching the buckle of her seat belt. There was bright red nail-polish on her small, wrinkled fingers.

'Not to worry,' Paul said reassuringly. 'Spoke to the pilot. Any minute and it'll subside.'

'Since when,' the old lady said acidly, 'does the pilot drive the plane from the lavatory?'

Paul grinned and fastened his own seat belt.

While unseen forces still buffeted the plane, the pilot, a sociable type, came on again over the intercom. 'You might be interested,' he said chattily, 'in a newscast we're picking up from Charleston regarding the space probe . . . we'll patch it through.'

There followed a series of squawks attributable to atmospheric disturbance, and then the smooth voice of a professional broadcaster was piped into the system: '. . . as for more specific information concerning the distintegration of *Challenger 2*, there's still great reluctance from NASA to provide details.'

Bradley had fished the Orpheus Report out of the suitcase at his feet and was just turning to the first page. Now he dropped it to his lap.

'Our correspondent in Houston is waiting, as all America is, for some explanation of this tragic happening in which three astronauts have lost their lives. As soon as we have that explanation . . .'

The plane did a slight, shuddering dance, then settled into droning, steady flight.

'Sorry we lost him,' the pilot said presently. 'But apparently he had nothing more to tell us. Stewardesses will soon be serving a snack. And you'll be glad to know the weather's clear in the capital.'

The 'Fasten Seat Belts' signs went off. The little old lady reached for a fresh cigarette. She puffed aggressively, then bent towards Bradley, ignoring the bound pages in his hand, the hunching of his shoulders that signalled, 'Leave me be!'

'They shouldn't have been up there. We shouldn't be up here! It isn't natural. I wanted to take the train. But my son insisted, so I said, "All right. I'll fly, but only first class!" I always think the rich are safe, don't you? And here I am. Those poor boys in that spaceship. And now they're dead. Who cares about Mars anyway? With all the mugging going on in our parks . . . don't you think I'm right?'

'Absolutely,' Bradley said, his tone as resolute as Nelson on the bridge of his flagship.

And, daring the little old lady to so much as address another syllable to him, he dug back into the NASA papers on *Challenger 2* and the fatal path of the comet.

4

He had reread Mason's conclusions on the Orpheus affair and had to admit that the calculations might well be correct. As a matter of principle, he would want to recheck them on NASA's Washington computer as soon as possible.

Now, stretched out on the bed in the hotel room, he glanced through the second top-secret volume Harold Sherwood had given him before leaving Houston. Since Bradley himself had edited this particular volume – the Hercules Memorandum – five years ago, and had been using the nonconfidential sections in his work at Columbia, he was able to whip through it, merely familiarizing himself again with some of the more obscure and relatively unimportant data.

The third piece of material in his suitcase, the Icarus Project, he set aside. He was simply too weary to tackle it; he remembered its conclusions well and he just didn't have the stamina to slip back into the *sturm und drang* that reading it now would entail.

It would conjure up memories of March 1967. Boston . . . Jamie had been born, Nancy was on the way. Helen had been up at M.I.T. with him; he'd been wonderfully happy . . .

He pushed up from the bed, getting a glimpse of a big, surly, unshaven stranger in the bureau mirror. On the bureau was the room service tray, a steak dinner only barely nibbled, a half-filled Pyrex pot of coffee. He poured a cup. It was tepid. He set it down.

He walked to the window and gazed out at the city. It was still early in the evening. There was little to be seen – few pedestrians below; above, a fine, star-filled night sky.

He tried the TV, idly flicking channels. On one of the networks, a woman newscaster was discoursing knowledgeably about the *Challenger* disaster. He listened a moment. Now she switched to the latest on Wall Street and the plight of the dollar, just as competently. Sports, too; she knew all about the morning's Admiral Cup Race on the Sound, the strange case of *Blithe Spirit*'s lead abruptly aborted by the Coast Guard. No comments from the owner, Charlie Snowden. Or, for that matter, from the rest of the crew.

Sherwood's security force had been active around the Yacht Club, Bradley mused. He placed the reports on the floor in the darkest corner of the closet, then grabbed his coat and went out, locking the door behind him.

The hotel lobby was full of talk and laughter, guests gathering for a fund-raising dinner for Third World Relief – prominent legislators in dinner jackets, a handful of world-famous fat cats with their dazzling women, a sprinkling of foreign blacks, diplomatic people with their handsome wives, some in elaborate native dress.

Bradley slunk around the stream of guests. He could spot a few old friends, but he sure as hell didn't want recognition tonight.

At the side entrance, he climbed into a taxi. For a moment he had no idea what to tell the cabbie; then, not for any particular reason: 'The Mall. Lincoln Memorial.'

'You got it, sir.'

It was one of those startlingly clear, cold autumnal evenings. The Capitol, seen from the Lincoln steps, gleamed luminously and, as always, he was struck by the beauty.

He strode along the Mall, hoping the exercise would have therapeutic value, clear his brain, cleanse the muck there. He tried to dismiss the events of the day, tried to think instead about not being mugged, tried to pretend he was an ordinary tourist enjoying Washington on a wonderful fall evening.

It wasn't possible.

The stately marble edifices on all sides, the architectural splendour, could not erase from his mind the real path he was treading. If the snuffing-out of the lives of three outstanding young men in *Challenger 2* was to have any meaning, if a far greater tragedy was to be averted, he, because of an unforeseen set of circumstances, might have to make a strong personal commitment.

Was he ready for it? he wondered.

Involuntarily, he looked to the sky again. A small white cloud was edging against the pale gold of the moon. The purity of space as it appeared this minute, this extraordinarily lovely, pristine night, was, he knew, a terrible fraud. Up there lurked a monster that could destroy half the earth.

He stopped at the hotel coffeeshop, ordered a club sandwich and coffee, and ate in peace. The public rooms of the hotel had settled into the grim, late-hour mood that veteran travellers found so familiar and depressing.

A message at the desk: Limousine would be waiting for him at 8:00 A.M.

Leaving an early call, Bradley retired to his quarters. The Hercules Memorandum, the Orpheus and Icarus papers were where he had left them, on the floor in the back of the closet. He undressed and put on the pyjamas Sherwood had supplied – finest quality Egyptian cotton. He tried to look at TV again, gave it up, thought of calling a woman friend in New York, Cathy Elliott. But while Cathy had a smashing figure and was a marvel in bed, in the 'sympathetic ear' department she had the potential of a pinball machine. Besides, what really could he tell her?

He found himself on the phone, dialling Connecticut.

In the house they used to share, Helen Bradley picked up the kitchen extension. She had done the final evening cleaning and was ready for bed.

'Paul!'

He understood her surprise. He didn't phone often these days, and usually, if it was about the kids, he called at dinnertime.

'I know it's late,' he said. 'I just wanted —'

'Paul, where are you? I saw the shots on television earlier at the yacht club. Why did they stop the race? Even the children are asking questions. Darndest thing! I tried to reach Charlie Snowden, but he's not taking any calls!'

No sense ever trying to stop Helen, he thought, amused, until she ran down of her own accord.

'Charlie's just goddamn mad,' he said.

'I'd be too. What on earth happened? I called your apartment. Where are you, Paul?'

'Washington.'

'And then that terrible thing with *Challenger 2*. Is there any connection? I mean with you and Uncle Hal?'

One thing was sure: You could never accuse Helen of being slow to grab onto things. He hated to lie to her but . . .

'No. Well, around the edges, with Sherwood maybe. I came here for the university. NASA is suggesting we tackle some problems in tandem.'

'Oh, wonderful, Paul. Be great if you and Uncle Hal could work together again.'

'Right,' he said vaguely. Then, 'How's Nancy?'

'Miss Wenty says she's the smartest in the class, she may even skip her next year.'

'Great. Jamie?'

Helen hesitated. 'Parker isn't sure. But the hearing is deteriorating. I can tell, even though Jamie won't admit to a damn thing! He's just as stubborn as you are. Parker's beginning to talk surgery again. Only as a slight possibility, mind you. Oh, Paul . . .'

'Yeah,' he said.

She kept on about Jamie: Parker was thinking of trying a new hearing aid, an improved model.

'I wouldn't worry too much,' Bradley told her when he could get a word in. 'Soon as I'm back, I'll have Olsen at the university take a look at him. Olsen's as good as there is. And surgery isn't the worst thing in the world; it may be the right answer.'

'Do you think so?'

In matters like this, Helen trusted him implicitly. Knowing this, he built up Olsen's reputation. Probably the best in the country! Soon as he got home he'd have Olsen on the phone – they had mutual friends.

The load had been lightened, he could tell. At least he had made someone feel better today.

'How are *you*?' he asked finally.

'Oh, not bad. You know . . .'

The silence between them had become uncomfortable. Really a difficult thing. Helen was a fine woman, had actually made him a good wife. But the bridge games and the tennis tournaments at the club that she enjoyed so much, that he had put up with so determinedly when they were first married, had become more and more painful for him as the years passed. And Helen's friends – all perfectly nice, decent people like herself – came early, stayed late and bored him to distraction.

On the other hand, he knew, his scientific pursuits and his intellectual friends were just as boring to her.

There came, of course, as it had to come, that unpleasant day when the fact had to be faced: Aside from the children, they had nothing in common, nothing to say to each other any more.

Bradley tried to recall. Maybe they never really had had anything to talk about. Once they got out of the sack . . .

'Helen . . .?'

'Yes?'

'Tell Nancy and Jamie I love them.'

'I will.'

The phone call was over and he felt more lonely and desolate than ever.

He got into bed and stared at the ceiling. Couldn't do much to help his own family, his own condition. But, in perspective, how important were his personal problems at a time like this? But he was human, damn it! And besides, what was happening up there was not real – just an absurd exercise invented by Harold Sherwood of NASA and a handful of astronomers, his own colleagues, designed to scare the shit out of people!

It took quite a while, but at last Bradley dropped off to sleep.

5

As it hurtled through space, a great black jagged island of matter, the bulk of Orpheus did not appear to have been materially reduced by the impact of the comet. Actually, of course, the asteroid had been considerably diminished by the shattering off of one huge, irregular fragment, along with a considerable number of small splinters.

The enormous fragment had become a separate body, independent of the asteroid from which it had been wrenched. It was a meteor now – with its own orbit, its own velocity, its own accompanying train of lesser fragments.

These splinters – some the size of a football, some as large as a ten-room house – were black and irregular, and just as awesome in their way as the monstrous bulk of the major fragment itself.

Telescopes around the world were beginning now to zero in on this menacing cavalcade of potential destruction.

It was not imaginary anymore. It was reality – an inescapable juggernaut heading for the planet Earth.

The alarm had gone out, very quietly, to as few as possible. These men and women were at work on their computations, checking and rechecking orbits, distance, speed, diminishing time to impact, in days, hours, minutes, and seconds.

But the meteor would not wait for this work to be calmly and properly completed, with ample time for scientific study, for careful evaluation. The meteor, with its attendant group of ugly black fragments out ahead, was plunging towards Earth at a speed of thirty thousand miles an hour!

6

The capital, in all its innocence, woke up to its first order of business – politics – with a secondary interest in pollution, crime, the market, the Redskins.

The *Washington Post* did have a headline that indicated another area of potential concern: MYSTERY SUR-ROUNDS PROBE DISASTER. There were photographs of the three smiling astronauts. Why in hell, Paul Bradley wondered, did they always pick photos of dead victims smiling? To sledgehammer the public with the wilfulness of fate?

What Went Wrong? the subhead on the paper asked.

'Okay,' Bradley asked of the bright, sunny morning. 'What did go wrong?'

The hotel doorman, if he heard, wasn't interested. A neatly dressed young man with a chauffeur's cap was at Bradley's side.

'Mr Bradley?'

'How'd you know?'

'The suitcase, sir. Size, colour, your initials on it. Here, let me carry it.'

'No, thank you.'

The young man nodded politely and led the way to a limousine.

'We picking up anybody else?' Bradley asked.

'Not that I know of, sir.'

Bradley climbed aboard. Traffic was already considerable. In Washington they might not be able to move mountains, but at least they started trying early in the day.

NASA headquarters hadn't changed. Fewer people, perhaps,

fractionally more modest – an effort in these economically difficult times to present a lower profile.

Room 402, the young driver had said, was Bradley's destination. Room 402 was apparently a corner suite. Bradley hesitated in front of the door. Then, face set, he plunged in.

A big room with big windows surveying the Hill, a big conference table, and not a damn person in sight. 'Yahoo,' he wanted to call.

He sat down and waited.

Harold Sherwood entered. Sherwood didn't look exactly fresh either. Times had indeed changed, Bradley thought. Sherwood wore a striped rugby shirt and a large beige sweater with a shawl collar. No proper shirt and tie.

Sherwood dropped his briefcase on the table, gave Bradley a weary, tentative smile, and sat down beside him.

'I'm late. Sorry.'

Bradley glanced around the room. 'You and everybody else.'

'Oh – we're not meeting here.'

Bradley flashed him a questioning look. 'Why not?'

'We're meeting the others at the Defence Department at eleven. In the Secretary's office.'

'Why not here?' Bradley asked, the anger beginning to rise in him. Up to your old tricks, are you, Sherwood?

'Because you and I need to get some things straight between us first.'

Sherwood was silent for a moment. Then, 'You talked to Helen lately?'

'Last night,' Bradley said evenly.

Helen was Sherwood's favourite relative, and he had always taken a proprietory interest in their marriage. It was he who had introduced them, and he had considered it a personal affront as well as a major tragedy when the marriage broke up.

Bradley spoke with slight impatience. 'I thought we'd exhausted the subject of Helen some time ago.'

Sherwood paused only a second, then shifted gears smoothly.

'What I really want to talk about is Hercules. You originated the project; you developed it. All I did was try to implement it.'

Bradley's voice was flat, accusing. 'That how it got screwed up?'

Sherwood got to his feet, on the edge of ripping into Bradley. Then, restraining himself, he fought for and achieved control.

'Let's cool it, Paul. There's too much at stake here and your knowledge is indispensable. This is no time to dredge up old animosities!'

'Don't have to dredge up old anything,' Bradley told him. 'I'm still living with it. I can taste it again right now!'

'It wasn't my decision to turn Hercules into a —'

'What, Hal? What *did* you turn it into?'

Sherwood's voice boomed out loud and resentful. 'Goddammit, I didn't do it! *They* did!'

He paused abruptly and settled back into his chair with a helpless shrug. *Okay*, the weariness in him said, *you've shot across my bow. I'm hove to.*

'Hercules,' Bradley stated coldly, 'in case you've forgotten, wasn't designed to be a weapon with fourteen nuclear warheads pointing down on Russia!'

'Not just Russia,' Sherwood managed to interrupt weakly.

'Or China, or wherever the hell! Its rockets were supposed to point outward, *not in!*'

They were both silent briefly, each envisioning the monster satellite, a doomsday weapon with its menacing rockets, moving in space, its orbit synchronized with Earth's.

Bradley came out of it first. Damn it, he didn't mean to hurt this man! On the other hand, he couldn't let him completely off the hook. 'Hal,' he said quietly, 'you know it as well as I do: Hercules was designed to defend us against the exact damn threat we're facing now.'

Sherwood was smart enough not to use any tricks at this juncture. Everything must be put on the table, no cards hidden.

Bradley mustn't have any doubts about that. 'Paul, what the first report didn't say was that that chunk of meteor's five miles wide! We've gone over the readouts a hundred times and it's definitely going to hit us! It'll make a hole big enough to put the Atlantic in.'

'Five miles?'

Obviously shaken, Bradley could only stare.

'Now walk out!' Sherwood dared him.

Bradley crossed to the window. He stood there, staring out, seeing nothing, figures leapfrogging in his head. He hadn't expected a meteor that size. While the elements of danger he had been told about in Houston remained constant, the key component of the equation had now been altered radically. Five miles wide! A behemoth! The possibilities were unpredictable – and too terrible to contemplate.

He turned towards Sherwood, who had lit one of his rope stogies and was looking with the concentration of a child into the curling smoke.

'What about General Adlon? Isn't he running Hercules?' Bradley asked.

'Adlon's a good man technically. But he's two-dimensional. We're going to have to move him out. That's one problem. Second, there'll be a hundred men in this town stupid enough to resist using Hercules because of what it might mean politically.'

'What am I supposed to do about that?'

'Help me ride over them,' Sherwood said.

'Hell, when it comes to politics, you don't need any help. You wrote the book.'

Bradley came back to the table. He fished one of Sherwood's cigars out of the tin case. He lit it, pulled at it, coughed.

'Okay, you sonofabitch,' Bradley said at last. 'I'm with you. But I want it straight up and down. No double talk.'

'Straight up and down. You've got my word.'

Sherwood had opened his briefcase and was taking out a

document. 'Just so we're clear, you and me, I'd like you to read this.'

Bradley's eye hit on the date first. Five years ago. The time of the Hercules hassle.

The document was a letter addressed to the chairman of the National Security Council. From the chief of NASA, H. Sherwood. It was an angry denunciation of the use of Hercules for defence purposes. It advised of the imminent resignation of Paul Bradley because of the committee's action. It stated that the loss of Bradley to NASA and the space programme was a serious blow and warned that if the reasons for it leaked out, other scientists, in other vital projects, might react similarly. Finally, it pleaded for reconsideration of the council's decision and a return of Hercules to the peaceful purpose for which it was intended: protection against an errant body from outer space.

The tone of the letter was direct and uncompromising.

Bradley placed it back on the table. He met Sherwood's glance.

Sherwood smiled wryly. 'The bastards never answered,' he said. 'Days later I got a telephone call from an aide, suggesting that I forget it.'

'I take it all back,' Bradley said, grinning. 'You're a *lousy* politician.'

Sherwood removed a fat manila folder from the briefcase. He shoved it towards Bradley.

'Hercules,' he said, 'Your original formulating data. You might need it. But I don't know. A wise-ass like you probably still has it all in his head.'

'For sure,' said Bradley.

'Well, those rockets have to be realigned. We've got exactly five days.'

7

It was tumbling remorselessly towards Earth, still millions of miles away, but for all its shapeless bulk, aimed as precisely as a marksman's bullet.

And no longer was it a nameless assassin on a darkened street: The proper authorities all over the globe had its record and mug photos out of the files.

In addition to Japan and Australia and the United States, observatories in England and France, in South Africa, in Israel, were tracking its course.

Later on the amateurs would be aiming telescopes at it . . . and the fear of its arrival would spread by radio and telegraph, even by drums. Cults would arise to claim it as their own. It would become the anti-Christ, on its way to destroy the world.

8

The brutal early storm had passed, but the snow still swirled down softly, no longer tormented by the wind.

The cold persisted, however. And the sky remained a patchwork of dirty grey clouds with only tiny glimpses of blue.

In its clearing in the forest, its dish antennae aimed into the overhead gloom, its buildings banked high with snow, the observatory looked like an old wreck of a car abandoned to rust in the elements. But during the last twenty-four hours, reports from across the world had been confirmed by the observations of the scientists inside.

This data had been telephoned at once to Moscow, with supporting information for the heads of the institute there to study. Alexei Dubov, director at Yaroslavi, who had personally initialled all the computations, had made a point of offering no opinion as to how the Soviets should respond – if indeed a scientific response was at all possible.

Moscow had reacted by ordering Dubov and key members of his group to headquarters at once for consultations.

Moscow had made no attempt to disguise its alarm.

The Chairman himself had been alerted and would be on standby.

Two snow vehicles with special insulation awaited outside the observatory centre to take the scientists to the airfield.

Fur-hatted, enveloped in a sober black woollen coat (Dubov was not about to venture to Moscow in one of his sporty bearskin jackets), he stood for a moment outside the observatory, gloomily assessing the heavens.

'It will clear, Alexei,' Tatiana Nicolaevna Donskaya said. She was Dubov's assistant, thirty years old, quite attractive – and today she was the only one who could make Dubov smile. There was nothing between them except friendship, though it was said that Dubov, for all his good qualities, was an incurable womanizer.

'It will not clear up here,' Dubov replied, pointing to his head.

Tatiana laughed.

The other members of the group waiting with them included Stutkin, who was party chief at the observatory. Bundled in his heavy coat, with a scarf tied around his head under his wool hat like a babushka, Stutkin resembled a hawk-faced peasant in drag.

Stamping their feet, they all waited in the swirling snow while the drivers warmed up the motors.

Dubov's gloom was still evident.

'It took the Germans three years to destroy Stalingrad,' he said, gesturing towards the sky. 'It would take our friend up there two seconds to turn half of Russia into one huge Siberia. And as fond as I am of Siberia . . .'

'No frivolity, Dubov,' warned Stutkin.

Dubov grinned at him, not in the least intimidated, and Stutkin stormed off towards the first of the vehicles, followed by two older scientists.

At a more leisurely pace, Dubov and Tatiana, along with Brochen, Dubov's second-in-command, proceeded to the other car.

'You are really worried?' Brochen asked, when he thought they were out of hearing of the others.

'Put it this way,' Dubov said – one could never be sure if he was making a joke or not – 'if our national budget can afford it, we should make a telephone call to NASA.'

Both Tatiana and Brochen broke into laughter, causing the other group, some distance away, to turn towards them reprovingly. It was clear they had heard. Dubov having made no effort to lower his booming voice.

The drivers signalled that they could proceed now.

Before climbing inside the first snow car, however, Stutkin, stung by Dubov's contempt and already planning his anti-Dubov strategy for the Moscow meeting, turned to Anastov, an astronomer, his one real crony in this damnable frozen wilderness.

'Tell me, Anastov, you've checked behind Dubov. There's no chance he's wrong, that this is a lot of fuss about nothing?'

Anastov shook his head. 'Sorry. I will have to confirm it. It's up there, Comrade, and it's coming down.'

Stutkin stared into Anastov's fat, sincere face, wiped his own runny nose with his sleeve, and grunted. When he spoke again, they could not tell whether he was speaking to them or proclaiming the law for himself and the others.

'Under no circumstances,' Stutkin said in a severe tone, fully as loud as Dubov's had been, 'must contact be made with the United States until the ramifications of this have been discussed with the Chairman.'

The two snow cars were filled. The doors slammed shut. The journey through the thickening white curtain had begun.

9

'I hope no one has been foolish enough to make contact with the Russians about this,' said the Secretary of Defence, Abe Holland.

Holland was not in the image of his office. He was a small, doughty man who never looked clean-shaven. And he scorned the sober dark suits that would have pleased the generals, preferring casual, Ivy League sports jackets. On occasion, during late-night sessions, he had even been caught wearing sneakers.

But he was considered to be one of the brightest men ever to head the great office of defence.

He hated war. And so, in all wisdom, he prepared for it in order to preserve peace.

Now he turned a cold, cynical eye on Harold Sherwood.

'No one would inform the Russians without your approval,' Sherwood assured him.

They were not a large gathering. Sherwood and Bradley, General Easton, in his position as Air Force Director of Space Systems. Across the table was Easton's counterpart, though ranking him by a star, General Barry Adlon.

Adlon had played fullback at the Point, and he still looked as if he could blast through a phalanx of tacklers. He was the present head of Project Hercules. Sherwood had warned Bradley that Adlon was not to be underestimated. Though he made a practice of bulling through opponents, terrorizing the enemy, Adlon was not unsubtle. He could be a wily opponent.

Next to General Adlon sat the deputy head of NSC; the Assistant Secretary of State, Steven Powell; and Andy Grant, the President's chief of staff.

'But, Mr Secretary,' Sherwood told Abe Holland, 'we can be sure that the Russians know all there is to know about the meteor by now. The only thing they wouldn't know is what we're planning to do.'

'What we're *discussing* doing. I sincerely hope it is still discussion.'

It was Adlon who had spoken, and Bradley knew that he would not be an easy man to move. To back him up, he had the authority of those four hard-earned stars.

The Defence Secretary was used to these intimidating voices of authority. Leaning back, he said without any particular emphasis, 'General Adlon, I assure you no decisions have been made. That's what this meeting's been called for. To decide what to do.'

Bravo, thought Bradley. Bravo, old Abe! At least we're still in the ball game.

The Secretary went on. 'Heads together, right, General? Now you're in charge of Project Hercules, and if the result of this meeting is to make use of —'

'There's nothing else we *can* use,' Sherwood interrupted. 'All we've got out there is Hercules.'

The Secretary flashed a little fire at the intrusion. But Sherwood, Bradley saw, wasn't about to let it bother him. Sherwood, from the beginning, wanted them all to know that talk was okay, but that there was only one way to go. Good for Sherwood – but would the tactic backfire?

Adlon fought back strongly. 'Damn it, Hercules isn't even out there as far as anybody but us knows, and it's got to stay that way! We've never admitted to Hercules!' His eyes were on Abe Holland's. How many other secrets, Bradley wondered, did they share in the freemasonry of the military? 'Mr Secretary, if we did admit to this now . . .'

'We have to!' countered Sherwood. 'You can't keep the whole world in the dark about what's happening!'

'All right, gentlemen,' the Secretary said soothingly.

Sherwood quieted. Adlon appeared to be holding his breath, like an engine ready to steam down the track. The Secretary glanced from one to the other, an appreciative glint in his eyes. The bastard was enjoying the fight! Bradley thought.

'Yes?' Abe Holland said to Sherwood.

Sherwood's tone was calmer now, but no less firm. 'What's more,' he said, addressing himself to Steven Powell and Andy Grant as well as to Holland and Adlon, 'once it's known that five miles of rock is going to hit somewhere at 48,000 miles per hour, people are going to want to know what the hell we intend to do about it!'

'So you tell everybody we've got nuclear rockets orbiting out there? In direct contradiction to every international agreement we've made?' Adlon was on his feet now, shouting, his face beefy-red. 'It's an invitation to being called liars and warmongers by every shitty little tenth-rate power with a folding chair at the UN!'

Sherwood rose. 'We'll be international murderers if we don't! Or maybe you'd like us all to get out there with slingshots and B.B. guns . . .' He, too, was shouting, and as a consequence, perhaps in reaction, a sudden quiet fell upon the others in the room, as though the meteor had already struck and they were watching the dust settle in shocked silence.

'I think we ought to be able to reason this out with a semblance of order and respect for each other's opinion,' Abe Holland said with a degree of melancholy.

General Adlon nodded as if he – the injured party, of course – agreed completely.

Sherwood made a noise in his throat and folded his arms, looking neither right nor left. Bradley, who knew Sherwood's ability as a thespian, also knew that Sherwood was quite content with his performance, and with the progress of the meeting up till now.

It was the President's man, Andy Grant, who now took the floor. He didn't seem too bothered by the ruckus one way or the other, Bradley thought. Probably a tea party to him. Voice very firm; a need to get at the actual facts before proceeding.

'Dr Bradley, would you please tell us what would happen if this meteor struck?'

Bradley hesitated. Please describe Armageddon in three simple declarative sentences.

'Well,' he said, 'let me start this way. A mass of rock a mile in diameter, travelling at 30,000 miles an hour, would blast a crater fifty miles across and approximately five miles deep.'

The other men – even Adlon – stared at him blankly, trying to visualize this appalling prospect.

'This meteor is *five* miles in diameter. Its striking force is equal to two million five hundred thousand megatons of TNT.'

Bradley paused to let the figures sink in. 'That's ten orders of magnitude larger than the largest earthquake ever recorded. It would hurl into the atmosphere five billion tons of earth and reduce solar radiation for decades to come. It could be the start of another ice age.'

There was a stunned silence, broken finally by General Adlon.

'Suppose this thing doesn't hit?'

Sherwood's face wore a thin, impatient smile. 'If it doesn't hit us it can't hurt us, can it, General?'

Adlon's resentment met Sherwood's more than halfway. 'You scientists have been wrong before. You were wrong sending *Challenger 2* off its flight plan. Cost us three fine astronauts.'

Sherwood's face grew livid, and he wasn't acting now. 'Damn it, Mr Secretary, I don't have to sit here and listen to that kind of —!'

But the Secretary had already intervened, banging his hand loudly on the table.

In the ensuing silence, Bradley spoke very quietly, his eyes fixed on Adlon.

'General Adlon,' he said. 'We've checked our orbital calculations with every important observatory in the civilized world. They confirm our data. The probability factor of a collision with Earth is 96.7 percent.'

Bradley rose and turned to Abe Holland, whose normally sharp eyes now looked glazed. 'If you'll excuse me, Mr Secretary – I'm afraid that's all I can tell you.'

He started out of the room, but stopped at the door. 'Before I go, gentlemen, let me say this: I couldn't care less what Russia says about America, or vice versa. I've told you what's going to happen when that meteor hits, and if you think you can prevent it by hiding your heads under a blanket, fine. If you reach a decision, I'll be in the bar of my hotel.'

Bradley gave them all a curt little nod, opened the door, and walked out. What a superb performance. Sherwood thought. He could hardly have done better himself!

The others in the room sat in stunned appreciation.

Sherwood did think for a moment that he had glimpsed a slight twitch on Abe Holland's face but he could not be sure.

Holland stood up. 'I'll have to discuss this at the White House. I'll get back to you.'

'In time, Mr Secretary, please!' Sherwood said hastily. 'Because there's damn little time.'

The meteor continued its fall, still far from the Earth, from the gravitational pull that would determine its final point of impact.

But another concomitant of the incident in the Asteroid Belt was now apparent.

The smaller fragments detached from the asteroid by the collision were travelling on a parallel course with the main chunk, actually out ahead of it.

It appeared certain that one or several of these splinters would collide with Earth before the larger and more lethal body, which was now a full-fledged meteor. And these splinters were not insignificant. Each was capable of inflicting enormous damage.

II

Bradley returned to the hotel, enduring a lifetime in the back of a taxi while the driver battled his way through the traffic funnelling out of the Pentagon.

Showering, he wished he could change clothes, but all he had was the same outfit he had worn yesterday morning on his way to the yacht club.

It didn't seem possible that only a day had passed.

What he needed, he decided, was an alcoholic infusion. How long since he had got really swacked? He could hardly remember. Too damned responsible a citizen lately. Must put on his calendar: 'Screw 'em all, and get drunk daily!' And daily remind himself to curse all bureaucratic midgets, all lamebrained hacks like Adlon; even the bright but arrogant political godfathers like Abe Holland.

The hotel bar, the Phoenix Room, was not empty as he'd hoped but filled with other desperate souls . . . like himself, he fantasized, frustrated beyond hope by the futility of their legitimate efforts in this land of Nod.

But another thought intruded: None of them in the crowded bar was even aware of the impending catastrophe that would disrupt their anthill labours here in the capital – that might destroy the anthill itself!

It occurred to him that the room was unnaturally quiet. Then, as he looked around, it became apparent why: all faces, without exception, were turned to the large television screen bracketed above the bartender's head.

A news broadcast – an interruption of the usual daily provender – had captured their attention.

A familiar, avuncular newscasting figure, himself of national prominence, was speaking gravely from the tube. '. . . and although we have finally been informed why the space probe was diverted, and how it was subsequently destroyed, our government has been reluctant to tell us what's been happening *since* that catastrophic event.'

Two men close to the door consulted watches and abandoned their places at the bar, agreeing reluctantly that they'd miss their appointment if they didn't leave now.

Bradley captured their seats and the ear of the bartender, a double triumph.

In the corner of the screen above him, behind the announcer, appeared a small image of Big Ben, the logo of London, England.

'We have now received further information about this mystery, but we had to get it from the British Broadcasting Corporation. Here is a recording of a broadcast made by them earlier today.'

Bradley's drink arrived, as above him the Big Ben image expanded, filling the screen. Gone was the trustworthy familiar American. In his place stood a young female BBC announcer. She was standing, it soon became apparent, in front of the Houses of Parliament, a microphone in hand. Her voice was clipped, contained, very British. 'The Cabinet met this morning to discuss the announcement made by Jodrell Bank Observatory that a piece of an asteroid broken off by a comet is on a possible collision course with Earth . . .'

All around Bradley, the murmur rose. It was intermingled with the clinking of glass and a certain amount of nervous laughter. Then the bartenders and the waitresses serving the booths were suddenly even busier.

Harold Sherwood slipped onto the bar stool at Bradley's right.

'In God's name,' he demanded. 'What have we here?'

'Took you long enough,' Bradley said. He nodded towards the TV screen. 'What did you expect? Can't keep a thing like this a secret.'

'You really did a number on the Secretary,' Sherwood said. 'He was furious – not used to that kind of treatment.' Then he grinned in wry approval. 'But he got your message.'

Now Sherwood was being shushed by people around them. The Englishwoman was speaking again: 'Should Jodrell's computations prove correct, it would seem that in less than a week this giant object could strike our planet, causing untold damage and great loss of life.'

No nervous laughter now. An uneasy silence, broken only by the soft *phizz* of the bartender's soda-water spigot. The customers, it seemed, were turning inward, stunned, soberly reflective.

Actual terror would come later, Bradley guessed. Disasters of such enormity could not readily be imagined. The initial reaction would be – must be – that this meteor, or whatever it was, would surely slip by harmlessly in the night.

'It is understood,' the young woman continued, 'that the Prime Minister is in close consultation with the American President, and has volunteered any assistance the British government can give to him or to any other nation . . . should such a catastrophe take place.'

'Like sending us a load of umbrellas,' said the man on the stool to Bradley's left.

Somebody snickered.

The Phoenix Room, however, was no longer a place for laughter, no longer a place in which to drown one's sorrows and resurface the lighter for it.

The famous newscaster was back full-screen again, rocklike, stern, not concealing his displeasure. 'We consider it strange' he said, 'that the American people should be dependent on BBC to supply us with these grim facts. We will, of cou return during the day with more bulletins as we receive them. Thank you.'

He was gone.

'I find it strange,' Sherwood said, 'that I haven't got a drink.'

'Two double Scotches,' Bradley told the bartender.

'Aren't you going to ask me what happened after you left?' Sherwood inquired.

'What happened after I left?'

'They're calling the President.'

'What if he says no?'

Sherwood considered that briefly, helping himself to an olive from a dish on the bar.

'Some years ago,' he said reflectively, 'my kid, Artie, started complaining that he had pains in his stomach. With all the junk food kids eat, that wasn't a big surprise. But he kept on complaining, so I talked to my wife and we took him to a doctor – just for an opinion, you understand. "Appendix," says the doctor, and my wife says, "We'll wait until tomorrow, the pains'll go away." You know what Miriam's like, can't stand the thought of an operation.'

The drinks arrived. Sherwood took a long slug, straightened his shoulders, and smiled.

Near them, a booth emptied out. They picked up their drinks and headed for it, narrowly beating out three middle-aged drinkers, the leader in a black silk suit.

'Congressman Peters, Oklahoma,' Silk-suit said. 'Government business to discuss. Hope you don't mind.'

Sherwood was at his smiling best, polite as a maitre d'. He motioned Bradley to sit. 'We're just discussing broads, Congressman,' he said. 'But I believe that's our democratic right.'

He slid his elegant frame into the booth alongside Bradley. 'Now,' he said, 'back to Miriam . . .'

The Congressman turned on his heel. 'Sh-ee-it,' he said.

'That night,' Sherwood went on, 'after she's cried herself to sleep, I go into Artie's bedroom and pick him up and drive him to a hospital. Six hours later, appendix is out, he's fine and having an ice cream, and Miriam's all smiles.'

Sherwood finished his drink in one more swallow. He looked satisfied with himself, but not smug – that wasn't in his character.

'You get my point?' he asked.

Bradley was doing his best to catch a waitress's eye. 'Yeah, but how do you sneak me into a position where I can fire off a dozen nuclear warheads – without Miriam knowing?'

Sherwood shrugged. 'I wish our military characters were as easy to fool as my wife. Or as sensible.'

They sat, the two of them, and thought about it.

'Wish we could be sure where it's going to hit,' said Sherwood.

'Could land right on this city.'

'Washington? It wouldn't dare,' said Sherwood. But he was clearly thinking about it, about Miriam and Artie a few miles away in Virginia.

Bradley's silence, too, was family-oriented – Helen, Nancy, Jamie. His face was grim. 'We're making jokes,' he said, 'but it might well be this country, Hal.'

Sherwood stared at him, frozen into position. 'Do not ask for whom the bell tolls,' he muttered bleakly.

Bradley was trying to separate the father from the scientist. 'What concerns me this minute are those goddamn fragments,' he said. 'They could hit anywhere, well ahead of the big piece.'

He tried to flag down a passing waitress, who ignored him, and then saw that the bartender was waving, trying to get their attention. 'Mr Sherwood —'

The man was holding a telephone receiver in the air. 'Telephone,' he called.

Sherwood left, but instead of heading for the bar, he walked towards an alcove in the rear. Bradley followed his progress, then found the waitress at his side.

'Refill?'

'Please.'

Sherwood, he could see, was in earnest conversation at the alcove phone. The Congressman and his party had finally taken over a booth nearby and the Congressman's voice was taking over all available air space: 'The Attorney-General, in my considered opinion, doesn't have sense enough to pour piss out of a boot.'

Laughter.

Opposition party, thought Bradley.

The waitress brought his drink and a fresh plate of olives.

Sherwood had replaced the phone in its cradle and was now moving slowly through the crowd back towards Bradley. He had been doing some heavy thinking, Bradley could see; he looked worried.

Towering over the booth, not sitting down, Sherwood said, still deep in thought: 'Better put those olives in your pocket. You're not going to have any dinner.'

The Oval Office was as advertised, Bradley thought. There must be more impressive chief-of-state workrooms in the world – he could imagine grand expanses in the Kremlin – but he doubted whether any, except perhaps Winnie's old digs at 10 Downing Street, had the aura of this one.

This President was a railroad buff, and paintings and etchings of famous trains ornamented the walls. The first open carriages used in England. The Flying Scotsman, Orient Express, *Le Train Bleu.* Photos of trains that opened the West. The various 'Chiefs' that spanned the continent. Early locomotives, sleek diesels. On a console near his desk, a model of the train that had carried Lincoln to Washington for the first inaugural, aboard which an assassination attempt had failed.

But the President, this late afternoon, was not thinking of trains. A man without the youth and charisma of many of his predecessors, a short, shrewd, tough veteran of the Senate, he was staring at Sherwood and Bradley with scepticism contoured into the very slant of his body.

'You're telling me that even if we admit to Hercules, we still need more firepower, more nuclear megatonnage, more rockets?'

The Secretary of Defence, Abe Holland, ready on principle to supply a layman's answer to almost any question, was about to take care of that one, but the President's right forefinger shot out, pointing at Bradley.

'Him!'

'That's right, Mr President,' Bradley said immediately, 'More rockets, more of everything.'

He felt himself being studied inch by inch. The President's grey eyes searched his face.

'What's your background, Dr Bradley?'

The President's question had been anticipated. Sherwood brought several sheets of paper over to the huge desk – Paul Bradley's dossier, including, among many other pieces of information, even Bradley's weight at birth.

The President didn't use spectacles; his boast was that he still had twenty-twenty vision. He scanned the sheets before him with absolute concentration.

At length he looked up, gave Bradley a curt nod. That was all. His searchlight eyes were now on Abe Holland.

'Well, Mr Secretary, do we *have* more rockets?'

The Secretary's tone was regretful. 'Not already deployed in space, sir.'

Scornfully, the President asked, 'Then what the hell are we supposed to do? Conjure them out of the air?'

The Secretary knew when to retreat; the army had taught him that. 'Sir, Mr Sherwood would like to ask you a question.'

Sherwood was no stranger to the President. On several occasions, there had been high-stakes bridge games.

'Sherwood,' the President had told Abe Holland once, 'may

look like he's got a ramrod up his ass, but Abe, don't under-estimate him — he remembers the cards and he's no bullshit artist!'

'Go ahead,' he told Sherwood now.

It was the bottom line, the President understood from all he'd heard today. *I'll have to make a decision. Better get the boys in from Congress, or I'm out there on a limb. Hell, what if I am?* he decided with an inward grin. *Goes with the territory, doesn't it?*

Sherwood was taking his time. On his feet, he threw a quick glance at the always alert Abe Holland; at General Adlon, sit-ting back on a couch, until now, at least, just taking it in — but a big brown bear ready to drop a paw in the swirling stream and pull out a trout; at Paul Bradley, who suddenly looked sleepy.

Then Sherwood faced the stubby man sitting at the desk with the American flag beside it.

'Mr President, would you confirm what I'm about to say? The Russians have their own equivalent of Hercules out in space — with rockets aimed at *us*. True or not true?' Sher-wood's tone was quietly insistent.

The President smiled thinly. 'Do I have to answer that?'

'It would be helpful, Mr President.'

'Well, it's true,' the Chief Executive said.

Sherwood nodded. 'We're going to need that extra firepower. We're going to need their rockets in addition to our own.'

The President's gaze touched every player in the game, land-ing finally on Adlon. Speak now, the gaze said, or forever hold your peace.

Adlon spoke. 'They'll never admit they've got the thing,' he announced flatly.

'We have to make them admit it,' Sherwood said.

Adlon's posture was disdainful. 'How?' he asked, sarcastic-ally.

The sides were drawn, and the President was well aware of it. He deliberately permitted his body to go slack in his chair, letting them stew while he weighed the pros and cons, the options.

Unknown to Sherwood and Bradley, but not to Abe Holland, he had had Adlon submit a written analysis of *his* position prior to the meeting. The President found such manoeuvring valuable, especially in situations like this, where it was risky to shoot from the hip. He had read Adlon's paper. He was more thoroughly briefed on the facts than any of them surmised.

Adlon, he thought, gazing at the General now – a man not to be underestimated, a valuable man in certain situations. But this, the President concluded, was not one of them.

'General Adlon,' he said in a cool, impersonal voice, 'for the time being, until this crisis has been resolved, I'm going to put Dr Bradley in charge of Operation Hercules. I rely on you to give him every aid and assistance.'

Adlon was clearly surprised. He would have wagered any amount on the opposite decision. You damned old fool! he thought. But Adlon's lengthy career had not made him a stranger to setbacks. He knew when you had to pull back and regroup.

'Mr President,' he said with a wry smile, 'I hope I'm public-spirited enough to do whatever —'

'I'm sure you are,' the President said quickly. 'Now listen, I have some ideas on this myself. Make sure you hear my broadcast at ten o'clock.'

He shook hands briefly with Sherwood, with Bradley, with Adlon, but indicated to Abe Holland that he should stay. He startled Bradley by telling him that he had witnessed the aborted end of the Admiral's Yacht Race yesterday on television. Damn shame Bradley had to be pulled away . . . !

Leaving the White House, General Barry Adlon told his driver 'Pentagon,' then changed his mind and told the man to take him to his apartment in Alexandria.

The General sat back in the car, opened the window all the

59

way and let the cold, crisp November air wash over him. The General liked the cold. He never wore an undershirt, even in the dead of winter.

Like many of his military colleagues, Adlon was a patriot – a zealous guardian of his country, single-minded, dedicated. Damn it, he said to himself, he knew the Russians, knew they'd take advantage of Harold Sherwood's woolly-minded scheme. The only remaining hope for global peace rested on mutual terror, on the nuclear rockets of Hercules and Peter the Great being aimed at the vitals of their respective adversaries.

The drive to Alexandria gave Adlon time to think, to plan his next move. His adversaries were liberals, but not fools. Harold Sherwood was an experienced Washington hand, knew the terrain, was not likely to make any judgemental errors. The problem was where to find allies, and how to counterattack, and when.

Adlon was convinced of one thing: he must avoid ordinary channels. Chief of Staff, the usual Air Force colleagues were out. The President would be there ahead of him; certainly the Chief's hands would be tied.

One way or another, it was up to him to act, to protect the country against Sherwood and his people. Meteor crisis or not, the other side, the Russkies, would not fall into the same trap. *They'd* be protecting their flanks! He'd bet his life on it!

Adlon was a lifelong bachelor – no need for women to complicate a military career – and his apartment was ground-floor in a lovely eighteenth-century house. He had the use of the garden.

He changed into civilian clothes, but was dissatisfied with himself in the mirror. (Why couldn't he achieve the casual elegance of a bastard like Sherwood?) He went outside where the gold-brown leaves needed raking and burning, smoked a cigarette, came to an inevitable conclusion, walked back in and made a phone call.

Satisfied, he went outside again and dismissed his driver, giving him a message for Adlon's office and his aides. Forget me for the day.

He waited for the car to be out of sight before strolling downtown, just to be sure he wasn't being watched – he wouldn't put it past Sherwood to have a spook covering him. Then he hailed a taxi back to Washington.

The building was a highrise and reasonably new, and Adlon's man was on the eleventh floor. On the door to the suite of offices it said, 'Jacob Pierce, Attorney-at-Law. Veterans' Affairs Advisory.' It was one of several Washington annexes of the Defence Intelligence Agency.

A secretary ushered Adlon inside at once. Jake Pierce listened to Adlon attentively. He himself was a bird-Colonel, but he was never in uniform – a tall flask of water with pale cheeks and premature white hair.

'We've tried to keep in touch, of course,' he said, 'but this has developed very fast.'

'Too damn fast,' Adlon swore. 'But Jake, we can't let our pants down just to keep that Sherwood group happy!'

'Sure,' agreed Pierce, 'but you yourself admit we don't have another Hercules ready.'

'Won't for at least another two years,' Adlon said.

'So we've got to find an alternative.'

'How? Where?' asked Adlon. 'We were in good shape until this fucking thing happened.'

Pierce queried Adlon about the President's attitude. Any chance of effecting a change there?

'Negative.'

Pierce said it was his opinion that a plan independent of the White House must be formulated, a counter to the removal of Hercules.

'Right,' said Adlon. 'Maybe some atomic subs on permanent station in the Baltic. Let the bastards howl!'

Jake Pierce smiled. 'We'll have to be a little smarter than that, General.' Then he added quickly, 'But you're perfectly right. We must do *something*.'

Mollified by Pierce's concern, Adlon rose to go.

'Of course,' Pierce put in, 'I'll have to advise my chief. You can be sure he'll come up with an answer . . . he's pretty good at that.'

Adlon agreed, somewhat cheered.

'And General,' advised Pierce, ushering him to the door, 'from now on, I'd play along with Sherwood and the others. Oh, an occasional harrumph to keep you in character. But don't forget, we'll be right on the ball!'

12

The network makeup man was at work, with the President bitching at every daub. He was no goddamn pansy; let the public see him warts and all!

Andy Grant signalled the makeup man to ignore the insults, get on with the job. His boss behaved this way at every TV session. So the makeup man kept at it, not easy with the Chief of State bolt upright in a straight-back chair, a white towel around his neck, squirming at every touch.

A fire had been set in the grate; the lighting men were fine-tuning the spots. A young aide, Kelly, acting as a double, sat in the big, comfortable fireside divan. The director was almost satisfied; the cameraman had given his okay. Baker, the President's press assistant, was watching the time, along with the network coordinator.

Stiffly, hating them all, the President moved towards the fireplace, and as Kelly hastily rose from the divan, sat down.

'Goddamn circus,' he said.

'Ten seconds, Mr President,' the director said.

The President nodded glumly, waved, and the voice of the network announcer was heard.

'Ladies and gentlemen – the President of the United States.'

The President confounded them. Unexpectedly, he got to his feet – they had rehearsed him on the divan – and leaned on the fireplace mantel. Looking straight into the number one camera, he began to outline in his slightly high-pitched, cranky voice the crisis caused by the comet's unexpected flight into the Asteroid Belt.

63

To the consternation of his staff, he abandoned his prepared text completely, relying on his own simplified version of the situation.

He was doing remarkably well, Andy Grant thought; you'd have to be a moron not to understand.

Now the President did sit – perhaps a kind of reverse dramatization; he was pretty good at that in his own way. The cameras moved in.

The President took out a handkerchief and unabashedly swabbed his face. 'Now you're going to ask – and properly – what steps have been taken to make sure that this meteor never comes anywhere near the earth's surface. And I'm happy to tell you that your government – under my direction – has already anticipated that an emergency such as this could arise . . .'

The number one camera was tight on the President now. He closed his eyes wearily, an old trick of his, then opened them. He could have been chatting from a park bench; his faith in his audience, in himself, in their country, was palpable on every TV screen.

Andy Grant gave the President a slightly worried look. Was that smart, indicating a previously concealed space operation? The press would be damn curious, sure to jump on him: Jesus!

The President, it was clear, couldn't have cared less.

'. . . and so, in collaboration with the best scientific brains at its disposal, your government developed a project which is now equipped to deal with this emergency, and that project is named Hercules.'

Sherwood had commandeered a small Air Force passenger jet – Adlon appeared only too eager to cooperate at this point – and, speeding to New York, he and Bradley and Adlon listened to the speech. Without that mobile, intelligent face to animate it, the words came over the radio in a flat, nasal cadence. But there was a country vigour to the voice, an affinity to the earth. A latter-day Odysseus, Bradley thought; the President could probably plant kernels of corn and missiles would spring up from the soil to turn away this threat to the world.

'What is Hercules?' the President was asking. 'Hercules is an armed, orbiting satellite, its nuclear weaponry aimed towards outer space.'

Bradley, sipping black coffee from a thermos, smiled wryly at Sherwood. 'He's got the name right and the direction wrong.'

'Old mirror trick,' said Sherwood, shaking his head in admiration. 'Smart as they come!'

General Adlon, who had deliberately taken the seat behind them, didn't comment. Remembering the advice of the white-haired Colonel he had visited, he kept his mouth shut and went along. But deep down, Adlon could not accept any of it. Damn it, they were *creating* this thing – this monstrous danger! There might be a meteor up there – collision with the earth might even be possible. But America – no! Why in hell America? Why not Tanganyika? A big flap about nothing, and these bleeding-heart liberals blowing Hercules on account of it! Treason, that's what it was!

'Coffee?' Bradley asked him.

'No thanks.'

Adlon closed his eyes, pretending to sleep. He had his orders from the President, the man now speaking, and like a good soldier he would go along. But there was the old army maxim: as long as you obey 'em, they can't stop you from thinkin'. No, thought Adlon, orders will be carried out meticulously, but they will not stop me from thinking!

'What can Hercules do? It was designed to send, at the press of a button, enough power to destroy a foreign body on a collision course with our planet.' The President paused for emphasis.

'But in this case a special circumstance has arisen. The meteor is of such size and velocity that even the powerful weapon cannot do the job alone.'

'Here comes the crunch,' Sherwood said, a football

commentator foreseeing the inevitable third-down pass.

'Fortunately the Russians, with the same foresight we ourselves possessed, mounted their own weapon for the same peaceful purpose.'

There was a sound from Adlon like a curse hastily throttled, which the two men seated in front of him ignored.

'Pretty good,' Bradley said.

'You don't get to be President for nothing,' Sherwood grinned.

'We do not know what the Russians have called their weapon,' the President said, 'but we know it exists.'

In the Kremlin, in the Premier's Office, the picture and voice of the American President came over with some distortion, transmitted by a recently installed nuclear-powered satellite.

The Russian Premier, in his late sixties, was a new man on the job, a former heavyweight in the Politburo. A broad-faced Georgian like Stalin, he listened to the translator while he watched, his expression telling the others in the room nothing.

There were two other Politburo members – the Director of the Moscow Institute, and Ditroff, paper-thin, bespectacled, actually head of all Soviet science – and, to the side, privileged spectators: Dubov, Stutkin, and Tatiana.

The translator kept up a rapid-fire pace, seeming to insinuate his own words even as the American President was enunciating his.

'And we are going to ask them to add their nuclear power to ours, so that, together, we will be able to deal with the meteor, to strike it with irresistible force and end forever its potential danger to us all. I will myself be speaking to the Soviet leaders as soon as I have finished this broadcast.'

The Russian Premier was playing with a letter opener. It had a jewelled handle and had once belonged to a tzar; it had been a gift from a party council in Leningrad. In years gone by it had served as a dagger.

'Yes,' the Premier said softly.

He might have meant yes *or* no. The man often confused his colleagues as well as his staff with his non-committal remarks. It was always better, they had learned the hard way, to wait until the Premier was ready to throw out at least a hint or two ... otherwise you could really end up looking like a fool.

'One last thing,' the American President was saying, 'I ask you not to panic. You must go on with your lives as you normally do. Your safety is in our hands, and I promise you, they are capable hands. Goodnight, and God bless you.'

The President's smile at the camera was a picture of sober confidence. It said: 'Be of good cheer; you've got *me* on your side!'

No commercial at least; the President had foreseen and vetoed that. Now came commentary by the network pros. ABC had employed the top man at the California Institute of Technology for its panel. CBS had got Rodney from M.I.T. NBC captured Stoker from the Nuclear Regulatory Commission. Each network was deep into technical explanations.

The Russians weren't particularly interested. The Premier motioned to Ditroff. The transmission was terminated; the screen went blank. The Premier put the letter opener aside and faced the people before him.

'Well, Ditroff?' he asked.

Ditroff removed his spectacles; automatically placed them in their case, and shrugged at the Premier, smiling slightly. He had long since mastered the invaluable art of the shrug.

The Premier smiled back, but with reluctance; it was the hard smile of a farmer pulling out a stalk of weevil-infested wheat.

'The Americans elected an alchemist for President,' the Premier said. 'He can turn hypocrisy into diplomacy.'

67

They laughed – the man from the Politburo, Ditroff, Stutkin, Dubov and Tatiana – even though they weren't absolutely sure what the comment signified.

'Now, any minute, the Alchemist will be calling us. Suggestions, please.'

Ditroff spoke with appropriate caution. 'We can hardly ignore the situation.'

The Premier nodded. 'Evidently. My suggestion is we permit him to initiate discussions which you – Dubov, is it? – will attend. But be quite clear, they are only to be discussions.'

Someone from Communications entered the room, a young major obviously with the authority to interrupt. He whispered something in the Premier's ear. But that was unnecessary. They all knew what the Major was reporting.

The Premier stood to reach for the receiver of an ordinary-looking white telephone at the far end of the colossus of a desk. He sat down again, listening, the other Politburo members like palace guards at his side.

Ditroff nodded to Dubov and Stutkin and Tatiana to leave, as silently as possible.

On the way out, Dubov, contrary as always, couldn't help whispering to Tatiana. 'The Volga is about to overflow its banks,' he said, 'and we are discussing swimming lessons.'

13

The President had promised a press conference following the broadcast, and he honoured his word.

The questions came thick and fast, as Andy Grant had known they would. Why hadn't the public been informed about Hercules and the implicit threat of meteor danger? And the Congress? Had *it* been informed?

The President asked the country to bear with him. Key Congressional leaders had been briefed on the danger, had concurred that Hercules should be kept secret, that the reason for its presence would be too alarming, a nightmarish possibility to adults as well as children. But perhaps it was just as well that this crisis had occurred. The government would now be able to show that it was prepared to deal with random objects from outer space.

Bradley, on the plane, marvelled at the man's verbal dexterity: he had managed to tell truthfully the original reason for Hercules – his, Bradley's, reason – and at the same time had been able to conceal, without actually lying, the ultimate military use to which Hercules had been put.

The press, like sharks nosing a sinking ship, sensed fresh meat but could hardly attack a steel hull. So they just circled, waiting. The President was content with that. 'They'll be on me soon enough,' he told Andy Grant, smiling.

On the plane with Bradley and Adlon, Sherwood was weighing the effect of the speech abroad, particularly on the Russians. It was his opinion that the Russians had little choice – their scientists had surely presented them with the unalterable fact that the meteor was on the way.

'Seat belts,' the pilot of the jet was saying. 'The Big Apple.'

There was New York under them, a weak afternoon sun fighting shifting clouds to give the great expanse of the city a dull metallic sheen. Then they were shooting over the stagnant pools edging the Sound and into La Guardia for a landing.

Bradley had his own dun-coloured army sedan and a sandy-haired young driver, Corporal Horace Drew. The car and chauffeur, Sherwood said, were Bradley's for the duration of the emergency.

Bradley, Sherwood, and Adlon went their own ways, with a time and place set for a later meeting.

Bradley gave Drew his address and settled back; it seemed to him he'd been away for weeks. Corporal Drew, obviously an old city hand, drove skilfully, and Bradley was able to relax. He noted that no one in the streets seemed the slightest bit worried about any impending disaster. At least, it wasn't evident in the pace of traffic, in the internal rhythms of the city. The Big Apple was frantic, impossible, dynamic – but no more so than ever – just too busy and involved to give more than passing thoughts to any little old meteor that sure as hell wasn't going to fall near New York!

In his apartment on Central Park West he showered, changed into fresh clothes and opened a tin of ham for lunch. Then, at the small kitchen table, he commenced a series of phone calls.

When his marriage broke up, he had leased this single bedroom flat, part of one of those huge, high-ceilinged multiroomed apartments no longer viable for economic reasons. On the fourteenth floor, it looked out on Central Park, which, though it still had patches of its autumnal colouring, in the main seemed like a great shaggy rug beginning to show the grime.

The first call was to the university, to Ed Copley. Copley, a bright, pleasant man, noted that NASA had already contacted him, asking to borrow Bradley. Copley had okayed it, naturally.

'How long do you think you'll be tied up, Paul?' he asked.

Hesitating, Bradley said, 'A week or so, Ed. Not much more. Let's hope . . .'

'Yeah.' Pause. 'Don't want to pry, but anything you can tell me – like where she's headed? In Washington, they're playing it pretty close to the vest and I've gone to cabinet level.'

Ed Copley would, Bradley ruminated; Ed was a man with a need to be totally informed.

'It's because they don't know, Ed. *We* don't know yet.'

'That's what our own people tell me,' Copley sighed. 'I've arranged for Peterson to take over your seminar. The Institute doesn't want a substitute for your speech – they'll postpone and wait for you. Keep in touch, boy.'

Bradley called the Columbia University Medical School. Dr Gerald Olsen was busy – who wanted him? Bradley left his name and number, asked that the doctor call back as soon as possible.

He telephoned Helen in Larchmont. Helen was out. Supermarket time, he guessed; the kids would still be at school.

He finished the ham, found some stale cookies and washed them down with a cola drink he found in the fridge. Ho for the bachelor's life, he thought.

The phone rang.

It was Dr Olsen's secretary. Was this Paul Bradley, of the university?

It was, Bradley said.

The secretary's voice was dripping with respect, and Bradley remembered that the President had mentioned his name as the new head of Project Hercules.

Dr Olsen came on the phone. 'What can I do for you, Bradley? Don't tell me you want to *hear* that thing approaching?'

Bradley laughed politely. Nothing like that, he told the specialist. It was about his son, Jamie. He explained Jamie's hearing problem.

71

Olsen was charming, eager to oblige. 'Bring him in. No, you'll be busy! Have your wife bring him in. Tomorrow morning?'

'I'll call back to confirm the time,' Bradley told Olsen.

He tried Helen again, and reached her.

'Paul' – she was worried stiff, shrill – 'I heard the President this morning. You didn't tell me . . . When will it happen? Shall I —'

'Sit tight, Helen, please,' he said. 'No danger to you, believe me. Listen, I've just contacted Olsen at Columbia . . .'

She was considerably calmer when he'd finished. She would bring Jamie into town in the morning. Would he keep in touch with her? Promise?

Of course, he said. Daily. He hung up, drained.

He went downstairs to where Corporal Drew waited with the car.

14

The American Telephone and Telegraph Company building is windowless, a great, imposing block planted like an ancient ideogram, its meaning lost to the ages, two blocks from the Hudson River.

On the north side, towards Fulton Street, is St Paul's Church with its little cemetery, the gravestones weathered, the names faded – yet, somehow, a small, lighted candle to the spirit of old Manhattan.

To the south, towards Dey Street, the World Trade Centre towers reach optimistically but blindly to the sky, as if the hoary adage about man's reach were true.

Bradley and Sherwood, men devoted to promptness, arrived together at the AT&T Building.

The elevators were bustling with closing time activity. Bradley and Sherwood bucked the tide.

At the far end of the marble-floored lobby was a semicircular counter at which a security guard sat with a large book of names before him.

The guard recognized Sherwood at once and nodded to him. He waited patiently until Sherwood produced his photo-pass. The guard made a time notation on a sheet on the counter.

'Has General Adlon come in?' Sherwood asked.

'Half an hour ago.'

'This is Dr Paul Bradley.'

The guard hit a button somewhere, a gate behind him opened, and the two men stepped through it. They were in a small private lobby, facing two stainless-steel elevator doors. The chatter from the main entrance was muted here; the voices had a tomblike echo.

Sherwood touched the elevator panel and one of the doors opened at once. They stepped inside.

Sherwood touched another button. The elevator only went down from here, he told Bradley. One stop.

'How far down?' Bradley asked.

'Next to the old subway station, the section that runs under the Hudson. Made it easy to bring in all the equipment. Nobody saw us and it saved millions. It would have been your baby if you'd stayed aboard.'

Bradley thought Sherwood should stow that kind of talk; it brought up unpleasant memories. Anyhow, ironically, it *was* his baby again.

'Why not some sensible place like Houston?' he asked.

'Easy access to a total telecommunications setup right over our heads, and nobody in their right minds would put their most important emergency striking power under the busiest city in the world.'

'Nobody,' said Bradley, smiling. 'Except Harold Sherwood. Say, where do we come out? Australia?'

The elevator finally came to a stop; the door opened, and they stepped out into another world.

The lobby before them was circular, with passageways running off it. It was not overly large, but like everything Sherwood had a hand in, Bradley thought, it was aesthetically pleasing as well as functionally effective. The colours were muted but not sombre; one did not have the claustrophobic feeling of being far below ground level.

'The passageways?' he asked.

'Offices in front of you – the rest sleeping quarters. Mess included. Got a damn good chef, too.'

'I'll bet you have,' said Bradley with a laugh. 'What happens if there's a power failure?'

'Plenty of ways out down below.'

Another guard sat at a desk opposite the two elevators. Behind him was a steel door with a small slot in it.

'How are you, Mr Sherwood?' the guard asked.

'Fine, Hodges. This is Mr Bradley. He's taking over direct command.'

The guard took a good look at Bradley, nodding. 'You still have to use your pass, sir.'

Bradley did not understand until Sherwood inserted his plastic pass card in the door's slot. The door opened and Sherwood entered. Then, about to follow, Bradley discovered it wasn't possible. With a hiss the door instantly slid shut, leaving him with his nose to the steel.

The guard was grinning. 'Your card, sir.'

Bradley inserted his card into the slot and the door opened for him, revealing an amused Sherwood on the other side.

'Sorry, pal. We run a tight, secure ship.'

But Bradley was staring past him.

They were standing on the top landing of an open staircase that led to a great work area below. Elaborate banks of huge late-model computers lined the circumference. Built into the four sides of a 10-foot-high cube were a cluster of closed-circuit TV monitors that tied in with NASA ground stations all over the world. Blank at the moment, the TV screens stared out starkly, like blinded eyes.

In carefully ordered array there was radio, teletype and telephone equipment, some monitored by civilian technicians, some by uniformed army and air force personnel. The technicians went about their business with quiet, purposeful dexterity, and the room was pervaded by an audible but unobtrusive electronic hum.

Doorways led off from this master chamber. Support rooms, Sherwood said, as the two men descended the stairs – canteens for snacks, glass-enclosed booths with smaller computers for private computations.

And the ceiling! Bradley stopped short, noticing it for the first time, and Sherwood relished his reaction with the delight of a kid. The ceiling was dome-shaped, with a slowly revolving inner core, similar to a Disney-inspired cyclorama, that showed the position of the earth, the planets, and the stars in their constant movement.

The lighting itself, Sherwood explained, was designed to conform with the lighting outside at any particular moment, giving the workers below an exciting ambience and a sense of spatial freedom. The effort was well worth the expense – it made life in this sterile, windowless underground environment acceptable.

At the bottom of the steps, a tall, thickset figure waited to greet them. It was General Barry Adlon.

Adlon wore a stiff but resolute smile. 'Welcome,' he said to Bradley. 'Sorry I don't have the military staff to transfer command properly.'

Bradley was friendly. If Adlon was willing to let bygones be bygones and play on the team, so much the better. Nothing could be more dangerous at this point than a jurisdictional fight between them.

'Thank you anyway, General, for the thought. We can sure as hell do without the formalities. And I don't need to tell you your help will be warmly appreciated.'

Adlon merely nodded. Sherwood didn't comment, and Bradley got the feeling it would be a mistake to put too many chips on the General's cooperative stance.

From somewhere overhead and far to the right of where they were standing came a muffled rumbling noise which grew in intensity, then slowly diminished.

'What's that?' Bradley asked, cocking his head.

The others seemed unaware of the noise. Not one of the technicians had so much as turned.

'Subway trains. We hear them all the time.'

'No interference with the electronic gear?'

'Marginal,' Sherwood said, 'and we're calibrated for it.'

Bradley took another wondering look around. The array of equipment, the quiet efficiency with which the staff was functioning, the technological feat of assembling all of this, making it work . . . It impressed him. Sherwood again – perhaps Adlon to some degree, to give credit where it was due – but all originating from his, Bradley's, own blueprints. God, how many years ago?

He should be proud, he thought. Instead he was touched suddenly with the fear that it wouldn't be enough, that the devastating force nature had unleashed could not be turned aside, even by the united efforts of these superbly trained men and women with the most sophisticated equipment at their command. But not for the want of trying! Goddammit, no!

'I'll want a tour, General, if I may,' Bradley said. 'Meet your personnel. But I don't mind telling you, I'm impressed. Quite a setup.'

'Thank you,' Adlon said. 'Normally we work with twenty-five, but since it's been called an emergency, I've brought in the full crew.'

The full crew, Bradley saw, included at least ten women. There might be more in the side workrooms.

Adlon had turned to include Harold Sherwood. His face was closed; it was impossible, really, to tell what he was thinking.

'I have this message here,' Adlon said. 'It arrived shortly before you did, special White House transmission.'

Sherwood took the note, and Adlon watched expressionlessly as he read it. Bradley glanced around. Another subway train was rumbling in the distance and, despite Sherwood's reassurance, the slight structural quiver worried him. The only weakness, perhaps, in the place.

'Good news,' Sherwood said. 'The Russians are coming.'

He handed the note to Bradley, who read it quickly.

Adlon, apparently unable to contain himself, broke out harshly. 'I would like to go on record that I consider allowing the Russians to come into this centre to be a grave error which one day the United States may bitterly regret.'

Several people working nearby turned their heads. Sherwood wore one of his patented smiles, as though he were allowing a rush of winter air to blow past him. Your position is stated and noted, it said; now, sir, may we proceed?

Bradley had lost his benign schoolmaster air. He looked suddenly as if he could chew nails.

'I'd like to meet some of your people,' he said evenly.

Adlon, who had automatically drawn his shoulders up, presenting a four-star posture, now managed by sheer willpower to ease himself from it.

'Of course, Dr Bradley,' he said. He tried, but could not manage, an accommodating smile.

'While you two are doing that,' Sherwood put in hastily, 'I'd like to use your office for a moment, General.'

Not bothering to wait for a reply, Sherwood moved towards what appeared to be the main corridor leading from the central chamber.

Outranked by civilians, ordered about in his own domain, Adlon felt his jaw tighten. 'This way,' he said to Bradley.

The console dominating the centre of the chamber was the heart of the system – the monitor of monitors, as it were, keeping its finger on the pulse of the complex.

In a large chair across from the console sat a bearded man with a thick head of hair flecked with grey. He was making little marks on a pad, analysing the readouts before him. Sensing their presence, he broke away from his pondering and looked up.

'Rolf Manheim,' Adlon said brusquely. 'Our chief technician. Dr Manheim, this is Dr Bradley, who is taking over.'

Manheim rose with an effort; he had a pendulous beer-belly. He squinted at Bradley with the same concentration he had been devoting to the material on the readouts.

'Ah,' he said. 'Dr Bradley, you have been teaching a nephew

of mine at Columbia University . . . he thinks you're a very intelligent man.'

'You have a very perceptive nephew.'

Bradley smiled; Manheim smiled back. He had a gold front tooth.

Manheim beckoned to the two other people working with him at the central console. One was a young woman – in her late twenties, Bradley guessed, although he was always poor at women's ages. She was prettier than a serious scientist ought to be. How should a female scientist look? he asked himself. Male chauvinist pig!

'Our Trajectory Analysis Officer, Jan Watkins,' Adlon was saying.

'Hello,' Jan Watkins said.

Bradley got a firm handshake.

'I'm going to be asking you and your computers a lot of questions,' he said.

'We'll try to give you a lot of prompt answers.'

'Triple-checked,' the red-headed young man at her side commented.

'My assistant, Alan Marshall,' Jan Watkins said.

Marshall was as broad as he was tall and evidently the kind who thought it a sign of sincerity to crush fingers when he shook hands. Withdrawing what was left of his right hand, Bradley made a wild stab. 'Like to pump iron?'

The young man stared. 'How'd you know?'

'So do I,' Bradley said, 'when I get the time. Have a set of weights at home.'

'Dr Bradley,' someone called behind them.

They all turned.

A few paces away was a lanky, good-looking black man wearing a fringed leather jacket and cowboy boots. Another individualist, Bradley thought. Like Manheim. Did this kind of work breed them?

This one said, 'Sorry to interrupt, but I've got Sir Michael

79

Hughes at Jodrell Bank on the monitor. He wants a word with you.'

'Bill Hunter,' Manheim said. 'In charge of tracking.'

'Excuse me,' Bradley said. He followed Hunter towards the bank of TV monitors at the far side of the big room.

'Who else are you linked with besides Sir Michael?' Bradley asked as he walked, almost trotted, beside Hunter, whose natural pace resembled a jogger's run.

'Hong Kong, Tokyo, Arecibo, New South Wales . . .'

They arrived in front of the tracking station monitors. Positioning himself in front of a locked TV camera that operated in conjunction with the monitors – it would transmit his image out to the stations – Bradley gave the okay sign to Hunter.

Hunter adjusted several dials and the image of a man appeared on the screen. Not satisfied, Hunter tinkered a moment and the image became superbly clear; the man could have been in the Centre with them.

'Good morning, Michael,' Bradley said.

Michael Hughes was tall, with a prominent Roman nose and a typically British understated manner. He and his wife had entertained Bradley far beyond the call of duty on Bradley's last trip to England, had had him at their country home for a long weekend, had introduced him to some of the best brains in their mutual field.

'Morning, Paul. I wasn't expecting to see you before Wimbledon – assuming, of course, there's going to be a Wimbledon.'

Bradley had forgotten Sir Michael's passion for tennis. He had been a prominent amateur and was usually a linesman or referee at the centre court matches.

'Or anything else, for that matter, Michael. What have you got for us?'

Sir Michael asked, 'Security your side, Paul?'

Bradley glanced up at Hunter, who didn't move a muscle.

'We're absolutely solid this end, Michael. You can trust us with the crown jewels.'

80

'Good. Well, this is it. In twenty-four hours we can expect the first small splinters. Almost impossible to track unless they arrive in clusters – then their density will register.'

Hunter was leaning over, making notations on Sir Michael's report.

'You'll want to doublecheck, but I think our findings are sound.'

'I'm sure of it,' Bradley replied. He motioned Hunter to step before the camera with him.

'Sir Michael, this is Bill Hunter. He'll act as liaison if I'm tied up.'

'Very good,' Sir Michael said. 'But don't go wandering too far off. No sailing!'

Bradley grinned. 'I hear you, Michael. Anything else?'

'Not for the moment. I'll be here until it's over. We'll keep in touch.'

'Day or night,' Bradley said.

Sir Michael made his exit with a gracious wave, and Bradley became aware that Sherwood had arrived and was waiting for him to finish.

'You heard?' Bradley asked.

Sherwood's face was grim; he had heard. 'Met Sir Michael once. Not exactly an alarmist.'

'No.'

'I presume you'll want to do your own calculations.'

Rolf Manheim had joined them. 'As soon as our own observatories begin sending in their reports,' he said.

Bradley said, 'Stick with it, Manheim. And thanks.'

Sherwood, Bradley could see, was excited, anxious to impart some news.

'They're arriving at seven-thirty this evening, Washington.'

'Why Washington?' Bradley frowned impatiently.

'They've got to touch base with the Russian embassy first, Paul. I'll get them here as fast as I can.'

15

Adlon made the call from a booth in the lobby of his hotel, first making sure that he was unobserved.

He used the Washington number the Colonel had supplied for such occasions. Actually, of course, nothing had happened that hadn't been expected, but the Colonel might want to speed up whatever response was being planned at that end.

'Adlon here,' he said when the voice answered.

'Yes, General.'

Adlon summarized the news of the day: Bradley's takeover, and the information that the Russians were actually coming.

The Colonel said, 'Yes, we've been so informed.' And in a voice that had the tiniest flicker of reprimand in it, 'You mustn't be concerned about us down here, sir. We're hooked into the main circuit, if you know what I mean. There's also another factor, General. We'd prefer that all communications between us be kept to a minimum. You understand . . . never know when these lines are – private.'

'Yes, yes!'

'That doesn't mean you're not to touch base when you think it's important. We don't want you apprehensive about that.'

'I understand.'

'And you can be assured we're not asleep down here. Far from it.' The Colonel's voice had dropped almost an octave. 'We're set for a goal-line stand.'

'Excellent,' the General replied.

'Goodnight then, sir.'

'Goodnight.'

Up in his room, Adlon went over the events of the day. Somehow, in a way he could not quite understand, he felt even more diminished than he had in Washington. The call he had just made was not, he perceived, much help. In fact, that white-haired sonofabitch of a Colonel actually had the effrontery to put him down . . . well, almost. Those damn little spooks were all the same.

Removing his jacket, reaching for the bottle of vodka — funny how he liked their drink — he came to another decision. Putting the bottle aside, he walked over to the bed, sat down, and reached for the hotel phone. 'Washington,' he told the operator. 'The Pentagon, The Secretary of Defence.'

The airfield lights picked up the red star of Russia emblazoned on the tail fin of the military jet.

After touchdown, the pilot followed the airfield jeep, which guided the jet immediately across several runways to where a group of people, bundled up against the chill of the night, waited beside several black limousines.

A tractor towed a stairway into place. Out of the plane, now bathed by floodlights, came two passengers — Dubov, a scarf wrapped around the upturned collar of his coat and a fur hat on his head, and Tatiana Nikolaevna Donskaya. Tatiana, apparently unafraid of the autumnal weather in North America, wore a dark leather coat with its wide collar open at the neck; her suede boots were fashioned from a current Paris model. She drew a discreet whistle from the tractor driver. Hearing it, she waved good-naturedly.

It was the only casual incident in what was otherwise a sombre, deliberately low-key welcome.

Swerdlov, the Russian embassy official assigned to greet the scientists, shook hands with Dubov and Tatiana and introduced them to the State Department's man, Reynolds, who welcomed them to the United States. Reynolds then called over Pete Watson, representing the Hercules Project. Watson was the only one present who seemed at all happy to see the visitors.

'Hope your trip was comfortable,' he said. 'I'm sure what you both want more than anything is a good sleep.'

'What did he say?' asked Dubov in Russian.

'He says we probably want to go immediately to bed,' Tatiana translated.

'Definitely,' Dubov said. 'With you.'

'Idiot!'

To Watson she said in English. 'Yes, we're tired, Mr Watson ... but the work, Mr Dubov says, comes first.'

'First thing in the morning, Miss Donskaya. Eight o'clock. I'll be picking you up at your hotel, putting you aboard a plane at Dulles. That's our civilian airport.'

'Thank you. Goodbye until then.'

She and Dubov followed their own embassy man to one of the limousines. Watching her, Watson was suddenly sorry that as Harold Sherwood's aide he would be spending most of his time here in Washington. New York could be so much more interesting.

'Hey, are you coming?' Reynolds called from the other limo.

Adlon's office at the Centre, now Paul Bradley's, had been fashioned to be more than an executive workshop. It was, actually a sales pitch. A large circular room, it had walls of shining aluminium interrupted by shafts of dark weathered wood; the furniture, of the same wood, had been built by one of the country's most prominent designers.

The lighting, emanating from hidden spillways, could be soft and warm or hard and illuminating. Fine contemporary abstracts, borrowed from the National Gallery, graced the wooden wall panels.

Several important Senators had been brought here by Sherwood. The office, they had admitted, was a fitting symbol of the Centre's importance and its role in the country's future adventures in space. They had voted in committee to substantially increase the agency's budget.

The pièce de résistance of the office was a great model of the world, fully ten feet across. In the middle of the room, it at once attracted the attention of visitors, and at this moment, shortly before a Thursday noon, it was being observed with wonder by Dubov and Tatiana. They had just arrived from Washington and had been welcomed by Sherwood, since Bradley was deep in conference with Manheim, collating information gleaned from the observatories that were now reporting regularly.

The globe had been turned to the vast land mass of the U.S.S.R. Projected over this area by a thin metal spike was a replica of Hercules, with its fourteen rockets facing down.

Dubov stared at it, amazed that they had been brought into this office and were being shown the model of the giant missile. The Americans, he immediately understood, were obviously not pulling any punches – all their cards were being placed on the table.

Nevertheless, he felt impelled to say severely, 'I presume this is an accurate replica of your satellite and its alignment? Or is the direction of the rockets just accidental?'

Immediately Tatiana and a young U.S. army specialist began translations into English, their voices running together. The soldier, Sergeant Turner, apparently a bit overwhelmed by the place and the company, looked to General Adlon, who had produced him magically from Washington just a few minutes after the arrival of the Russians.

But Adlon motioned for Turner to start his translation over again. When he was finished, Adlon said without any particular emphasis, 'I am not prepared to volunteer such strategic information.'

Sherwood, at the back of the room, made no effort to interfere, but whispered to Hunter at his side. Hunter left the room immediately.

Tatiana was busy translating Adlon's answer for Dubov. Adlon, his head following first Tatiana, then Dubov, asked Turner, 'Is that what I said?'

'Yes, sir.'

Dubov, ignoring Adlon's openly hostile manner, faced the General with a stubbornness of his own.

'What striking power does it carry?' he demanded.

About to translate this into English. Tatiana paused, allowing Sergeant Turner to handle it. The Sergeant did so, speaking directly to Adlon.

Adlon looked for a moment at Dubov. Then, shoulders squared, clasping his hands behind his back, he swung away from the Russian. 'I would prefer you got that information from Dr Bradley.'

'Fourteen rockets, each carrying a one-hundred-megaton bomb,' a voice said from the doorway.

Bradley stood there, with Hunter behind him. Bradley was slightly out of breath. He wore no tie and a quick shave had left him with a cut on the chin.

Adlon winced at his statement, turning away as if washing his hands of all of them.

Tatiana had translated for Dubov, who now stared at Bradley as if by sheer force of intellect he could plumb what manner of man operated beneath the skin. Then he came forward to meet Bradley, aware that the appraisal was not one-sided.

They met by the globe, shaking hands soberly. There was little warmth in the meeting. And too much was at stake for the usual social amenities, although Bradley made a decent effort. 'Welcome to New York, Dr Dubov. I'm glad you're here.'

Tatiana translated for Dubov, but this time Sergeant Turner translated it back into English for Adlon.

Bradley was frankly confused. 'What the hell is this?' he asked Sherwood.

Sherwood said gravely, 'This is Tatiana Nikolaevna Donskaya, astrophysicist and Dr Dubov's English voice.'

'How do you do?' Tatiana said.

'How do *you* do?' said Bradley.

She wasn't exactly too beautiful, he thought. The mouth was a little wide. The nose had character; one could say with certainty she'd never had a nose job. But all this was quibbling, he knew damn well. She looked great.

'And this is General Adlon's Russian voice, Sergeant Turner,' Sherwood said, trying to keep it all light.

Adlon came out of his sulk long enough to state coldly. 'It's the recognized procedure. To assure that we're being properly interpreted.'

Another series of translations – Tatiana serving Dubov; and, when she was finished, Sergeant Turner retranslating it for Adlon.

Christ! Bradley fumed, looking to Sherwood for relief. But Sherwood, behind Adlon, shrugged helplessly.

Bradley ventured to solve the problem. 'I think we all trust each other here,' he said, avoiding Adlon's glare. 'If we don't there's no point. So – if it's a matter of choosing one or the other – I'll take the pretty one.'

Tatiana tried not to laugh as she translated.

'Did she give it all?' Bradley asked Turner.

'Yes, sir,' the Sergeant said. 'All.' He did not look at Adlon, and he did not look amused.

Dubov had no such inhibitions. But remembering abruptly where he was, he buried his amusement in a hasty frown, pretending to be fascinated with the representation of Russia on the outsize globe.

'Since we're redundant here . . . please excuse me,' Adlon said. He gave Dubov a stiff nod; he ignored Bradley. To Sherwood he said, 'I'd like a word with you.'

The General strode out, followed by Sergeant Turner.

Unused to being commanded, Harold Sherwood lingered for a long moment, his tall, elegant frame hunched as he removed a silver cigar case from his pocket, selected one of his stogies, lighted it carefully, and blew a thoughtful puff at the ceiling. Then, with a charming smile at both Dubov and Tatiana, he strolled out to join Adlon.

Dubov broke the tension, speaking suddenly to Tatiana.

'Dr Dubov says he does not believe General Adlon is pleased to see him,' she translated for Bradley.

'Tell Dr Dubov he does not understand the American military mind. General Adlon is ecstatic to see him.'

She so informed Dubov in Russian.

Dubov grinned at Bradley. He had found out what he needed to know; he could work with this man.

Adlon, smoking a cigarette, was a few paces from the door of his former office; with Sergeant Turner standing near him, when Sherwood emerged from the meeting. The General hesitated, then curtly told Turner to have lunch and report back later.

When the Sergeant was out of earshot, Sherwood spoke. 'General, I know this isn't easy for you.'

'Mr Sherwood,' Adlon said at once, 'last night I felt it my duty to call the Secretary of Defence, who seems more aware of the complexity of this situation than you do —'

'General, please —'

'His orders are, and I quote: "There will be no change in the direction of our rockets until the Russians admit they've got their own rockets, and until they agree to realign them! Is that understood?" '

Sherwood, who had jammed his cigar into his mouth in frustration, moved closer to Adlon, glaring at him.

'Dammit, why don't you xerox a hundred copies of those orders and send them to a hundred guys in Washington, and then take a hundred meetings to discuss them, and then the meteor will have hit — and there won't be any more problem!'

Adlon was a tank, impervious to such small-arms fire; he even managed a lopsided smile. 'Nevertheless, I would appreciate it if you would pass that information on to your friend Dr Bradley!'

Sherwood took a deep breath and tossed his cigar into a nearby wall container. 'I believe Dr Bradley is aware of the problem you discussed with the Secretary. But I'll remind him, General. I promise. In the meantime, why don't you and I walk over to the World Trade Building, take an elevator to the top floor restaurant and buy ourselves a nice, expensive lunch?'

Adlon said, 'Trying to get around me, Sherwood?'

'Jesus, Barry!' Sherwood exploded. 'What are you military bastards made of – just gunpowder?'

Despite himself, Adlon laughed.

Dubov would speak – interminably it appeared to Bradley – then Tatiana would translate, and it would turn out to be a few simple declarative sentences.

But Bradley glimpsed comprehension in Dubov. He wouldn't be surprised if the Russian understood more English than he was letting on. An old diplomatic trick, of course; Sherwood had warned him of it.

They were back at the model now, and Tatiana was translating, 'I don't mean to criticize, but you will find it difficult to hit a meteor with your warheads pointing towards the U.S.S.R.'

'Quite right,' Bradley told Dubov. 'We call ours Hercules. What do you call yours?'

Not batting an eyelid, Tatiana repeated this for Dubov's benefit. The Russian was as unabashed as the woman.

'How can we have a name for something that does not exist?' he asked blandly.

Tatiana translated, giving it exactly Dubov's inflection.

Bradley gave them both a half-smile, then crossed to a large panel opposite his desk. He pressed a button; the panel slid back to reveal an illuminated map the size of the wall. Tiny lights showed all the acknowledged orbiting satellites put up by the major powers – and a few minor powers also. And not all of them acknowledged. In one corner was a brightly glowing red dot.

'Then who in hell put up this thing called Peter the Great,' Bradley demanded, 'with its warheads trained towards the United States?'

Dubov walked slowly over to the wall, taking in the whole spread of the heavens, centring his attention finally on the dot in question.

'This one?'

'That one,' Bradley said firmly.

Dubov looked to Tatiana with a shrug, pleading for help in answering an unanswerable question.

'Chinese perhaps?' he said in heavily accented English. Once before he had used an English word, as if to demonstrate that he was not totally ignorant.

'I didn't know they had anything up there,' Bradley said.

Dubov answered at once, Tatiana translating, with: 'You can never tell with them. They do not say much, do they?'

He met Bradley's look and held it. Bradley caught Tatiana glancing at the Russian. It's a minuet, he thought, but we have to stop dancing, have to stop the music.

He sat down behind the desk and motioned for Dubov and Tatiana to sit also. He tried to put it as reasonably as he could.

'Dr Dubov, we've got a slight problem. If Peter the Great *did* exist, I'd have to know what weapons it would be carrying and its exact position. What we've got up there on the board is only an approximation. Now, for purposes of discussion only . . .'

He paused, giving Tatiana time.

Tatiana turned it into Russian. Dubov listened and reflected. He was on his feet. He walked the length of the room and returned.

'I can see the importance of your questions,' he replied, through Tatiana. '*If* I had been involved in the construction of such an illegal weapon – for the purpose of discussion only – I could theorize answers to those questions.'

The fog was beginning to lift slightly, Bradley realized. He pressed on.

'Then would you be prepared – this is academic, of course – to work out the details with me as to how we would link the satellites?'

Tatiana went to work, and once more Dubov considered at length. There was a lot on his shoulders, and Bradley was aware of the load.

'Academically' – Dubov replied suddenly in English, and as quickly lapsed back into Russian – 'Yes, I would be prepared.'

Bradley understood, without Tatiana. The relief showed on his face as he leaned towards Dubov. There was still a key point to be resolved.

'Before we go any further, what would you have designed your striking power to be?'

Dubov's mind had been made up. Now his answer came quickly; he and Bradley were on the same wavelength, both committed. 'Sixteen rockets. Each carrying the same mega-tonnage as your own.'

'That would have given us – a billion plus. Too bad it's only academic.'

'Yes,' Dubov said.

'I'm starved,' Bradley said. 'Don't know about the two of you, but suppose we all go out and get something to eat?'

16

The group had been in session in Kalintov's dacha outside of Moscow for hours. Marshal Kalintov, hero of the Soviet Union, chief of the army, was flushed with vodka, but his capacity was prodigious. He had, it was said, literally drunk himself to power – by valour in battle when drunk, by ferocity of political action against rivals when drunk. Some of his earthier enemies had secretly pointed out that shit floated to the top also.

Kalintov was, nevertheless, a capable officer, with a realistic appreciation of geopolitics.

Marshal Valnow, airforce chief, was, as always, absolutely sober. Dark, saturnine, he looked more like a priest than a military man, but he was equally as famous as Kalintov, if for different reasons. Valnow was known to be a cool, calculating strategist with a violent hatred for the West – his mother and father, two sisters and a brother, had been shot to death by the White Army during the revolution.

For Stutkin, this was high company indeed. He had had a few vodkas but was careful, realizing this was no time to risk even the slightest loss of equilibrium. For all their apparent affability, these two men would crush him like a gnat should their mood change.

He had detailed the situation of the oncoming meteor, including the moves secretly instituted by the Premier – the sending of the dove, Dubov, to the United States and the hotline exchange between the Premier and the U.S. President.

'You are certain they spoke?' Kalintov asked.

'Absolutely.'

'And the subject of their conversation?' Valnow put in sharply.

'A course of united action,' said Stutkin, although with not quite the same assurance. 'What else could they have been talking about? The Premier picked up that white phone and ordered us all out of the office.'

'He's quite right,' a voice drawled. This was Sergei Ditroff, of the Moscow Institute. 'Major Mackili verified it for me later. It was the President calling from Washington. Mackili, naturally, was also dismissed right after the rest of us.'

Thin as a rail, with a perpetual nagging cough, Ditroff was something of a mystery, being one of the few 'old Bolsheviks' still active. As a young man – he was now in his seventies – he had been a favourite of Stalin. The most powerful man in science in the country, Ditroff was unique, and not only as a survivor. It was conceded, even by men like Kalintov and Valnow, that he knew where all the bones were buried. The better part of valour was to leave him strictly alone.

'What is your analysis of the situation, Sergei?' Kalintov queried.

Ditroff coughed, spit into a dirty handkerchief, and grinned at them with surprisingly white teeth – recently acquired, and of which he was very proud.

'I would say that our very wise Premier will oblige the Americans . . . that Peter the Great will be turned to face the heavens, along with the Americans' orbiting missile launcher.'

'You are in agreement?'

Ditroff shrugged. 'Certain facts are inescapable. The meteor *is* headed for us. This would seem to dictate a cooperative posture, if we, along with the rest of the world, hope to survive.'

Valnow, like a prosecutor, continued to press the old man. 'But suppose this meteor does not hit the earth. Suppose it misses it? And that is a possibility, too, I gather.'

'A possibility, yes,' said Ditroff, coughing again. 'I haven't got the latest calculations. Without them, I'm not only old, I'm blind.'

'But, if it should slide past the earth,' continued Valnow stubbornly, 'and we've released those missiles, we'd be left without our primary defence against our principal adversary —'

'China . . .' mumbled Kalintov. 'Don't forget China.'

'For the moment I exclude China,' said Valnow impatiently. 'As I said, we'd be left without our number one weapon, vulnerable to a devastating, crippling attack!'

Ditroff laughed unexpectedly, like a child. 'You gentlemen are the military geniuses. You did not ask me here for my advice on such an important strategic question. Presumably you wanted my scientific judgement, along with that of my colleague, Stutkin here. I've given it to you.'

He laughed again, coughed, and was silent, looking round the big, comfortable room of the dacha, wondering where the bugging equipment was hidden. This Premier was no Stalin, he thought. The KGB was not absolutely under his control, things were not quite the way they used to be. It was barely possible that the report of his presence here would *not* reach the Premier. Still, as always, he must be cautious.

He need not have worried; Stutkin had jumped in with both feet.

'As Comrade Valnow has said, there is always the chance the meteor will not hit,' Stutkin announced in his high, positive voice. 'If Comrade Ditroff will forgive me, it is not unusual, in the face of possible natural disaster, for panic to develop — even within the scientific community.'

'What do you say to that, Ditroff?' Valnow demanded.

Ditroff wagged his head in what could have been either assent or dissent.

'Comrade Stutkin's thesis has merit,' he said gravely. 'Like the military, the scientific community can sometimes behave like a bunch of scared rabbits.' He finished with a cough-laugh.

'You will excuse me,' he said to the two Marshals. 'I am due back in Moscow for dinner.'

He rose, looking unsteady on his feet – it was part of his act – and glancing around as if for his coat, which, of course, was in the vestibule.

But Valnow would not let him off the hook completely.

'We will have to devise countermeasures to the Premier's move if we cannot get him to cancel it. We will want to meet with the Premier and explain our position. Can we count on you to be at that meeting?'

Ditroff's answer was, 'Where is the toilet?'

Kalintov motioned with a thumb. On his way out, Ditroff turned. 'If the Premier asks me, how could I decline?'

The Premier had it in mind to give a negative response to the request of the two Marshals for a meeting, to shove it over to a colleague on the Politburo – or at least postpone it. He was buried in work and was to leave on a trip to Yugoslavia within the week.

But, in view of the exchange with the American President, and of the unspoken but strong disapproval of some in the Poliburo of his having sent Dubov to America, he decided it would be expedient to give Kalintov and Valnow the opportunity to blow off steam. Valnow, in particular; his hawkish position was well known in the inner circles. Kalintov was considered more or less a moderate. Yes, Valnow would need placating.

The Marshals had also requested that Ditroff be invited, and that the meeting be restricted to the four of them.

The Premier had had few dealings with Ditroff, but didn't dislike him. In fact, the idea of having Ditroff present gave him some comfort. While many considered him senile, and perhaps all the more dangerous in that condition, the Premier knew him to be remarkably keen and, in the final analysis, someone with the best interests of his country at heart.

The meeting was scheduled for the following afternoon. The three men were waiting in his office when the Premier arrived, having put in a long morning with the Yugoslavian experts. His spirits had been somewhat revived by a light lunch and a brief nap.

The two Marshals were in full uniform, all decorations displayed, which was ominous. Ditroff wore his usual shabby grey suit and his shoes were cracked and unshined, as if by his anti-sartorial bias to remind them all of their proletarian beginnings.

The talk was inconsequential at first, the Premier giving them the latest news of the preparations for the Olympic Games, which were fast approaching. Kalintov, who had once been a weight-lifter, medium division, talked of a young soldier named Sokol who was an incredible sprinter, already breaking records for the hundred-metre, a certainty to give the American blacks a run for their money.

Then there was an awkward silence, broken by Valnow, who stated that news had reached the military of the approaching meteor, of Dubov's being dispatched to the United States, and of the possible retargeting of the missiles.

The Premier glanced briefly at Ditroff who, having been in the initial meeting, was probably the source of the leak.

But Ditroff, realizing what must be flashing through the Premier's mind, spoke up immediately. 'I have not communicated with either Marshal Valnow or Kalintov,' he said. 'Nor to any of their associates.' Then he added, through a spasm of coughing, 'I can't, of course, speak for Comrade Stutkin – though his patriotism has never been questioned.'

Kalintov frowned, Valnow's lips compressed, and the Premier wrote the name down on a pad.

'The source of information is unimportant,' he told them. 'But my time is not. Proceed, please.'

Marshal Kalintov set out their position for the Premier. Simply put, it was that they did not trust the Americans. The realignment of the missiles would put them at a huge disadvantage. Better to take their chances with the meteor.

'But if it can be turned away?'

'Let the Americans do it alone,' Kalintov rumbled.

'Possible?' the Premier asked Ditroff.

The old man shook his head. 'Not by our present calculations.'

'As military men, Comrade Premier,' said Kalintov evenly, 'we are used to weighing risks.'

The Premier eyed him coolly. 'You would rather risk the meteor than the Americans?'

'We know what the targeted American missiles can do to us. About the meteor we can't be sure. Even if it struck the Soviet Union, we could survive. This is a big country, thinly populated.'

'You forget that the Soviet people are my responsibility! I am sworn to protect them!'

'We forget nothing,' Valnow put in. He too was on his feet now, and his voice was cold, penetrating. 'We are sworn to protect against the imperialists!'

The Premier realized suddenly what he had on his hands. At best it was an open, full-fledged threat to his authority; at worst, a possible takeover by the military.

He was consumed with a cold fury. He came from around the desk prepared to summon the Kremlin guard, to stamp this thing out before it could go further. But his political instincts, his keen knowledge of where this insane talk could lead, took over. With a great effort he managed to throttle his anger. He was, after all, a political animal. He placed a broad peasant's hand on Valnow's shoulder.

'Comrade,' he pleaded. 'Let us calm down, talk sense . . .' To Ditroff he said, 'Tell them where we'll stand in world opinion if we turn our backs. All our hard-won gains lost. Explain it to them, Ditroff. The world will despise us!'

'Forgive me, gentlemen. I'll be right back,' Ditroff said. Grinning with the new teeth, he added, in an attempt to lighten the atmosphere, 'Sometimes, at my age, pissing is the most important thing.'

And he trotted into the Premier's bathroom.

'World opinion,' Valnow said, 'can go to hell. We'll survive it. And we'll survive the meteor as well.'

The Premier poured himself vodka from a silver decanter. He motioned to the others, and Kalintov needed no second invitation. The military men had the whiphand, no question about that.

'Suppose I agree,' the Premier said. 'What do I tell Washington?'

'Very simple,' said Kalintov. 'Because of violations on the part of the United States, France and England, our military commander in Berlin puts into effect a new blockade of all access roads into the city.' Kalintov grinned. 'Berlin is once again cut off from the outside world. Shall I go on to step two?'

Hardly, the Premier thought bitterly. The Americans would scream bloody murder. The resultant crisis in United States–Russian relations would effectively prevent any possible agreement on a joint nuclear attack on the meteor! And there would be the threat of a third world war – equal to or possibly more lethal than the threat of the meteor.

It was quiet in the room. They could hear Ditroff banging around in the toilet, then the muted sound of the flush. The Marshals watched the Premier, not really hostile, it appeared. Kalintov was already on another vodka. Valnow displayed no particular elation, just a look of quiet satisfaction.

It wasn't a clear-cut victory yet, the Premier decided, though the bastards had him by the throat.

He walked back around the desk and sat down. He felt immensely weary; perhaps he had been too long at this job.

Ditroff emerged, zipping his fly, coughing.

Ditroff never managed to hear anything political, the Premier realized. Such a very clever man.

'I will give it every consideration,' he told the two Marshals. 'I will not act alone.'

They knew that; they'd already prepared their ground with his opponents in the Politburo.

'I will probably call a full meeting tomorrow. I'll expect you to attend.'

They both nodded. There'd be hell to pay, they knew, but they had confidence they would win.

The Premier's aide entered with a note for Ditroff from the Moscow Institute of Science. Urgent.

Ditroff carefully took out his bifocals, read what was written, coughed, spat into his handkerchief, and faced the Premier.

'A splinter of fairly good size, one of those broken off from the asteroid, speeding ahead of it, is about to hit northern Russia. Perhaps by tonight.'

17

The place was called Zaisan, in central Siberia. It was hardly on the maps, and preliminary geological studies, brief surveys by the minerologists and the oil engineers, had indicated little of value in the area. Veins of ore, perhaps, but not worth the money and time that would be required. At a later date, perhaps. For future generations.

And so it remained a desolate, barren region of ridges and crags, swept by piercing arctic winds, its tough vegetation good only for goats – and even the goatherds were migrants. Usually, at this time of year, they were moving miles to the south.

It was night, so the landscape was difficult to make out. But, gradually, certain features could be distinguished, an unusually large ridge here, a bare rock escarpment there. Behind the escarpment, somewhat protected from the winds by its geological placement and by a smaller ridge on the other side of it, was a flat piece of ground about the size of two football fields. In the centre of this protected terrain, a dim light flickered.

The light was coming from a makeshift shelter, a thing constructed of goatskins and wood, in which, like a wounded animal kept barely alive, a fire sputtered.

Around the fire were the goatherd, a young-old man with a brown beard, and his wife, shapeless in her layers of wool robes. Her high cheekbones revealed her Mongolian ancestry. She was not yet seventeen. Huddled close to the fire were their two children, asleep.

The man and the woman were eating from bowls, ignoring the low howl of the wind that periodically swept around the escarpment. Here they were protected; here even the goats were quiet, sleeping outside in the darkness.

They were spooning up a thick mixture of goat's milk and bread from the bowls. As their stomachs began to fill, they became fairly content, the man even making a small joke, something he would tell the other goatherds when they met on the trail south the following day. The woman giggled, and when one of the children stirred, she laid a comforting hand on its brow.

Outside the rough shelter, the wind abated slightly. The bitter cold was constant, but nothing to what it would be in the coming winter months. The sky, unseasonably free of threatening clouds, was a dark canopy speckled with pinpoints of stationary lights.

But one of the pinpoints was moving!

The pinpoint also seemed to be growing larger – although, of course, the goatherd and his family were unaware of this phenomenon.

Now it was no longer a pinpoint, but a glowing thing, changing colour.

Suddenly, it seemed to generate its own light as it shot through the sky, heading as if deliberately aimed towards this cold, bleak land.

The goatherd and his wife stopped eating, aware now of the growing light from outside that had begun to shine through the skins of the shelter.

The woman put down her bowl slowly, looking at her man's face. He, too, had placed his bowl on the ground beside the fire; he was on his feet, muttering under his breath.

The man removed the door flap, allowing the icy wind to sweep into the shelter and waken the children, who instantly began to cry. Outside, the man looked up at the sky.

He could not believe it.

The sky was brightening rapidly, turning white. In his memory, or in the old tales of his people, he could not recall a similar happening. He continued to look, frozen in place, a terrible fear constricting his bowels. Then he called out loudly to his wife.

She joined him instantly, also gazing upward, paralysed by the light which had become almost pure white – glaring, infinitely frightening.

There were no questions to be asked now. The woman understood that at once and dived back into the shelter. The goatherd could hear her talking to the children, piling clothes on them.

'Hurry, hurry!' he called, although he sensed with an awful sureness that time was unimportant, that they were imprisoned in the irrational grasp of nature. The goats came awake and set up a low, shrill clamour that scared him as much as anything else.

The object in the sky could be seen with dreadful clarity now, heated by friction to incandescence as it plummeted into the earth's atmosphere.

The woman bolted out of the shelter, carrying one child, dragging the other by the arm.

Too terrified to open their mouths, the children, along with the man and the woman, gazed at the sky which was now pink. Even as they stared in disbelief, it was turning a bright, incendiary red, until it seemed that a terrible summer had come to this bare winter landscape.

Wild with fear, the man and the woman, dragging the children, ran down the grade of the small plateau as fast as they could, the terrified goats plunging around them.

The fragment was very close now, its light blinding, and the cries of the little family and the piteous bleating of the goats were lost in the rush of air and the swirling, gale-force wind.

With the concussive impact of an atomic explosion, the fragment struck the earth. The man and the woman, the children, and goats, all were swallowed up in the gigantic mouth torn open by the blast. Flame and smoke and billowing clouds of stone-filled earth shot up into the atmosphere.

The escarpment, the plateau, even the mountain above, had disappeared.

The Premier took Ditroff's call shortly before he read the final evening's news briefings.

It was interesting, the Premier mused, that the splinter had landed in Siberia and that the casualties were so light.

Whose case would it support, he wondered – his, or the militarists'?

18

The weather in New York was rotten above and rotten under-foot. It had snowed, wet stuff that at first clung to the side-walks and then slowly became slush.

Grey-black clouds still hung over the city. People hurried along in that head-down, upturned-collar condition that under these circumstances characterizes urban behaviour everywhere.

At the United Nations, the afternoon session of the General Assembly had been called to order after a long lunch break. The President had been conferring right and left without tangible results, and now found himself finally in a position of relative helplessness. It was without enthusiasm that he addressed the international body.

'I give the floor,' he informed the Assembly, 'to the first speaker on my list, the distinguished representative from Canada.'

The Canadian was big and impressive. He took his time about adjusting the microphone in front of him, fixing his seat, waiting for the buzz of conversation to drop to a slight, acceptable hum.

Then he addressed the Assembly.

'We have information,' he said, his honest concern apparent to all, 'that a disturbance of earthquake proportions has occurred somewhere in Siberia. Would the Russian delegate kindly tell us what was the cause of the disturbance?'

Although there was scarcely a delegate who wasn't prepared for the question, an immediate hush fell over the big hall, and all eyes went to where the Russian delegation was sitting.

The chief Russian delegate, Rotinsky, heavily built, with flushed cheeks, sat still, his mouth locked. From behind him, an aide whispered in his ear; Rotinsky's nod was so slight it was barely perceptible. He reached across his desk for a cigarette, which was lighted at once by the aide. Puffing, he leaned back and stared straight ahead. No response to Canada, it was clear, would be forthcoming.

The representative from Zambia, a handsome man, impeccably dressed, had been waving his hand.

The President of the Assembly spoke again. 'The representative from Zambia has asked for the floor.'

The Zambian spoke Oxford English, purring but precise: 'Two days since the President of the United States made his appeal to the Soviet Union, and we still have silence from them. Are they facing imminent catastrophe with equanimity? *They* may be, but the rest of the world is not!'

Rotinsky puffed on moodily. Behind him, his aides sat expressionless with folded arms.

Henderson, of the United States, whispered to no one in particular. 'He's a stubborn mule . . . a goddamn stubborn mule!'

Hands were shooting up all over.

The Assembly President leaned into his microphone. 'The Representative of the United Kingdom has asked for the floor.'

The British delegate, who looked startlingly young, with a brushed guardsman moustache and a splendid drawl, turned towards the Russian on his right. 'You could at least tell us, since it was in your country, whether that disturbance was caused by an earthquake or by a fragment from the meteor.'

There was applause, short, sharp. It cut off instantly as everyone waited for the Russian reply – if, indeed, there was to be any.

Rotinsky sat like a statue in his chair. There was activity behind him. Someone came down the aisle and whispered to one of the aides. The aide rose and approached Rotinsky, spoke into his ear. Rotinsky immediately put out his cigarette and raised him arm.

The silence in the great room became, if possible, more intense.

'The Russian delegate asks for the floor,' said the President.

Rotinsky looked pale, but his voice was firm. 'Mr President, I am authorized to tell you that it *was* a fragment from the meteor. And I request a recess while I consult further with my government.'

The newspapers were already on the street as the delegates emerged into the cold, wet, miserable city. 'ORPHEUS SPLINTER HITS SIBERIA.' 'FIRST STRIKE FROM OUTER SPACE.' 'WHAT NEXT?' 'HERE THEY COME – ARE WE PREPARED?'

The media, it was evident, had not waited for the Russian answer. The media had their own sources.

The newspapers were snapped up. At home, people stayed glued to the television news programmes. Terror was beginning to grip them all.

Working at a computer, feeding into it a mathematical analysis she had just finished, Jan Watkins stripped out the instantaneous, stuttering reaction.

'Good boy,' she said automatically, scanning the readout. She could never understand why she considered computers male; probably she was just another victim of the male superiority syndrome.

Rolf Manheim, at the central console, took the readout from her, ran a pencil down it, and handed it back.

'I could eat you today, liebchen,' he said.

'You're a dirty old man.'

'Ach! If only I were . . . that was my last stage!'

Grinning, Jan headed for the corridor leading to Bradley's

office. She was intercepted by Alan Marshall, who walked beside her.

'Get any sleep last night?' her assistant asked.

'Couple of hours. How about you?'

'Played gin rummy and lost. What's the Russian woman like?'

Jan gave him a shrewd look. 'Very nice. And very bright. And forget it!'

They had come to Bradley's door.

Alan laughed, 'I miss you,' he said.

Jan knocked and went in. One of Bradley's first memos had stated that he would be instantly available to the staff – none of the business of going through secretaries.

Bradley's office hardly looked like anyone's idea of a scientific nerve centre in crisis. It was inordinately quiet. Styrofoam coffee cups littered all available surfaces – the detritus of successive catch-as-catch-can meals on tin trays.

Dubov sat beside Tatiana, who was typing on an IBM machine at a desk against one wall. Bradley, in his shirtsleeves, feet on his desk, was scanning a batch of reports from abroad, sailing them into an out basket as he finished.

Jan, who had waited patiently, watched a sheet flutter past her, then picked up the errant paper from the floor. She placed her own report in front of Bradley.

He put down what he was reading, took a quick glance at what she'd brought him – a projection of possible splinter hits – and realized that he'd asked for the impossible. There were too many variables. Any prediction at this stage was nothing but a computerized guess.

'Thanks, Jan.'

She nodded, turned to go, saw Tatiana's head swing towards her.

They were sharing one of the tiny bedrooms in the dormitory wing of the Centre.

'Hi,' she said to the Russian. 'I've had them strip the army blanket off your bed and put on some proper sheets.'

'That's very kind,' Tatiana said.

'I've also got some decent soap for you, because the stuff they give you here is like washing your hands with a rock.' Jan nodded towards the men. 'Got to watch them, you know.'

'I know,' Tatiana said. 'That's a very pretty scarf.'

'Thanks.' Jan touched her neck. 'Takes a woman to notice.'

In a friendly voice, Bradley said, 'Go on, scram.'

Bradley looked awfully tired, Jan thought. Probably hadn't been to sleep since he'd taken command. One thing she was sure of – she wouldn't want his responsibilities.

She left.

Bradley went over the projection she'd given him for a second time. It came down to the fact that it was simply too damn early to predict anything about the remaining splinters. They could crash to earth anywhere.

The White House would have to be told that. No sense handing out crap to the President simply because he was the man in the Oval Office. As the fragments came close to the earth's atmosphere, they could be plotted, but not before.

Bradley handed Jan's readout to Dubov, who received it with a nod and a cavernous yawn. Christ, do I look as bushed as he does? Bradley wondered.

But Dubov was going over the information, frowning, shaking his head. Then, looking up, he gave Bradley a perplexed, comradely shrug. They were in this together . . . in this frustrating hell together.

Dubov walked back to Tatiana, handed her the readout, and told her to recheck the computations. This was something he and Bradley had agreed on hours ago – all readouts were to be put into the grinder at least twice. Any error at this point, no matter how slight, was unacceptable.

Tatiana went to work. Other than being a bit pale, Bradley thought, she looked wonderful. Fresh as a daisy. Makeup? Or did women have more stamina than men?

Dubov had walked over to the large contemporary leather chair in the corner of the office and fell on it like a big tree crashing in the forest. Even as they watched, he fell asleep.

Tatiana pivoted from her desk. 'Jet lag,' she said to Bradley. 'And he had little rest before we flew here.'

'How about you?' Bradley asked.

'I'm all right.'

She began to feed Jan's data into the computer.

Bradley walked to a table with a large coffee jug and a platter of sandwiches on it. Making up a small tray with a sandwich and a cup of fresh coffee, he carried it over to Tatiana.

She paid no attention to him for a moment, intent on the computer until the readout appeared. She scanned it carefully, comparing it to Jan's, then glanced up at Bradley.

'It checks.'

She gestured towards Dubov. 'Shall I wake him?'

'Let him sleep; he's earned it. It doesn't tell us much anyway.'

'No.'

Glancing at the food on the tray, she gave him a weary smile. 'Sorry, too tired.'

'You don't look it.'

Tatiana was leaning back drowsily in her chair. She closed her eyes briefly, opened them again. 'You could do with some sleep, too.'

Bradley took the chair alongside hers. There wasn't much coquetry in her, he decided. And there was infinite pride in the way she carried herself, in the respect she gave and obviously demanded. He wondered about her relationship with Dubov – it could hardly be just a platonic arrangement between colleagues. They both gave off sparks.

He motioned towards Dubov. 'How long have you been with him?'

'I've known him for ten years, but I have only worked with him for five.'

Bradley sipped the coffee he'd brought for her.

'You're nervous,' she said. 'You're waiting for the next splinter.'

'No,' he said without hesitation. 'I'm waiting for my employers to give me permission to retarget the rockets.'

Tatiana said nothing.

He gave her a curious look. 'What about Dubov?'

'Perhaps he's waiting for the same thing.'

They smiled together.

'Why did you choose astrophysics?' Bradley asked.

'It chose me,' she said.

Sighing she reached for one of the sandwiches on the tray. She bit into it with zest, he observed, like a man, unashamed to discover she was hungry after all.

'I was a telephone operator,' Tatiana went on. 'It was at the Centre for Control of Flight in Kalimin, near Moscow. I was bilingual, because even when I was a child, my mother kept giving me books in English and saying, "One day you will be grateful for this." And I suppose I am. Would you like a sandwich?'

'Thanks, no.'

She finished the sandwich and seemed to be thinking back – reliving moments of pain, he sensed. She sighed again.

'What's this got to do with astrophysics?' he prompted.

'About ten years ago, some British scientists came to talk to some of our people. Alexei – Dubov – needed someone to translate for him. And they asked me.'

She crossed her legs. How lovely she was, Bradley thought.

'Dr Dubov's English voice,' he said.

'Yes.' She smiled. 'When I finished, he asked me to stay on with him as interpreter and secretary.'

She gestured towards the slumbering Dubov, who obliged by moving restlessly but not waking.

'He was married to Eva then, his first wife.'

'How many has he had?'

'He's on his fourth,' Tatiana said. She gave Dubov a dis-approving but maternal look. 'He's sleeping alone now, but it's not often.'

Bradley poured himself more coffee. 'You know,' he said, 'it's nice talking to you.'

'Thank you,' she answered, puzzled. 'But we've been talking for almost two days —'

'No,' Bradley said. 'I've been talking to you-Dubov. This is you-you. Very attractive.'

'Oh. Thank you again.'

He was pleased to note that she had coloured slightly, turn-ing involuntarily to her work. He wasn't about to permit that.

'Then?' he asked.

'Then?'

'Astrophysics,' he reminded her.

'Ah. I found out that space fascinated me. Alexei saw this, and he encouraged me. He arranged for me to go to school. And when I came back, I was his second assistant.'

Dubov's reading glasses had fallen out of his extended hand. Tatiana picked them up and placed them gently on his chest.

'What wife was he on then?' Bradley asked.

'His third, Elena.'

'Beautiful?'

'All of them were beautiful,' she said reproachfully. 'He has exquisite taste.'

'I'm sure.'

'Elena danced in the ballet, very graceful, very good, but he once said, "In most people, the brain occupies all of the cranium. In her cranium, there is still room for a football field!" After a while I became his first assistant.'

Dubov had begun to snore, sputtering like a small motor.

'Promotion for brilliance?' Bradley suggested.

Tatiana chose not to answer that. She refused to allow him to be cute with her, he realized. Now she was having other thoughts, going back.

'I met my husband then.'

He said, startled, 'Your husband . . .?' He gave her his full attention.

'He was an astronaut,' Tatiana said. She spoke without emotion, as if she were reciting a memorized series of facts. 'Three years . . . then he went on an exploratory flight . . . and he didn't come back.'

'Sorry.'

'Yes. I was sorry. He was a nice man.'

Tatiana's eyes, dusty grey, lifted to Bradley's face as if she wanted to add something. Then she seemed to reconsider, as if what she wanted to say to him, or to ask him, would have to come later.

She picked up her story. 'So I went back with – with Sleeping Beauty there. He was just leaving the ballet dancer.'

'And now? I mean, with you?' he asked lightly, trying to make it sound unimportant.

'Nothing serious. Not really.'

Abruptly, from the Centre's intercom, a sharp voice broke in.

'Rolf Manheim speaking. Will Dr Bradley and Dr Dubov join me at the main console, please. Immediately!'

Manheim clicked off.

Dubov had awakened and was staring groggily at the ceiling.

'Come on, Dubov,' Bradley said. 'Trouble.'

Tatiana translated.

At Manheim's console, the readouts were as plain as the nose on your face, Bradley realized. So did everyone else clustered around the big computer – Manheim, Dubov, Tatiana, Jan Watkins, Bill Hunter, Alan Marshal. Meteors were coming in over central Europe – small splinters, actually, from the asteroid.

Bradley asked Hunter to get Sir Michael Hughes at Jodrell Bank.

The group crossed to Hunter's territory, where they were joined by an anxious General Adlon.

'Just heard,' the General said. 'What's up?'

Bradley told him. Adlon made no comment.

Hunter, who had been manipulating the keys of his console like a virtuoso, nodded to Bradley. 'Here he is, sir.'

And there was Sir Michael coming into focus, calm, unruffled. 'You have something, Paul?' he asked.

Bradley gave him a rundown.

'Hold everything,' Sir Michael said.

He spoke to his staff offscreen, and there was a snap to his tone. Sir Michael, Bradley noted, was not always the relaxed Britisher.

Now he was reporting back. 'Righto, Paul. We show them coming in, too. Perhaps we were a bit tardy interpreting the readout.'

There was a flurry of talk behind camera on Sir Michael's end, and someone handed him a teletype sheet.

'Another moment, Paul,' Sir Michael said. 'We've got something on the wire.' He read the message. 'Ah . . . Yes. The Observatory in Frascati is reporting a cluster – I repeat – a cluster big enough to track, coming in over Italy, south of Pisa.'

He scanned the paper again.

'They're approaching at close to fifteen thousand metres per second. Impact time, seventy-four minutes.'

Someone near him, on the other side of the ocean, made a comment.

'Make that seventy-three now!' Sir Michael said.

'Jesus,' Jan Watkins muttered.

Rolf Manheim cursed under his breath, then stomped off back to his own domain.

Manheim's action more or less summarized the feelings all around. There just wasn't much anyone could do except pray, and this was not exactly a praying group.

Dubov had been speaking quietly with Tatiana.

'He would like to call Moscow,' Tatiana said.

Bradley nodded and led the way back to his office. The atmosphere in the Centre had become suddenly constrained, hushed – as if they were trapped together in a submarine.

19

It was Friday evening, dusk. The sky above Pisa had become blood red, silhouetting the famous Leaning Tower. Below the Tower, the crowd was still increasing; it numbered thousands now – perhaps out of religious fervour, or some belief in the sacredness of the Tower, people gathered beneath it. Thousands of others were scattering into the countryside, even though they had been warned that it would be impossible to outrun the oncoming meteors.

The roads in all directions were already clogged. The airport was empty of planes, all private and commercial aircraft having already departed. In the mobbed terminal, announcements were being made periodically, begging the public to leave – no additional commercial planes would risk the flight into Pisa.

All of Italy, all of Europe, had been alerted to the situation, with radio and television stations broadcasting bulletins by the minute. But there was little hard news to report other than the countdown – and even that was imprecise; the cluster was approaching the southwestern portion of Italy at a speed exceeding the transmission capabilities of the media.

The menacing cluster, coming closer and closer, small but potentially lethal splinters, was being tracked by observatories in every corner of the globe.

In Rome, St Peter's Square was packed with people. A sudden crowd-roar split the cool evening air – a small, familiar figure clothed in white had appeared on the distant balcony.

The Pope allowed the shouting to continue for what seemed an interminable period, as if the terror and fear below him might lessen by virtue of the verbal release. At last, slowly, he raised his hand. Like a record grinding to a halt in the middle of a composition, the noise squawked to silence.

The Pope spoke. He urged the people assembled below him to remain calm; he reminded them of His compassion. They were in His hands as always, and must accept His acts with open and willing hearts. Perhaps, the Pope said, in time this thing which was about to happen would be understandable to them, like the Great Flood and other calamities which had befallen mankind. For now, they were to be of good heart; they were to pray . . . and ask for His infinite mercy.

The Pope made the sign of the cross and blessed them, and then was gone. The people below crossed themselves and reluctantly, like children being dismissed by an all-knowing father, began to disperse.

In Pisa, the deep red in the heavens was changing colour, growing lighter, pinker. A soft moan went up from the crowd at the Tower as this change became apparent – any alteration of the external characteristics of the phenomenon added to the fear.

A television mobile unit had pushed its way into the centre of the crowd, the technicians hurrying to set up their camera. The presence of the crew with all its paraphernalia was accepted without comment, such being the average citizen's concept of the importance of the media. Only a few hooted at the cameramen, asking if *they* expected to survive. But no one paid attention to the loudmouths. Of course this had to be recorded – this was an event!

The announcer, a handsome fellow in beautifully cut jeans, began to speak excitedly into a microphone, describing what was happening.

The pinpoints of light in the sky were beginning to define

themselves. Dozens of them, flowing with the seconds, were changing colour, deep pink to orange to yellow to white, as the temperature and apparent size of the fragments increased with the rush into the earth's atmosphere.

The people became more restless, some crying out, some trying to butt their way out of the crowd. Families clung together, praying. Over the entire area below the Tower, a kind of melancholy singing murmur could be heard.

Many people had transistor radios turned up as high as they would go, the hysterical voice of the announcer informing them of what they could see quite well for themselves. But still they relied upon the radio voice. In a curious way, it made them spectators, not participants.

And then, suddenly, a strange thing became apparent: the dazzling lights over the city were beginning to fade in intensity.

The announcer, noting this, became incoherent, not knowing how to interpret the change.

But the reason for the dramatic shift in light was soon clear to every knowledgeable observer. Rushing into the earth's atmosphere, the cluster of small meteor fragments had begun to burn up, as giant fireworks propelled into the night sky will explode into brilliant colour before expiring meekly and losing themselves in the darkness.

The night sky over Pisa slowly became darker and darker, and the people below began to realize that the danger had passed.

'Saved!' the TV announcer was now yelling ecstatically into the microphone. 'We are saved!'

It was over.

Someone tried, unsuccessfully, to organize a mass prayer. But individuals here and there were kneeling as the crowd, as if dispersing from a sports rally, began to flow away from the Tower.

All over the city, people appeared from fields, from church

cellars, from doorways – mothers and fathers and children – all quiet, subdued, filling the streets as they made their way home. Their radios could still be heard, but only as a faint whisper in the blessedly black night.

'They've burnt up! The cluster's evaporated!' Manheim was shouting.

They were receiving reports from England, from all the countries that had a night sky.

Manheim's excitement spread to the entire Centre. 'Frascati tells us not one of them has made it through. Everything's back to normal,' he informed the assembly.

Bill Hunter got Sir Michael for them on the screen.

'Good news, Sir Michael,' Bradley told him.

Sir Michael wasn't particularly euphoric. 'That was an easy one, old boy. May not be so lucky next time.' He glanced at his watch. 'I'm dashing home for a quick bite. Cheerio!'

General Barry Adlon was very much present at the Centre. Arms akimbo, he faced Bradley. 'Well, what about this one?'

Shrugging, Bradley said, 'You heard Sir Michael. We were lucky.'

'Why not wrong? Why can't we assume the emergency is over? This particular one, and the emergency in general? It's a pity the world has been sent into such a state of unnecessary panic. There's your threat, Dr Bradley – a fireworks display!'

Bradley, aware that the entire Centre was privy to this dialogue, tried to keep his temper.

'What about the meteor in Siberia?' he asked.

Adlon didn't even bother looking at Dubov. 'My opinion,' he said flatly, 'is that that explosion was caused by an underground nuclear test, in contradiction of —'

He didn't get any further. Sherwood had come in. He had been yo-yoing back and forth between Washington and New York; he was tired; the Italian scare hadn't helped any; he was in no mood for Adlon's shenanigans.

'General!' Sherwood shouted.

Adlon faced around, momentarily disconcerted.

Bradley spoke to Sherwood. 'Tell this asshole general once and for all that the main chunk will not burn. It's too damn big!'

What Sherwood told the General was not quite the same thing: 'We've got enough to deal with here, General Adlon ... we don't need any additional aggravation.'

Two dozen technicians had witnessed the confrontation, as had just about every man and woman in the vicinity of the central console.

Stunned, embarrassed, Adlon, struggled for a semblance of control.

'Not one promise of a calamity has come true, and as far as I'm concerned, not a single one will. When good sense is restored, when the President has returned control of the Centre to me, I shall return to the Centre!'

Eyes turned away in embarrassment. Trembling with rage, the General managed to contain himself. He shouldered his way through the onlookers, his footsteps heavy on the white rubberized floor, as he headed for the stairs to the elevators.

They waited in dead silence until he had climbed the steps to the lobby and was gone from their sight. Then quietly, not commenting, they started for their posts.

But now a new voice was heard. It was Dubov's. He had launched into a furious speech in Russian. Directed at Tatiana, it splattered everywhere, like an engine throwing oil. Dubov went on and on, never dropping the level of anger, and it seemed as if he had ammunition enough for the rest of the day. Then, as abruptly as he had begun, he stopped.

Everyone gaped at him in complete silence.

Tatiana broke in. 'Dr Dubov says he is very upset.'

The understatement brought a wave of laughter in which, curiously, Dubov joined. But now he turned to Sherwood.

'I would like to make a telephone call to Russian Embassy in

Washington,' he said in reasonably good English.

Sherwood didn't seem in the least surprised, either by the request or the language in which it had been couched.

'Follow me,' he said.

They moved off together, Dubov continuing in Russian his polemic against all the fools of the world, particularly those who dwelt in Washington and in Moscow.

20

The village, Zukstein, a picture-book group of chalets, nestled in a cleft in the snow-mantled mountains of the Austrian Alps.

It was Saturday, less than a day after the scare at Pisa.

Schussing down towards Zukstein, Sally Rivers, of Denver, Colorado, considered herself, for the moment at least, completely fulfilled. The snow was powdery, perfect. The run was not too crowded, and she was attaining that feathery inner feeling of perfect balance, of flying, that had made skiing her passion.

Though quite aware of the picture she presented – blonde hair trailing from a green helmet – Sally was not unduly vain; she concentrated on what she had to do to make the run memorable.

Hurtling past slower skiers, conceding nothing to the steepness of the grade, she held herself in complete command, though remaining conscious of the intense blue of the sky above her and of the postcard village below.

At last, out of breath, every bit of her body alive with the excitement and danger of it, she came to a stop, spraying snow, jamming her poles into the ground.

Some beginners, negotiating a tiny hill to her right, had stopped to stare. Their bronzed young instructor waved. Sally waved back. He had tried to date her the night before.

She removed her sunglasses and wiped a sheen of thin snow from her face. Then, taking up her poles, she commenced the gradual descent to the village.

It was Sally's first trip to this part of the world, and she was not disappointed. It was just as she'd dreamed it would be – the village, the skiing, even the crowd of young, friendly people. Employed in a Denver travel agency, she knew the ropes and had made damn sure that Zukstein was as represented, a popular but not too expensive resort with better-than-average ski facilities. This was her third day, and Zukstein rated an 'A.'

Skis over her shoulder, she walked along the snow-covered street, her boots crunching. Immediately ahead was her hotel and the outdoor terrace on which a dozen late-morning skiers were still breakfasting. Parking her skis, Sally climbed the short flight of steps and looked for a table.

Close by was a table taken by two young women and two men. She would have passed them by, but one of the women – Hilda something-or-other – called out, 'Sally. Come here. Eat with us.'

The young men had risen politely, careful with their women present not to be too openly admiring. They had both danced with Sally at the hotel disco, though neither had made any significant progress with her.

Hilda – pugnosed, small, nice-looking – said, 'The hotel has been trying to find you. There was a telephone call from Fenver.'

'Denver,' corrected her boyfriend. 'They left a number to call back.'

'Oh,' said Sally.

She had come here to this shallow little valley, to this absolutely foreign place, to make a decision between two men, each of whom wanted to marry her. She was startled to realize that she had to force herself now to remember either one of them! What she really hated at the moment was the idea of leaving this sun-drenched terrace.

'Keep him waiting,' said the boy called Helmut. 'Isn't that the first rule? Have a croissant first.'

Sally laughed. 'I am starved.' She pointed to the mountain,

to the ski run cutting down it like a shining scimitar. 'It's smooth as silk up there.'

'We'll show you one that's not so smooth, but much more interesting,' Helmut said.

The waiter approached. 'Hi,' Sally said. 'Bacon and eggs, and some sausages too. And loads of toast!'

'*Ja*, Fräulein.'

From above the terrace there came a roaring sound. Instantly the men and the girls were all on their feet, looking instinctively up towards the mountain.

The thing had come hurtling out of the sky without warning, its speed greater than that of sound. It was a black misshapen rock the size of a large house – one of the smaller splinters broken off the asteroid. Heated by friction with earth's atmosphere to an incredible temperature, it glowed even in the sunlight as it plummeted down into the side of the mountain, which was dotted here and there with immobilized skiers. Plunging through the whiteness of the snow, the huge rock found the earth beneath and dug its own deep crater from which, in a sudden explosion of enormous force, there burst into the air a geyser of earth and rock and snow.

With the ferocious impact, the mountain itself seemed to shudder. Then the falling debris loosened in several places the deep snow-pack that covered the mountainside. A great wall of snow began to slide down towards the town.

Cries could be heard all around the hotel's terrace, people calling and running from the chalets.

'Avalanche!' Helmut shouted.

Sally and Hilda and the others, impelled by excitement as well as fear, ran from the terrace to the street to get a better look.

On the mountainside trees were torn from their roots. Great crevasses suddenly appeared, and brightly clad figures, desperately trying to evade the opening craters, found themselves sucked down to their deaths.

To the side of the run itself, only moments before so pristine in the bright morning sun, the ski lift shot into the air, dismembered like a child's toy, and was engulfed by the rushing oceans of snow.

There was a continual cracking, rending sound; it seemed that the mountain itself, grinding up ice and snow, was moving onto the village of Zukstein, which lay supine before it. The tide of ice rolled down with steadily increasing speed, gathering size.

The villagers scurried in and out the matchbox houses. Since Zukstein was built in a cul-de-sac in the mountains, they could not escape to the south; there the mountains heaved steeply up again, sealing the town.

Sally Rivers had run with Hilda and Helmut, but now, as she began to realize the extent of the disaster, she lost them in the confusion. She stood helplessly in the main street. People too panic-stricken to shout were skittering past her in all directions, some towards the slide, others away from it. Many of them were driven by absurd notions of where they might find safety – behind a stone wall, inside a stoutly built house, in the shelter of a row of pine trees.

Her heart pounding, aware that the onrushing sea of snow and ice was close now, Sally began to run in the direction she imagined Hilda and Helmut had taken, back towards the hotel.

Behind her the flowing death slid inexorably over all obstacles, cracking the outlying houses, devouring them, covering them with rocks and trees and snow.

The hotel was midway in the village, slightly below the level of the main street, and even as Sally reached it, the avalanche, cascading down the other side of the ridge, reached it too.

Sally saw Hilda try to bolt away, only to be trapped and smothered in the pitiless wave of snow, and then she saw that she, too, was directly in its path. She screamed.

Helmut and the hotel proprietor and another woman were backed up against the wall of the terrace – it seemed foolish to

Sally, but then came the horrible understanding. There simply was no other place to go!

And even as she hesitated, knowing that she was going to die, trying to find a prayer and managing only a 'Dear God!', the avalanche reached her, burying her under the terrible whiteness. Then it swept onto the hotel terrace, over the tables, over everything. It covered Helmut and the proprietor and the others there, silencing their shouts, and continued its progress over the village until, except for here and there a chimney top, a tree top, there was absolutely nothing to be seen. Only an empty snowfield in a notch in the mountains ...

The sun shone down benignly; the sky was a poem, cloudless, cobalt blue.

Only the silence told something. It was absolute.

2I

In Bradley's office at the Centre, they were watching an ordinary television screen – Bradley, Dubov, Tatiana. Sherwood was in Washington.

'. . . five hours since the splinter struck in the Alps,' the announcer was saying, 'and the enormity of what has happened has only begun to sink in.'

They had no comment. The Zukstein splinter had been an aberration, coming in the daylight hours on the sunlit portion of the globe, untrackable by night spotters elsewhere. When the splinter did finally show on their instruments, it was too late; the little Alpine village was doomed.

On the screen now they could see Zukstein, or the grave of Zukstein. Helicopters, stretcher bearers with no one to carry – the task of digging out the dead would probably take months.

'Never been anything like this,' the announcer said. 'There have been avalanches, and storms which have destroyed whole villages, but nothing on the scale of what happened here.'

They could see for themselves. Salvage operations would be incredibly difficult; the approach roads were nonexistent.

'A mess,' Dubov muttered in English. Without excuse, he was now allowing himself the pleasure of speaking directly to Bradley. To hell with the KGB and the instructions they had given him in Moscow!

'For twenty miles around, not a tree stands,' the man on the screen continued. 'Not a tree stands, not a house can be seen.'

Bradley snapped off the set.

In Zukstein, the horror could not be turned off. A few giant army helicopters had been obtained and were beginning to lift bulldozers into the area. The television people who had skied into the buried town were already photographing the frantic efforts to dig below the snow blanket – perhaps a few souls were alive, not crushed, breathing. In the strong basements of houses? Who could know where?

The Austrian President promised the nation that the rescue operations would go on until it was certain any person alive was found. He stood in the snow in front of the cameras, stricken, haggard.

'Help is coming from every corner of the world,' he promised Austria. 'And we are grateful for it . . . helicopters, ambulances, supplies.' The President paused; his voice shook. 'But whatever help comes, this tiny village of ours is forever gone.'

He strode away from the cameras, shaking off a batch of newly arrived reporters, most of them poorly dressed for the cold wind now sweeping the shallow mountain valley. The Austrian President was bitter. Why hadn't they been fore-warned?

On one of the principal American networks, a famous announcer was posing a critical query: 'In the minds of people all over the world, the question is – "Where next?" And what about the big one closing in on the Earth at thirty thousand miles an hour?'

There was no one who could answer the query.

The Premier had requested that Kalintov and Valnow and Ditroff be in his office before the larger meeting with the Polit-buro began.

But first he had some business with a group of industrial commissars – a pet project, a great new hydroelectric facility on the drawing boards designed for the Far East, over the roof of China. In fact, he was in a mood to let the high and mighty military men cool their heels. He was almost an hour behind schedule when he called for the two Marshals and Ditroff to be ushered in.

The Marshals were confident, even a trifle arrogant, as they entered. Not Ditroff, of course, who walked with his usual head-down shuffle.

The Premier asked if any of them had heard the latest international news.

They had not, said Kalintov, mystified. And with something of rebellion in his voice, he pointed out that they had come early, had been waiting in the anteroom for almost ninety minutes.

Valnow was aware of other currents, more important than Kalintov's pique. 'What has happened?' he asked.

'A town has disappeared,' said the Premier. 'A village in the mountains of Austria, struck by another meteor fragment.'

The Marshals were silent momentarily, then Valnow said contemptuously, 'An Austrian village? Surely of no concern to us.'

The Premier toyed calmly with his jewelled letter opener. Unlike the two soldiers, Ditroff was aware of the danger in this demeanour. The Premier was not, on balance, a subtle man; this low-key approach was out of character for him.

'Of *great* concern to us,' the Premier said, not raising his voice. 'Churchill once spoke of not being willing to preside over the dissolution of the British Empire. I, Comrades, am not willing to stand by and see my country, leader of the Socialist world, stupidly dissipate the store of goodwill and the political advantages we have fought so hard to obtain since the Revolution. I will not, in short, for a momentary strategic gain, sign away the future.'

It was all said in an unstressed monotone, with absolutely no melodramatics.

The Premier placed the letter opener back on the desk top.

He smiled, first at Valnow, then at Kalintov.

Ditroff was on his feet. 'I am entirely and wholeheartedly in agreement,' he said to the Premier. 'But the news of the Austrian fragment demands my immediate presence back at the Institute.' He coughed, not getting his handkerchief out in time, as he waited for the Premier's reply.

Keeping his eyes on the two Marshals, the Premier waved at Ditroff, who scuttled out like a fast-moving crab.

'It is hardly a momentary gain,' sputtered Valnow. 'You are placing the Soviet Union in mortal danger.'

'Then it's on my head,' the Premier replied coldly. 'I have already sent instructions to Rotinsky at the United Nations. I've informed my colleagues in the Politburo. That will be all, Comrades.'

In the United Nations Assembly, the delegate from the U.S.S.R., Rotinsky, had gained the floor. The galleries were full, with not an empty seat, nor was there a whisper anywhere in the huge hall.

Rotinsky read from a prepared statement, enunciating slowly, giving the interpreters plenty of time to translate his words.

'The U.S.S.R. is not unaware of the seriousness of the situation,' Rotinsky said. 'We therefore have decided to add to the power of Hercules the considerable power that we ourselves possess – a satellite developed *before* the United States developed theirs, and which we designed and constructed for the purpose of defence against possible disasters such as the one facing us now – *and for that purpose only*.'

There was a slight movement among his listeners. Without reacting, Rotinsky allowed the Assembly to settle back before resuming his speech.

'Our scientists are therefore at this minute advising their American counterparts, and have now been granted permission to add the striking power of our satellite to that of the American one. To this Assembly we say: "As we have done before, and will continue to do, the U.S.S.R. will always support any exercise the primary object of which is to benefit mankind." '

The Assembly broke into sustained applause.

The world press, although reporting in full the U.N. proceedings, was now clearly making an effort to minimize the potential danger of the oncoming fragments. Some attributed this new attitude to governmental pressures, some to an awakened sense of responsibility on the part of the press itself.

Strangely enough, the public, all over the world, did not panic – a phenomenon that the World Psychological Institute found of prime interest. Basically, it seemed, people were unwilling to believe that it could happen to them.

22

Most of the personnel were in the mess. Minimum crews remained at their stations in case anything untoward should occur, or any of the observatories report in.

In Bradley's office, a victory of sorts was being celebrated. Dubov had insisted on it, having obtained by his own secret resources (obviously the Russian Embassy) several bottles of a clear liquid which he swore was the finest and most potent vodka on the market.

'To Peter the Great,' Bradley said.

They clinked together – Bradley, Dubov, Sherwood and Tatiana – and drank chug-a-lug, down in one gulp. Dubov refilled the four small, long-necked glasses he'd brought with the vodka.

Sherwood raised his glass. 'To our Russian scissors, for the cutting of the Red tape.'

They clinked solemnly with Sherwood, with each other, downing the fiery stuff in the Russian manner. Tatiana, Bradley noticed, asked for no quarter and showed no effects.

She caught his quizzical look and grinned. 'That's all,' she whispered. 'Two. Sometimes three. Then I fall on my face.'

Dubov had no intention of stopping. His glass full again, he rattled off something to Tatiana. As if programmed, she turned to translate.

'No,' Bradley said to Dubov. 'In English.'

'In English, yes,' Sherwood said.

Dubov stared at the two Americans, shrugged at Tatiana,

then drew himself up, looking grave. 'Where there is a way,' he said, the words accented but clear, 'there is a will.'

'Or words to that effect,' Bradley said.

Then they drank to it, Tatiana abstaining.

The satellite, its Russian markings fresh and new-looking in the purity of space, began to revolve, turning its array of nuclear weapons slowly up and away from the Earth, aiming them into the outer darkness at a still-invisible target.

This jagged target was continuing on its deadly course. Within days it would crash into Earth with an impact impossible to predict or imagine.

Unless it could somehow be diverted.

Another satellite, American markings visible on its silvery body, began also to turn its armament away from the land mass in the semidarkness below, positioning its sixteen great rockets to meet the oncoming meteor.

At the Centre, Rolf Manheim was at the controls. A row of privileged spectators, among them Bradley and Sherwood, were ranged behind him. Manheim was watching the indicators on his monitors. He tapped out a set of signals and waited until the indicators gave him a satisfactory response. Only then did he turn to Bradley and the others.

'Attitude correction complete. Situation nominal,' he informed them.

Hours before he had cornered Bradley alone in his office. He had to speak to him at once, Manheim had said.

'Shoot,' Bradley told him.

He liked Manheim. Occasionally, when he rolled up his sleeves, you could see the concentration camp number tattooed on his arm, but he obviously wasn't embittered, wasn't tight and brooding. On the contrary, he radiated confidence and kindness and good cheer. Kept the whole Centre loose, Sherwood had remarked once.

'Maybe you should use someone else,' Manheim said.

Bradley studied the bearded, battered face.

'Not up to it?'

Manheim growled, 'Oh, I'm up to it. Hell, I could hit that meteor with a .22.'

'Then what?'

'Suppose those rockets . . . suppose there's a misfiring . . . satellite thrown off course . . . God knows what! We *could* miss. . . . They'd blame it on the goddamn Jew!'

'If there's a misfire,' Bradley said, 'there may not be people around to blame it on anyone. I've got absolute confidence in you. But if you want me to replace you, if you're afraid of it . . .'

Manheim laughed suddenly, showing the solid gold tooth.

'Afraid? No! It's just that – forget it! I'm a stupid fool. Buck fever, maybe. Don't worry, I won't miss. I'll knock it out of the ballpark!'

He was gone from Bradley's office, not without a bit of a swagger. Moments later, at the command console, the very picture of a sedate, disciplined scientist, Manheim faced them unsmiling.

'Both satellites aligned?' Sherwood asked.

'Both.'

Sherwood nodded. 'So we wait until we see the whites of its eyes.'

'O-seven hundred, Sunday,' Bradley said.

The dinner, the President's foreign advisors had been told, could not be called off. The French Chief of State would be leaving the following day, and there were important trade matters unresolved as well as questions concerning NATO. Even though France was not a member nation, its cooperation, particularly with the nuclear missiles being repositioned, was more important than ever.

Finally, the Frenchman would certainly expect to be briefed concerning protective measures being taken with regard to the onrushing meteor – France could be the target as well as any other place in the world.

The President grew restive during the lengthy state banquet. To amuse himself, he identified the wine being served as a rare Burgundy. His French guest took a sip and nodded, as though recognizing an old friend.

Delighted with his own little prank, the President grinned. 'Actually,' he said, 'that bottle came from Sonoma County, north of San Francisco!'

The Frenchman showed not the slightest surprise as he took another sip. 'You had me completely fooled, Mr President,' he said with only the faintest of smiles. 'I was positive it was Napa Valley.'

A pretty bright guy, the President conceded, and he discovered during the evening that his guest had valuable notions on many perplexing international situations.

The Frenchman and his entourage went bananas, as the President's grandson would have said, about the entertainment the staff had cooked up – a jazz group from New Orleans, and a younger group that played the cool jazz the President himself fancied. And then the great American artist, Ella Fitzgerald.

Later, in the small, intimate room off the Oval Office, a different set of men awaited the President – Abe Holland, the Secretary of Defence; Harold Sherwood, head of NASA; and a third man, General Henry Pierson, Marine Corps, Retired, now head of the Defence Intelligence Agency. It was at Pierson's request, the President had been given to understand, that the meeting had been called.

Pierson, square-faced, square of figure, dove right in. 'We don't like the trade-off, Mr President.'

'You're referring, I gather, to Hercules?'

'Exactly. Turning those missiles around. Suppose we fire ours and they withhold theirs?'

'General. I don't think you understand. The meteor can pulverize all of us!'

'Matter of chance, Mr President. By our calculations, with their greater land mass and a spread-out population, the Soviets might be able to survive even a direct blow from the damned thing! Now, sir, stay with me another moment . . . Imagine, just for the hell of it, that at the crucial moment they don't fire their little babies: *they turn those missiles against us again.* Got us by the balls! Right, Mr President?'

The President looked to his Defence Secretary, who seemed to be fascinated by a painting on the opposite wall that depicted a railroad train traversing an arid stretch of desert and being attacked by hard-riding Apaches.

Sherwood, the NASA man, had crossed his long legs and seemed preoccupied with his fingernails.

'All right,' the President said. 'Considering the pros and cons according to your thinking, General, what do you suggest?'

Pierson smiled. It was more of a rictus, a humourless grin.

'Well, we've worked over a number of ideas, sir. Some flew and some, I don't mind telling you, we shot down ourselves. "Keep it simple," I told my boys, and I believe they have. What we do is this, sir: we move all our long-range bombers to advance SAC bases overseas, the planes to be nuclear-armed and kept on twenty-four-hour alert.'

The General paused; then the smile came again. 'And here's the kicker, Mr President. We make no attempt at concealment. Matter of fact, we leak it to the world press – let the Russians know in advance that one tricky move and they get our whole damn nuclear arsenal up their ass!'

My God! the President thought. He said to Pierson, 'Have you discussed this with the Chiefs of Staff?'

Silence.

Pierson looked to Abe Holland, nominally his boss.

Holland spoke, his voice dry. 'It's been discussed,' he said. 'There seems to be a divergence of opinion. What it comes down to is this: exactly what are we looking at in this meteor? I'm talking now in absolutes.'

The President turned to Sherwood. 'I thought that was settled. The ball's back in your court.'

Sherwood was on his feet, glowering at Pierson.

'For chrissake – total world disaster!'

The President said, 'Thank you. General Pierson, I'm rejecting your plan in toto. I'm sure your agency feels it's been acting with the best interests of the country in mind. I'm grateful to your people. Inform them of that.'

Pierson hung there a moment, breathing hard, not quite believing the President was dismissing him.

'Yes, sir,' he muttered.

And, as quickly as possible, he left.

The President found a decanter of whisky on a side shelf, a tray and glasses on another. He poured himself a generous shot. 'Help yourselves, boys.'

They did so.

Strangely enough, the President seemed relaxed. He laughed ruefully, as a man will after avoiding a nasty accident.

'Not exactly what you'd label a dove, is he?' the President said, half to himself. Then he turned to Sherwood. 'Tell us, please,' he asked, 'as briefly as you can, the procedure from here on in.'

'Yes, sir,' Sherwood said. 'The Russian and American satellites are orbiting the earth twenty-two thousand, five hundred miles out in space. Since they're in different orbits, in order to make the rockets arrive on target together they'll have to be fired at different times – Peter the Great first, Hercules forty minutes later. Two hours after that, they'll explode simultaneously at a designated distance from the meteor, knocking it out of its orbit and sending it away from Earth.'

The President pondered this. Sherwood sensed that he was picturing those two satellites up there, those two ponderous yet strangely beautiful machines of destruction in the pure, deep midnight blue of outer space.

'Can anything go wrong?' the President asked.

'Once the rockets are launched, they switch to their own decision-making systems. If these systems perform properly, everything's fine. If they malfunction —'

The thought brought a chill. The President poured himself a small shot, added water, and sipped slowly. 'What are the odds?'

Sherwood didn't want to hazard a guess. The President was being unfair. But the man *was* entitled to the truth.

'We've never done this before, Mr President. There's no saying.'

'If you fail —'

There was a long silence.

'The meteor will hit two hours later,' Sherwood said.

The President absorbed this, shook his head as if to make the awful problem go away, and got up from the desk.

Abe Holland asked, 'When will you know the area?'

'If you're asking will there be time to put out a warning and evacuate,' Sherwood told him, 'the answer is – no.'

The President was roaming the small room, examining the pictures on the wall as if he'd never seen them before. Then suddenly he turned back to Sherwood, his voice resonant and strong.

'Hit it, Mr Sherwood,' the President said. 'Get rid of it.'

23

Tatiana had spent the early hours of the afternoon with Jan Watkins at the big New York department stores – Bloomingdales, Bergdorf Goodman, Saks Fifth Avenue. Fresh from the Centre, she marvelled at the deliberate unconcern of the shoppers. Were they consciously pushing aside their fears?

Struck by the abundance of merchandise on the attractively arranged counters, Tatiana was ready for more, but Jan was not only due back at the Centre, she was absolutely exhausted. From here on Tatiana would have to carry on by herself.

She did so – very capably, she thought. She had tea at Schraffts, one pastry, then another. Gluttony, she thought, thy name is Tatiana.

Looking at her watch, she discovered that she still had almost two hours before the deadline Dubov had set for her return. Her only problem was her purchases, two gaily decorated, heavily loaded shopping bags.

She would not let them impede her! She was drunk with her day; the city was dazzling in the bright, brittle cloak of late fall.

A taxi brought her to the Metropolitan Museum of Art. Here she checked in the two bags and roamed the floors. She thought the paintings good, but inferior to those at the Hermitage in Leningrad. However, she was not in the mood to be critical. The plunge into the world of art, a relief from the stern mathematics of space, was exhilarating.

She explored the Egyptian Section downstairs. Inside the

beige stone walls of a reconstruction of a pharaoh's tomb, a man tapped her on the shoulder.

She turned without concern, thinking the touch had been accidental. The man, very average-looking – flat nose, heavy eyebrows, a touch seedy – spoke to her in Russian.

'Tatiana Nicolaevna, is that not so?'

It took her a long moment to reply. 'Yes.'

The man said, 'Will you please come with me.' It was more of a command than a request.

'Who are you?'

He looked upset. 'It makes little difference . . .'

But seeing the stubborn set to her face, he reached into his pocket and brought out a worn wallet. From it, he extracted a card. It was expensively embossed, and he handed it to her with a flourish. 'Ivan Prokomi,' the card read. 'Office of Stephan Luchec.'

Tatiana was well aware who Stephan Luchec was. He was the Russian Ambassador to the United Nations, its representative on the Security Council.

She held her ground, however, her eye on the wallet.

With reluctance, as if his pride were at issue, the man pulled out a dog-eared ID. It identified him surely – there was a small photo – as the Ivan Prokomi mentioned so splendidly on the embossed card.

Annoyed by this mysterious interruption of her wonderful afternoon, Tatiana looked the ID over from all sides, openly comparing the photo with the man before her. She returned the card, nodding.

'But why should I go with you?' she asked.

'He wants to see you.'

'About what?'

'He will tell you, I'm sure.'

'And where can Stephan Luchec be found?'

'At this hour, where he lives. In his apartment. Where else?' the man said, exasperated. 'Please don't make trouble.'

In the black limousine, clutching her precious purchases, Tatiana asked, 'You have been following me all afternoon?'

Ivan Prokomi gave her a disdainful look. 'I am not a policeman, young lady, or a spy. I am a diplomat. You were watched by others. When it was determined you would be at the museum for a period of time, I was informed.'

She sat back, smiling at him nicely. 'I see,' she said.

Stephan Luchec's apartment overlooking the East River would have done justice to a well-heeled capitalist statesman. The decor was rigidly contemporary, almost bare. A large brass samovar sat incongruously on the sculptured glass coffee table.

Stephan Luchec did not have a contemporary look. He was tall and slender, with a full head of silvery hair and a warm smile. He wore a green velvet smoking jacket.

Luchec greeted Tatiana by kissing her hand. Then, with a dip of his shoulders, he dismissed Ivan Prokomi, who immediately disappeared.

As if to reassure Tatiana that her presence here was perfectly proper, Madame Luchec appeared promptly. As handsome as her husband and equally agreeable, she welcomed Tatiana, expressing her unhappiness that Tatiana had to visit New York under such unfortunate circumstances, without a real opportunity to enjoy it. Not Paris, of course, but a vital, exciting city! After it was over, this dreadful meteor affair, perhaps there'd be time for them to get to know each other; she would love to be Tatiana's guide. Sandwiches and sweets were there on the side table, if Tatiana would do the honours with the tea.

Madame Luchec left.

Her husband, standing at the great windows, the New York skyline like a stagedrop behind him, said, 'Of course you want to know why I sent for you ...'

Why I was almost forcibly brought here, Tatiana wanted to add.

'Yes,' she said simply.

Obedient to Madame Luchec's wishes, she drew water from

the samovar for their tea and handed the Ambassador a cup and saucer, then politely drew a cup for herself.

As it happened, she knew something about Luchec. A woman friend of hers, in the Foreign Office, had characterized him as one of Russia's most valuable men – a dagger in a silken sheath, a man who could pronounce a death sentence with a charming smile, a superb practitioner of the diplomatic arts. And a womanizer.

Tatiana wasn't concerned with that aspect of him now. Nor, she sensed, was he. Yet he could not resist the obligatory compliment.

'You have surprised me, Tatiana Nicolaevna. One doesn't expect our country to raise, much less export, such lovely scientists.'

'Only capable scientists count, Comrade Ambassador,' she said dryly. 'Not their sex.'

'I'm sure you qualify.'

She shrugged without expression, sipping her tea.

He put down his cup and strode restlessly back and forth in the long room.

'Most delicate, this assignment they've handed me,' he said. 'I hardly know where to begin.'

'At the beginning.'

'No,' he said. 'That would take the rest of the afternoon. Let me put it bluntly: it naturally concerns your mission here with Dubov. That mission is very troubling to certain highly placed officials.'

Tatiana was not knowledgeable about the behind-the-scenes manoeuvring in Moscow, but Dubov had filled her in on a few elements of it – Stutkin's role, and Ditroff's.

'I was under the impression the Premier fully approved,' she said, hoping to forestall any involvement.

'Naturally. No choice. That doesn't mean he's happy with it. And there are changes one can always make in the field . . .'

Luchec's voice drifted off. The easy smile had vanished. He

walked around to a small chair directly facing her.

'Changes that would eventually please the Premier as well as . . . other leaders. You begin to understand what I'm saying?'

'What changes?' she asked directly.

'In the firing of the Peter the Great rockets,' he replied. 'It has been suggested to the Premier that this would leave us absolutely naked. At least, that is the fear. Do you comprehend?'

She'd be damned if she'd admit to anything. 'I'm merely Comrade Dubov's assistant.'

'A brilliant man, Dubov, but in some ways a naive one. And stubborn in the bargain. Unable to understand the pressure points, the necessities of power politics.'

'Comrade Ambassador, I would appreciate it if you would be more specific. Surely you can't be asking that our country withhold our rockets? The meteor would —'

'The meteor must be diverted,' he interjected firmly. 'No question. All that is being asked is that Dubov insist that the Americans fire their rockets *first*. To be *followed* by ours!'

Luchec smiled persuasively, leaned forward, and patted her knee. 'You now perceive that such a situation would afford us the protection we seek. It would totally prohibit them from allowing us to spend our ammunition, while they are free to shoot us down, so to speak, at will.'

Appalled, Tatiana did her best to make him understand the scientific ramifications involved. It was vital that the rockets arrive on target simultaneously. The Soviet and American satellites were travelling in different orbits, at different distances. If the order of firing were reversed, it would take hours – a full day perhaps – before the satellites were in position to synchronize the release of their rockets on their new schedule. That would be taking too much of a risk. The meteor might hit before then; the firing might come too late.

Luchec shrugged. He held his long graceful hands palms up, in a gesture of controlled helplessness.

'I am not a scientist,' he said. 'I know nothing of such things. But the people who have contacted me – people at the highest level – have the best scientific advice available to them.'

His eyes were suddenly cold. 'However, I do understand the world of politics. And this is something that has to be done.'

Tatiana was silent for a long moment, sitting very erect in her chair. Then she said, 'Even if such a change in plans was feasible, how would I get Dubov to agree to it? Obviously your people haven't been able to convince him.'

Luchec rose, emitting a small chuckle. 'I don't think a lovely woman like you has to be told how to get a man to do something . . . anything.'

His back was towards her. He was looking to the west, across the spiky skyline, towards the late afternoon sun.

Tatiana said, 'And if I don't wish to, or can't – then what? I'm sent home in disgrace? Harm comes to my son, my mother?'

This brought him swiftly around.

'Please, my dear! I'm not threatening you. Be at peace on that score. But unfortunately, I'm not the only one involved. I tell you that in all frankness. This matter deeply concerns – as I've said – others far more powerful than myself. If Dubov ignores their request, it is possible he will suffer.'

'How?'

Again Luchec's hands were raised expressively.

'An accident of some sort. A bad accident. It is possible. These people would probably consider it a supreme act of patriotism. Now you understand my unhappiness?'

He didn't look unhappy, she decided.

'Yes,' she said coldly, and rose to go.

Dubov had been napping in his tiny cubicle at the Centre. He came gradually awake, raising his head like a seal at the water's edge.

'So Luchec predicted I would end up with my blood in the gutter?' he barked.

'Unless you arranged it their way, yes,' Tatiana told him. She had given him only a bare outline of the conversation with Luchec.

Dubov slid from his bunk to the floor and pulled on a sweater. 'It can get cold here.' He gestured towards the door, raising his voice. 'Let's go to the canteen. I could do with something to eat.'

In the canteen, almost empty at this hour, they sat at the end of a long table. Dubov requested the mess orderly to bring them coffee cakes and tea.

'We can talk more safely here,' he said. 'Now tell me everything Luchec said.'

Tatiana told him, word for word.

'The bastards,' Dubov said when she was finished.

'What are you going to do?'

'What do you suggest?'

'I don't know. Perhaps . . . Is there *any* way to have the American rockets fire first?'

'Tatiana! You know as well as I do that's absolutely impossible. The orbits wouldn't be in phase until sometime tomorrow. We can't take a chance like that!'

She brooded, not touching her food. She hadn't eaten at Luchec's, either.

'I don't want you killed.'

'The rockets will be fired tomorrow. If I stay here, don't show myself, how are they going to get me? And after the firing, to kill me would serve no purpose.'

'Vengeance perhaps.'

Dubov shook his head, brushing this aside. 'Do you really believe what they say? That all they want is for the others to fire first?'

'What else?'

'My dear, we have cold-war maniacs just as the Americans do. Once the American rockets were off, they would point Peter the Great back towards the United States again, you understand? They would be willing to gamble on absorbing the shock of the meteor in order to have America by the you-know-what.'

'By the privates,' said Tatiana delicately, biting into a cake.

'Your logic is improving – and so is your English,' Dubov said with a grin. 'Now we forget it – the whole conversation with Luchec. You never saw Luchec, understand? We have only one concern, one enemy – that goddamn meteor!'

Earlier the same cold, windy, sunny November afternoon.

The Los Angeles Rams were in town and Yankee Stadium was filled to capacity. Todd, the Jet quarterback, had just thrown a third-down sideline pass, bringing the crowd to its feet.

'Wow!' Jamie Bradley shouted. 'See that, Dad?'

Nancy Bradley, who was six, was loving every minute of the afternoon – not the game, at which she hardly bothered to look, but the people, the banners, the pom-pom girls, the band. And of course the eating! Nancy was now on her second hot dog and Coke, and already she was thinking about a chocolate bar.

Huddling against her Daddy, feeling his arm around her, she licked at the mustard on her cheek and said, 'I'm still hungry.'

Paul Bradley knew he shouldn't. Helen had been very specific about that. Nancy was already too pudgy. 'Don't let the kids eat all that junk,' she'd warned.

'What do you want, Nancy?' he asked.

'Chocolate ice-cream stick.'

'Here,' he shouted to a vendor.

'I love you,' Nancy said.

'Love you, bunny . . .'

If things go wrong, God knows where it will strike, how much of the earth it will take, how many will survive.

The fear was in him like a knife. Not for himself alone. For them, these two bright-faced, affectionate kids.

Helen had taken Jamie to see Olsen early that morning.

Bradley had called Olsen before he'd picked up the kids for the game.

Olsen didn't sound concerned. 'An accumulation of serous fluid in the middle ear,' he said, 'based on a strong allergic component, blocking off the Eustachian tube. It's not too uncommon, Dr Bradley. We could go into a lot of allergy tests, although at your boy's age anti-allergic medication should do the trick. And of course, to relieve the immediate symptoms, a myringotomy.'

'Myringotomy?'

'Puncturing the eardrum. Really a conservative procedure . . . drain out the pus. I've made an appointment with your wife for next week. One night in the hospital, at most two, should handle it.'

'Thank you.'

'Don't mention it. And don't worry, please. How's our sick meteor coming?'

'Not too good,' Bradley had answered, relieved at the diagnosis. 'So what we're really trying to perform here is a meteorotomy.'

'Ha, ha,' laughed Dr Olsen.

The Jets rammed one through. Touchdown! Jamie screamed with delight. The Jets were only three touchdowns behind now, with a whole final quarter to play.

Bradley grinned at him. 'That's the spirit. Never say die!'

'What?' Jamie asked, giving his father his attention for the moment.

'We can still win it!' Bradley yelled into his son's ear. And he was on his feet, shouting, 'Go, team!'

'Go, team!' shouted Jamie. 'Go! Go! Go!'

The house was gracious but unpretentious, a split-level with pale blue siding and white trim. Bradley could never drive up to it these days without a twinge.

He parked at the kerb and turned to the children beside him, bending down to kiss Nancy.

Tears gathered in her eyes and she clung to him. 'I don't want to go, Daddy. I want to stay with you!'

It might be histrionics – she had always been a little ham – but her tears, as usual, moved him. 'I know, honey,' he said.

He went around to the other side of the car, opened the door, and pulled the two reluctant bodies to him in a big hug.

'Okay . . . inside! Both of you!'

They started across the lawn, stopping to wave to him. He had all he could do to keep from following. He waved back, watching them disappear between house and garage. They would emerge in a moment, he knew, at the kitchen door where Helen would be waiting – so that she and her former husband wouldn't have to meet.

The familiar depressed feeling returned, and it was like being immersed in an all-embracing fog. No openings anywhere. Should he go in? Helen and he could discuss Jamie and the morning visit to the doctor . . .

Bradley's eyes fell on the mailbox. One of the numerals was lying on its side. He straightened the errant number, pressed it into place, then went back to the car and got in.

There was no going back.

It was just before six when Bradley reached his apartment. It seemed terribly empty suddenly, only half furnished; he could use more chairs, lamps, a couple of good pictures for the walls. He was glad he had been able to keep the stereo; Helen had never cared much for music.

What he needed now was something big and meaty, something to fill in all the cracks, the emptiness. Brahms. Brahms Second.

He found it, put it on the turntable. It was very helpful. Listening to it, a drink in hand, did indeed help. He walked to the window and looked at the park below. Lamp lights gave the park a satisfying definition, while the lights of the cars winding through it supplied an inner rhythm, not unlike the symphony he was hearing.

It occurred to him that he was in need of more than music, more than the electrifying view. He went to the phone and dialled the Communications Centre.

It was quite a while before Tatiana came to the phone.

'Hello,' she said. 'I'm sorry, Mr Bradley. I thought tonight we were not working. I thought we were free —'

'We are.'

'Then why have you —'

He was not comfortable in such situations. He said abruptly, 'I thought we might have dinner together.'

There was a long silence.

I've put my foot in it, he thought. Christ, maybe in Russia there are conventions about things like this. Necessary to have tea first, or meet the mother . . .

'Have you lots of money?' Tatiana said. 'I'm hungry as a wolf.'

He laughed with relief. 'Pick you up at the Centre at eight . . . if you can hold out that long?'

'Yes,' she said. 'But Mr Bradley . . .'

'Paul.'

'Paul. I have no pretty clothes. You'll be ashamed of me.'

'That'll be the day,' he told her.

She didn't quite understand, but gathered it was a compliment. She'd be ready, she said.

He showered and shaved and – there was time to kill – tried to neaten up the apartment a little bit. Hell, they *might* come back here – he could dream.

The bookshelves, in particular, were a mess. In trying to bring a little order to the stacks, he came across a thick, unbound report. Project Icarus, the overleaf said.

Bradley sat down with Project Icarus in hand, feeling a little guilty about it. This was a duplicate of the report Sherwood had given him in Houston, to be reread at his leisure. He hadn't been able to get to it in Washington, and so far he had had no time here in New York.

Bullshit. He hadn't touched it because emotionally he wanted no part of it.

The Icarus Project had been set up at the Massachusetts Institute of Technology in 1967 to study the possibility of a large meteor – or portion of one, as in the present case – somehow being shoved out of orbit and heading for Earth. Evidence of such accidents in the past clearly existed, notably the Great Meteor Crater in Arizona.

The M.I.T. project envisioned an asteroid on collision-course with the earth, and proposed to study possible counter-measures, as well as potential damage to areas of dense population. In the course of this study, the idea of using nuclear detonation to divert an approaching asteroid was born.

As NASA's up-and-coming young man, Bradley was chosen to attend the extended series of seminars. Sherwood, his mentor, his uncle-in-law, told Helen and Bradley, 'Live well, eat well, enjoy yourselves. Can't think of a more worthy way to spend the government's money. You've earned it, Paul. Besides, gives me a chance to come up and visit you . . . see some friends at Cambridge.'

They'd taken a small apartment near the University and settled in. Helen, in her third month, hardly looked pregnant. They walked all over town; they bedded constantly; they made no pretence of trying to save a dime. It was really a honeymoon, since Bradley had been involved in a space launch when they'd been married six months earlier.

He was finding out about his wife. She was quite a wonderful person, sexually a bit on the shy side until aroused, but then enjoying it as much as he.

It was in other areas that differences popped up. Minor ones, to be sure, but indicative of future trouble. Helen, born and raised in Texas, often became uptight about the little things – money, manners, clothes – and even about some of the bigger ones, such as politics, education, the kind of friends they would choose.

And so he had resolved early on in Boston that spring (although it wasn't until later that he was conscious of actually having decided anything) that their marriage would have to be compartmentalized – on one side *his* work, *his* friends, *his* notions about God; on the other side *her* ideas about everything, *her* lifestyle.

They were happy. They went to theatres, to concerts, to small, highly touted ethnic restaurants. They dined formally at some of the best old Brahman homes, courtesy of Harold Sherwood. They drove to the Cape. They sailed, a first for Bradley, who found himself hooked and began to take sailing lessons. He had a rare talent, the doughty old Cape-Codder told him. Had there been a sailing master in his family?

It was during this season at M.I.T. that Bradley plunged into theoretical aspects of astronomy he hadn't found time for previously. The top people there – Eckstein, Thomas, Harris – on the other hand, found Bradley's practical knowledge of space, based on his NASA experience, invaluable.

The graduate students participating in Project Icarus found it valid as well as scientifically stimulating. No one expected an Icarus situation to happen – not in the foreseeable future, at any rate – but it *could* occur if the dice came up snake-eyes for the planet Earth. That was the bizarre and provocative fact.

There was endless speculation about ways of diverting this imagined monster asteroid from smacking head-on into Paris or Rome or London or Chicago or Tokyo. Or landing in the middle of the Pacific Ocean, for that matter, creating colossal tidal waves, destroying the ecological balance of the world.

Of the many solutions proposed and debated, all but two

were discarded. The first was the use of a powerful rocket to intercept the asteroid and nudge it from its course. The other was simply to blast it to rubble with a nuclear warhead. Either method would utilize multiple-booster vehicles and existing space technology. Gemini and Apollo hardware could also be used if a manned system was judged likely to enhance the probability of success.

Out of the endless bull sessions, some extending far into the night (Helen tried to be good about it when he dragged himself back to her, never quite understanding why he couldn't have called it a day at a reasonable hour), had come the germ of Hercules. Not right away. Not until Bradley had returned to Houston, had gotten Sherwood interested and made him aware of the very real potential danger, after which Sherwood had finally talked the then-President into doing something about it ...

Leafing through the pages of the report, Bradley suddenly looked at his watch. My God, it was almost eight! He thought of calling Tatiana to say he'd be late, decided against it, grabbed a tie and jacket, and ran for the elevator.

The taxi driver performed miracles in the Saturday night traffic. She was waiting in the upper lobby, just outside the security area, looking chic in the black leather coat she had worn the night she had flown in.

He caught her looking into his face as he arrived, not for approval – she was secure about that – but as if searching for other signs. Later, much later, she told him why: she knew he was terribly tired and had been concerned about his son's medical problem.

Greeting her, Bradley was cheerful, contrite about being late, and openly admiring. Did she know how beautiful she looked?

'No, please,' she begged. 'We are colleagues going out for something to eat, correct? Bradley, you must tell me something.'

'What?'

'How many hours have you slept in the last forty-eight?'

'Oh, plenty,' he lied. 'For God's sake, I'm all slept out.'

She was wearing Jan's scarf. 'Haven't I seen that somewhere before?' he asked, not liking the turn the conversation had taken.

'I can't think where. Bradley, perhaps —'

'Paul.'

'Paul, perhaps it's better if we just have a bite in the canteen here and you go home to bed. What about it?'

He took her arm, guiding her firmly towards the elevator. He'd kept the cab waiting.

Outside, the city seemed deserted, asleep. But across the street, down a ways, a man paused to light a cigarette before climbing into a yellow coupe.

Bradley gave the taxi driver the address of a small place, La Pomme Rouge, in the East Sixties, and he and Tatiana settled back in the cab.

After a few moments, he noticed idly that the yellow coupe had made a U-turn and was behind them. If Tatiana was aware of the coupe she made no comment.

Big City blues, Bradley thought — the constant fear of thieves, muggers, cutthroats.

They proceeded uptown, and soon the coupe was no longer visible. He relaxed. Tatiana, too, seemed at ease. Beginning to lose their strangeness with each other, they drifted into shop talk about the meteor.

'Tomorrow night,' Tatiana predicted. 'Do you think later, Paul?'

'No,' he said. 'By tomorrow night we should know if the firing's done the job.' Left unsaid was what would happen if the meteor could not be diverted.

But he couldn't hide his tension. He was trying to inhabit two worlds simultaneously — the everyday one, and the one up there in space. Mentally, Tatiana knew, he was continually tracking the oncoming asteroid.

She touched his hand lightly. 'Paul, let's forget about the Centre. Let's talk about something different. How many children do you have?'

He looked at her, and was unable to conceal the surprise in his voice.

'Two,' he said. 'A boy and a girl. How do you know I'm married?'

'I asked Mr Sherwood about you. He told me you and your wife are separated.'

'Divorced,' Bradley said. Then, with a wry smile: 'I'll have to have a talk with Sherwood.'

'I hope you don't mind that I asked him.'

An American woman, Bradley realized, would hardly be this direct. He questioned it a moment, then decided he rather liked it.

'I would have asked Dubov about you if I had known he spoke English,' he said.

'It was a stupid thing, the hiding of it,' Tatiana said, shrugging.

'It's okay,' he said. 'Part of the game. What else would you like to know?'

The wide grey eyes met his; there was amusement in her voice. 'It would be too rude to ask.'

La Pomme Rouge was crowded; though Bradley had made a reservation, they had to wait standing up at the bar. They had plenty of company. If it wasn't like this, Bradley told Tatiana, New Yorkers would consider the restaurant underpatronized and unchic, to be avoided.

Their table, when they were finally awarded one, was squeezed into a corner, but it had the virtue of privacy.

Bradley ordered appetizers and the house speciality, a veal dish, with a good red wine. Then, with what remained of their drinks, they settled back to contemplate each other.

'The maitre d' knows you,' Tatiana commented. 'You bring all your . . . your women here?'

'All my women . . . yes. Let's see, I was here two months ago.'

'You move around very much . . . you lecture?'

'Between University assignments,' he said. 'To keep on the run.'

The sommelier arrived with the bottle of wine. He opened it carefully and poured a bit for Bradley's approval.

Tatiana was still sipping her drink.

'Actually,' Bradley told her, 'I'm a very lonely man.'

She laughed. 'Even in America, the men sing the same old song. Perhaps it is a mother you need.'

'No, not a mother,' he said positively.

His eye was caught by the crowd still waiting for tables. A man had come in alone, a large man with dark bushy hair. He was giving his topcoat to the hatcheck girl. He was speaking to the maitre d'. Now he was sauntering to the bar.

There was something familiar about him, Bradley thought. Of course! It was the man he had seen briefly outside the Communications Centre, lighting a cigarette – the man in the yellow coupe.

Tatiana was asking, 'Why are you and your wife divorced?'

He might have resented the question if anyone else had asked it. He could not have said why he didn't resent it at all from her.

'It just happened. Came to a halt. No specific reason. No more talks together, no more interests together. It's what we here in America call incompatability.'

'We call it the same in Russia,' she said dryly.

'And probably in Swahililand as well,' he said.

Smiling she began the first course, a quiche. The man was still at the bar, Bradley saw. Was he looking their way? Bradley could hardly be sure; it was probably his imagination.

'Ever thought of living anywhere but Russia?' he asked.

Tatiana's plate was clean. She thought for a moment. 'Not often.'

'But sometimes.'

'Yes ... sometimes.'

He had the curious feeling that talk was really unnecessary. It was as if each of them could anticipate what the other would say.

'You'd like it here, you know,' he said. 'We've got power shortages, a terrific crime rate, strikes, droughts, unemployment and race riots. Never a dull moment.'

The maitre d' was escorting the man to a small table not far away, but still out of Tatiana's line of vision.

'Your country sounds lovely,' she said, smiling. 'Do you think my little boy would like it?'

'Aren't you full of surprises?' he said, returning the smile.

The waiter brought their dinners; the sommelier filled their wine glasses. They raised the glasses, clinked silently, drank, and began to eat.

The man from the yellow coupe, Bradley saw was ordering his dinner.

For the life of him, he couldn't have repeated to anyone what Tatiana and he talked about during the rest of their meal. It had all seemed to come very easily, naturally. Her boy was five, living with her mother in Moscow. Bright. Looked like his father, but she adored him. She too was lonely. Not many men. None serious, as she'd indicated before at the Centre.

Like Bradley, her thoughts were mainly focused on the meteor – on the safety of the people she loved, her fear for them.

Tatiana and he were front-line soldiers, Bradley realized. In the trenches, figuratively speaking, but not concerned with their own survival. They would do what they were trained to do, push the necessary buttons. But they were more aware of the consequences of failure – that was the difference.

When they left La Pomme Rouge, Bradley noticed that the yellow coupe man was just paying his bill, but he didn't give it another thought; not only was his belly full, but he was more relaxed than he'd been in days.

Tatiana and he swung off west towards Fifth Avenue hand in hand, hardly aware that they had taken a great intimate leap together. It had just happened.

They window-shopped, they had a brandy at the Plaza. Then, without discussing it, they took a taxi to Bradley's apartment.

They were too engrossed with each other, with minor but pleasant revelations, with the magic of finger-touching, to notice that they hadn't been alone for even one minute. The man from the yellow coupe had followed them every step of the way.

After watching them disappear into Bradley's building, the man drove to Columbus Avenue, where he found a drugstore with a public telephone. Here he dialled a number written on a card in his pocket.

At the Communications Centre, Dubov, a half-finished bottle of vodka before him, was watching an American crime show — a very exciting and well-made affair, he thought — when his extension phone rang.

Cursing, still watching the TV screen, he picked up the receiver, remembering in time to answer in Russian.

'Dubov here.'

'Comrade Dubov, this is Kroldi. I regret to disturb you, but my orders are to report any deviations in relations with foreign colleagues.'

'Deviations? What in hell are you talking about?'

'Your assistant, Tatiana Nikolaevna Donskaya.'

'Tatiana? What about her?'

'She is . . . she has spent the evening with the American scientist Bradley. I have been observing them for the last three hours. Their behaviour, Comrade Dubov, is hardly profes-

156

sional. You might even say their conduct is . . . intimate! At this very minute she is with him in his apartment!'

On the TV screen, the bald-headed detective who looked so Slavic was sticking his gun into the gangster's stomach and smiling his big-toothed smile, releasing the girl and her family from the gangster's evil clutches. The young brother who was on dope and had been the gangster's fall-guy was now told by the bald one to 'get the hell home and from now on stick to lollipops.' What was lollipops? Dubov decided he must remember to ask Bradley in the morning.

'You understand the danger, Comrade? In his apartment! A woman of such high security risk!'

Dubov tilted the vodka bottle, eyes still on the TV, an expression of impatient disdain on his face. You had to lie to these KGB men. It was the only thing they understood.

'Thank you, Comrade Kroldi. What you don't know is that she is there under my orders. To lure him sexually and discover his American secrets. That clear, Kroldi? Excellent. Goodnight.'

Kroldi got off the phone. Dubov took another slug of the vodka, placed what remained of the bottle on the bureau top, turned off the TV set, and stretched out on the bed.

Lucky Bradley! Hell, lucky both of them! He fell into a comalike sleep.

24

Her leg was over his when he awoke. He was trying gently to ease it away so that he could go and get breakfast started, and then she was awake, whispering, 'No, no . . .' And then they were together again as they had been at intervals all through the night. They could not, it seemed, get enough of each other.

This time, with the dawn light teasing the corners of the bedroom curtains, she was completely visible to him – slender, boyish, with lovely, small, upthrust breasts.

'American men like big bosoms, no?' she had asked him during the night. 'I am too small, nothing.'

She was far from 'nothing,' he assured her. Of course, a series of breast exercises might be advisable if she really intended to have many American lovers. This brought on a flurry of bites. She had very sharp teeth, he learned, but the biting inevitably turned into something else, something quite the opposite.

The insane part of it was that when at last they lay side by side in complete contentment, the clock showing only 6:00 A.M., he didn't feel tired at all. It was as if he had slept soundly the night through.

The telephone had no sense of propriety. It jangled now close to Tatiana's head. Reaching over her, Bradley picked up the receiver.

It was Hunter from the Communications Centre. 'Sorry to do this to you, Dr Bradley. God knows you need the sleep, but it's something of an emergency.'

'It's okay, Hunter. Shoot.'

'We've got Dr Yamashiro on the monitor from Hong Kong.'

'What's happening?' Bradley asked.

Tatiana, beautiful in the daylight, was scrambling out of the bed, hunting for his robe. Finding it, half lost in it, she moved back to the edge of the bed, watching Bradley's face.

At the Centre, Hunter held the phone in front of the monitor so that Bradley could hear. 'Here it is, sir,' he said.

Dr Yamashiro, a heavy-set fellow with luxuriant grey-white hair, was on the screen, speaking with great urgency.

'We have just received a transmission from a TWA passenger jet over the Pacific. There was an explosion somewhere at sea, heavy enough to knock out two engines!'

Yamashiro consulted a note just handed to him, then continued. 'The plane's heading for Taiwan to make an emergency landing.'

He cleared his throat. Across all the miles, his worry was apparent, his words heavy with it.

'They have reported a tidal wave,' he said. 'One hundred feet high. It is heading directly for Hong Kong.'

Hunter repeated this last message to Bradley, word for word.

'Thank you,' Bradley said. 'We'll . . . I'll be in as soon as possible. Tell Dr Dubov.'

He put down the receiver and looked at Tatiana.

'Splinter number four,' he said.

'Where?' she asked.

'Somewhere out in the Pacific.'

Its height did not seem so great from a distance, and if one was viewing it from far away there was nothing to measure it against, no scale of reference.

Up close, the wave was another thing. It was immense, of incredible energy, towering over the sea as if to suck the entire ocean up with it on its journey.

It was, as Dr Yamashiro had indicated, not too far away from Hong Kong. It was travelling towards that city in giant steps, an evil genie with the immeasurable power of the ocean in its loins.

The police launch moved at more than its usual speed among the boats vying for slips at the piers, weaving with great skill among the junks and other craft that made this part of the harbour a pilot's nightmare. As it proceeded, the launch's loudspeakers blared out over and over again the same message: 'Leave the dockside! Get inland! Get inland!'

The repeated warnings were, in a sense, counter-productive. Every boat within sight – from gleaming yacht to junk to scow to raft to rowboat – headed in as per command, creating a gigantic logjam. The docks were swarming with the newly arrived boat people, with relatives anxious to be of assistance, with sailors, dock workers, fishermen.

Shen Ti's rowboat, in which he made the rounds of the harbour peddling chocolate and cigarettes and sometimes opium (when the dealers would give him credit), was close to the docks when the government boat sounded its warning.

As a result, Shen Ti, who had been enjoying the warm afternoon sun in his new striped T-shirt, a birthday gift from his wife Tiang, was able to reach land quickly. Tying up next to a fishing boat, he hurriedly threw a tarp over his small remaining stock, jumped on the pier, and gained the street. Here there was pandemonium, people scampering in all directions, not knowing what it was all about but generally heading away from the waterfront.

Shen Ti, as mystified as anyone, was able to get to a side street, dodging in and around the growing mob and the cars that materialized from nowhere. Already it was almost impossible for vehicles to move, so great was the congestion ahead and behind. Much better, Shen Ti thought, to be on foot.

He still did not understand why all this was going on. He could hardly have been expected to envision the approaching tidal wave, now within several hundred miles of Hong Kong and still growing in size and momentum.

The wide thoroughfare before him had to be crossed, but at first glance this seemed impossible. The crowd had become even larger and more dense, and to make matters worse the entrance to the avenue was half-blocked by police vans, themselves immobilized, their loud speakers going full blast. 'Do not panic,' the loudspeakers bellowed. 'Move inland but do not panic!'

It was crazy, of course. As more and more people came within sound of those speakers, the greater became their fear and helplessness. Cars, trucks, taxis could not move an inch.

Shen Ti was pretty well frightened by this time, but he knew the quarter like the back of his hand. He managed to inch himself towards the entrance of an office building, push the door open a few inches, and slide inside.

He was in the reception room of a large ships'-supply emporium, probably the most important one of its kind on the waterfront. The riches within easy grasp did not tempt Shen Ti now. In the back of the store was a door leading to the first basement. In a moment he was dashing down the staircase to a second basement crowded with still-crated merchandise from overseas. At the rear of this dark, smelly cellar was a crawl-hole through which workers could get at the pipes and electrical conduits that fed the building.

The crawl-hole opened to a tunnel below the street. The tunnel ran under a bank across the thoroughfare and connected with a variety of shops. Its exits were as numerous as ratholes.

Shen Ti emerged in the cellar of a restaurant two blocks away, climbed some rickety stairs, and burst out into a narrow alley. His brand new T-shirt was covered with muck; his eyes smarted as the bright sunlight hit them.

But here there was comparative peace; the local residents had already joined the mobs seeking egress through the larger avenues.

Shooting up another side street, Shen Ti dashed into a decrepit building, climbed the stairs to the first landing, and threw open a door in the middle of the corridor.

His wife, was sitting on the floor, trying to cram the few belongings they prized – mostly wedding presents from their families – into a cardboard suitcase. Their four-year-old boy, Teng, was playing with a ball beside her. Delighted to see his father, Teng tossed the ball to him, expecting to have it thrown back.

Tiang had risen. Her soft, pretty face was frightened.

'Forget that,' Shen Ti ordered, indicating the valise. 'Get the baby.'

For a moment, reluctant to abandon the treasures in the suitcase, Tiang hesitated. Then she ran into the bedroom.

Shen Ti picked up his son, hitching him atop his shoulder, as Tiang emerged from the bedroom, their baby girl in her arms.

Tiang still did not understand what was happening. Neither did Shen Ti, not exactly, although on the street he had heard people talking fearfully about the oncoming great wave.

'We have to go – quickly! No time for questions, no time to take anything!'

Reading the anxiety in his eyes, seeing his dirty, mud-splattered body, the fear was transmitted to her and she obeyed without question. Carrying the baby, she followed him out of the room.

The narrow street below was jammed now up to where it joined a larger cross-street. There were many people that Tiang couldn't recognize, many of them old and infirm, being carried piggyback by sons and daughters. There was a constant keening, mostly from the old people. The young were hostile and aggressive, not minding whom they shoved as they fought their way through the bottleneck. The biggest problem for Shen Ti and Tiang was to stay together, not be jostled apart.

It seemed to take forever to reach the larger thoroughfare. Here, at least, was breathing space. But they still had no notion of where they were going, where they could find safety. They had no choice at this point but to allow themselves to be pushed along with the human current.

In the New York Communications Centre, they were gathered around Hunter's control screen watching Dr Yamashiro who, as harried assistants ran in and out with the latest bulletins, was trying to keep the world abreast of the situation in Hong Kong.

'Radar contact with the wave establishes height stabilized at one hundred feet plus,' Yamashiro told them, then read from a paper thrust into his hands. 'Speed is constant, six hundred miles an hour. Fifteen minutes before it hits us!'

'How far are you from the bay?' Bradley asked.

Yamashiro, not having the New York Centre's sophisticated equipment, couldn't see Bradley, but he did have voice contact. 'Twenty miles,' he answered.

In New York there was a dismayed, restless stirring.

'Do you have a way of getting out of there?' The question had been put by Sherwood, who stood next to Bradley smoking one of his odious ropes.

'Where would we get out to?' Yamashiro asked calmly. 'Hong Kong is an island.'

It was noted in New York that Yamashiro's staff seemed now to have diminished considerably. Only one woman and a young man could be seen in the background.

Yamashiro, however, showed no signs of testiness or fear. His smile on the screen was wry. 'I'm staying here. Keep tuned in.'

In Hong Kong, the mass exodus from the city had now reached the suburbs. All streets and lanes were clogged with people in headlong, desperate flight from the sea. The long lines of vehicles were worse than useless, creating additional blockages, smashing into each other, running out of gas, having to be abandoned by their frantic owners. Movement in some areas had become funerally slow. In other areas there was no movement at all.

Shen Ti and Tiang had made small progress; they were still within blocks of the waterfront. And then what Shen Ti worried about the most happened – Tiang dropped back in the crowd.

His son still on his shoulders, Shen Ti fought his way towards her against the stubborn, remorseless flow, at one point having to butt a monstrously fat woman who refused to let him by.

Reaching Tiang, who had fallen and was in imminent danger of being trampled with her child, he pulled her back to her feet, put the baby on his other shoulder, and managed to get his family into the slow-moving stream again.

He was aware now that except for the occasional cry of an infant, the huge crowd, packed solid in the street for miles, was almost completely silent. It was as if the premonition of doom had struck everyone at once. There was no hope.

The horrible wave came sweeping into the bay, unbelievably high, the force of the great ocean at its back. Its destructive power was incredible, and it roared like an enraged beast as it struck.

Boats were picked up and smashed into the docks. Buildings collapsed, driven from foundations, hurled against other buildings. Water spun through the canyons created by modern highrise structures, a huge tide that engulfed the midget people immobilized by their own numbers, drowning them where they stood.

In other parts of the city, farther from the bay, people scurried frantically towards higher ground, in most cases futilely. There were bizarre occurrences – a broken boat carried by the wave burst like a projectile through a department store window. Everywhere cars, bicycles and trucks were swallowed up, along with their passengers, in the watery horror.

Shen Ti and Tiang, having managed to burrow their way out of the compacted mass on the avenue, joined a smaller group trying to escape through a tangle of narrow back alleys.

It was as if the giant wave had eyes. Curling through street after street, it found Shen Ti and Tiang and engulfed them in its inexorable, thundering path. It continued on to the country-side, still a killer, uprooting trees and wooden buildings.

It had reached the Hong Kong Tracking Station. The staff people poured out into the street, joining those who still had the strength to run.

Inside the station, Dr Yamashiro, sticking it out in front of the camera, asked his watchers all over the world, 'Can you hear it?'

On the monitor, Bradley was yelling, 'We hear it! Get out of there!'

Yamashiro smiled. 'No use!' he shouted. 'Get the meteor, get it, kill it!'

Then, abruptly, the power was gone, and with it Yamashiro. Those who had been listening to him imagined the wave strik-ing the station, demolishing it, sweeping Dr Yamashiro away through the tumbling walls. And then only the sloshing water . . .

In New York, they stared in silence at the dark, silent screen.

Bradley spoke. 'That's what we'll do. We'll kill it.'

In the press all over the world, the Hong Kong disaster dominated. Several planes had circled over the city during the horrible event, and panoramic film was available. None of it included close shots; the pilots had feared to be sucked down by the fierce winds generated by the wave.

Many papers, however, included imaginative renderings by staff artists of the panic in the city, the mass drownings, the death and destruction. They also published fanciful drawings of the meteor itself – the five-mile hunk of black metal that was anything but fanciful – as it hurtled towards Earth, its course deadly and unwavering.

Newspapers, television commentators, astrologers, metaphysicians, fortune-tellers, Indian swamis and African medicine men – all gave their predictions as to the time and location of the approaching disaster.

A handful flatly prophesied a complete miss.

For the most part, the public went along with the accredited scientists, whose charts of the meteor, its orbit and its estimated arrival time, were accepted as hard truth.

Early Sunday morning, the President of the United States went on television, attempting to give some reassurance to the nation and the world.

'Fifteen minutes from now,' the President said to the bank of cameras and microphones facing him, 'the Russian rockets will be launched, and approximately two hours and thirty minutes later, our own rockets will be sent to join them. They will strike the meteor, sending it into harmless orbit, never again to menace Earth.'

The President paused, and his eye fell on the technicians. For once, he noted, there was no banter among them. They were as anxious as the public to hear his words.

He went on. 'On this Sunday, there is nothing we can do but wait and pray. Stay in your homes, have faith, and we will let you know when the danger is past.'

He gave his most reassuring smile, put his arm up in an easy farewell gesture, and was off the air.

There was a smattering of light applause from the staff.

'I need a drink,' the President said.

This had been anticipated. He was immediately handed a double whisky.

25

There was almost no vehicular traffic on Fifth Avenue, except for city buses. Although the morning was crisp and sunny, there were few pedestrians, even for that early hour, and these appeared to be headed for the churches. But the great houses of worship in the city reported small attendance. The majority of people, even the deeply religious, preferred to spend this fearful morning in the family bosom or in private session with their God.

In San Francisco, the bay was fogless. Its islands, its bridges, were limned in the first rays of dawn, perhaps the most splendid sight in America.

But something was missing from the magnificent canvas — boats. No early-bird commercial fishing boats, no private fishing boats, no yachts. By accident or design, the big freighters remained at sea — not one bucked its way home beneath the Golden Gate.

What gave the city a particularly desolate air was the bridges; almost no vehicles could be seen crossing. The city seemed isolated, subdued, a concrete island.

Each bridge, however, had a special guard of police. The Golden Gate had a double contingent. It had occurred to an important official that today the 'jumpers' would be out in force.

In all the great urban centres of the world, the story was pretty much the same. Tokyo's heart, the Ginza, was empty; the shops, normally open on Sunday, were closed and shuttered. The window-shoppers, tourists and Japanese alike, remained in the hotels or at home, watching the TV coverage of the awful event that threatened mankind.

In Rome, the Vatican, at the government's request, had decreed that the Pope would not appear as before – with St Peter's square packed, mass hysteria might result. Instead, it was decided, the pontiff would make a rare television address to the faithful.

Paris was somewhat different. Though its great boulevards were not deserted, nor the sidewalk cafes, one could stroll the length of the Champs Élysées without being jostled. But it was difficult to miss the gendarmes and the mobile police vans placed strategically throughout the city.

Instanbul, Cairo, Copenhagen, Brussels, Moscow, Amsterdam, Bonn, Vienna, Bucharest, Athens, Tel Aviv, Buenos Aires, Rio de Janeiro, Mexico City, Melbourne, Capetown, Washington – a similar story. Largely empty of pedestrians, of vehicles, but with soldiers or police patrolling the uneasy avenues.

Hyde Park, in London, had a pretty good turnout. The crisis, it seemed, had spawned speakers as well as listeners. Most prominent of the former was an elderly man, the image of an Old Testament prophet, wild-haired, wild-eyed.

'The end of the world is here!' the old man was screaming. 'The end of the world, ye hear me?'

They heard, and for the first time in memory they failed to laugh or rail at him. Some even shouted their amens. They were hip; they were with him; they dug it.

The old man grimaced at them, gap-toothed, exultant. It was his life's greatest moment. 'I've stood on this corner for years, trying to tell you that the end was coming. You didn't believe me, did you? Well, now it's here! IT'S HERE!'

'Our sympathy goes out,' the U.N. Secretary-General said, 'to the victims of these awful calamities. I am informed by scientific authorities that there may be more occurrences of this kind, but that where they may strike is not at present predictable.'

Sipping from a glass of water, he tried to exude confidence and decided that he was failing miserably. The damn television cameras picked up every eyebrow twitch.

He smiled wanly at his small studio audience, wondering if he would have time after the session to make the 9:00 A.M. plane to Copenhagen. At least if he could be with his family . . .

'I urge everyone, no matter where he may be, to remain calm, to avoid panic, to go about his daily business until official notice is given that he should do otherwise.'

He was aware, if only dimly, of the grave faces of his aides, his secretaries, listening intently as if he, by virtue of his high office and personal contact with the most powerful men in the world, could at this last moment produce a saving vision.

Alas, he could not. Only more empty words.

'This is an unprecedented time of great personal tension for all mankind. I ask for your courage, your understanding and your prayers.'

At the Communications Centre, they had no time to listen to the Secretary-General. Their attention was focussed on something more vital – the Russian firing of Peter the Great. For the first time in the memory of the Americans present, they were rooting wholeheartedly for the Russians. They had bet all their chips on Soviet science. Success or failure depended on their Soviet colleagues.

Surrounding Manheim's console, which was locked onto the Russian satellite by radar, were Bradley, Dubov, and Tatiana. Sherwood had left an hour earlier; he would be jetting to Washington, then back here before the day was out. Sherwood had to hold hands everywhere.

Bradley and Tatiana were careful not to be caught looking at each other. They were both private persons, neither caring

169

for public display. Yet, as happens so often in such cases, each gave their secret away; the entire Centre was aware of the electricity between them.

Manheim, wearing earphones, playing with his dials like an organist, was tuning in on the Russian satellite. Suddenly, with a dramatic wave, he indicated a small dial. Numbers were jumping on it, running down: 25, 24, 23 . . .

No one had to be told what the numbers indicated.

Without realizing it, Dubov and Tatiana moved closer together, as if by this physical proximity to give each other courage and to demonstrate a solidarity to the world.

Bradley, in a crew-neck sweater and jeans, tried to appear relaxed. He was aware that every technician on the floor had stopped work to watch. It was breath-holding time, and by his own demeanor Bradley wanted to display complete confidence.

He tried to get Tatiana's eye. But she, too, was staring at the tiny dial. 5, 4, 3, 2, 1 – ZERO!

A grunt from Manheim as his finger hit the lighted button.

A small, half-strangled cheer went up from the technicians, to be immediately stifled. Was it too early to tell, too early to be sure?

In space, the rockets were firing one by one. Ditroff, on the phone with the Yaroslavi Station – where Sergei Varentoi had been in charge since Dubov's absence – was getting minute-by-minute reports.

The exact timing had been worked out with Dubov in New York and with the Americans, but still Ditroff was nervous. Face it, he thought, our hardware is not as sophisticated as theirs. Should there be a misfiring, an accident, on whom would the blame for such a disaster fall? On innocent old Dimitri Ditroff!

Then, with Varentoi counting off in his ear, Ditroff cackled. A misfiring and there might be no Russia to come down on old Ditroff's head, no world at all!

Out in space, however, Peter the Great was performing flawlessly. Rockets streamed from their pods one after another, thrust forward on tongues of flame, reached out across the darkness towards the distant meteor.

'All gone! On their way!' Varentoi reported jubilantly. 'My respects to you, Comrade!'

Ditroff simply grunted and hung up the phone.

At the Centre, Manheim gave the spectators the thumbs-up signal.

Flushed, Dubov stepped back. He could almost feel the tension easing from the room.

Tatiana kissed him tenderly, as one does a child. Smiling slightly, Dubov accepted Bradley's handshake. He couldn't tell these Americans what he actually felt − a strange mixture of triumph and loss. Half to himself, he murmured, 'My babies . . . good babies.'

Bradley heard and understood. He would not have Dubov's ambivalence when the time came for Hercules to be fired, but then he and Dubov, like twins raised in conflicting environments, brought different emotional attitudes to the crisis.

Behind him, he heard an assortment of toasts. Dubov had brought out two bottles of vodka, someone had supplied styrofoam cups, and people were drinking and laughing.

'Hey!' Bradley called. 'One shot to a customer, right?'

They hooted at him. Spoilsport! Grinning, he held his ground. This was the beginning of the day. Just the kickoff.

He was handed a cup. He raised it towards Dubov, but his eyes were on Tatiana. She smiled at him.

Then Bradley was aware suddenly that the gaiety was gone. Everyone was looking past him.

Twisting around, he could scarcely believe what he saw. There, in full uniform, a short beige overcoat over his arm, was General Barry Adlon. He had entered unnoticed while they were toasting Dubov.

Adlon faced Bradley. He held himself very erect as he spoke.

'It's obvious I was wrong about the possible damage from the meteor, from its splinters. I've come to volunteer my services – in any capacity at all.'

Adlon's gaze moved past Bradley to Dubov, Manheim, and the central console, which was serving now as Dubov's vodka bar.

'That doesn't mean I've changed my mind about the Russians. I still think they'll withhold their rockets —'

Two dozen sets of astonished eyes were on him. A woman giggled.

'I think you should know,' Bradley said, 'that Peter the Great has just been fired.'

'Here, General.' Jan stepped forward boldly, holding out a cup. 'Drink with us on it.'

Adlon shook his head, but not impolitely. His glance moved past her to the console, to the silent group, then back to Bradley. He spoke slowly, uncomfortably. 'Please convey my compliments to Dr Dubov.'

Whatever Bradley was thinking, he allowed none of it to show. His big frame relaxed, he shrugged towards the console. 'Dr Dubov is right over there. Tell him yourself.'

Adlon held himself even straighter than before, turned, and was eye to eye with Dubov.

'Very good, Dr Dubov. Congratulations.'

Dubov nodded. 'Thank you.'

Adlon turned back to Bradley. 'Now sir, if there's anything I can do . . .'

Bradley nodded, genuinely pleased. 'You know more about the physical workings of this place than anyone. We're happy to have you back.'

Appreciation showed in Adlon's whole body. He tried to say something, but it died in his throat. Then he marched off to his office.

*

In California, in the early, still-dark hours before dawn, the Goldstone Tracking Station, its giant radar dishes slowly revolving, was sending and receiving signals, 'reading' the Russian rockets' trajectories. A constant beep-beep of radio signals could be heard in the station's scanning room where John Stewart, the director, was personally monitoring the readouts.

The results looked good, and Stewart asked, 'Anybody checked out Hercules' telemetry?'

A technician who had just been in communication with New York replied in the affirmative.

Satisfied, Stewart began to fill his pipe from a battered leather pouch. Before he could light up, his assistant, Howard Berman, who had been doing a routine scan of the heavens, came down from the observatory with a photograph. Wordlessly, he handed it over.

Stewart looked at it for a long time before commenting. Berman was brilliant, but a worrywart; Stewart wasn't buying this before double-checking.

On the photograph, Berman had outlined in red pencil a small dot.

'Another splinter?' Stewart asked.

Berman's sad eyes gave him his answer.

In New York they were still euphoric. Bill Hunter had three illuminated screens in front of him. Printed above one, on ordinary tape, was the legend: Peter the Great. Below it: Time In Flight – 36 minutes, 34 seconds. The other two screens were blank. One was being saved for Hercules, the other for the meteor, when its approach would warrant tracking.

Rolf Manheim had a duplication of Hunter's primary screen. On Manheim's, tenths of seconds were registering.

Manheim had just finished going over the figures with Bradley and Dubov and Adlon when Hunter signalled from across the room. They crossed into his territory.

A man was on the screen. It took Bradley a moment, and then he remembered – John Stewart, from Goldstone in California.

'I'm afraid I've got some rather serious news . . . Dr Bradley there?'

Bradley stationed himself in front of the locked camera. 'Bradley here, Stewart. What have you got?'

He saw Stewart hesitate, saw a readout in his hands.

'We've picked up another splinter, a big one.'

'Heading where?' Bradley asked. Stewart was being a little slow about this, he thought.

Stewart glanced down at the paper again before staring at them from the screen.

'The U.S.,' Stewart said in a choked voice. 'The eastern seaboard.'

Bradley glanced quickly around. Happily, only the key people were in on this – Dubov, Hunter, Tatiana, himself.

'You certain?' he asked.

'I'd say so. Yes.'

John Stewart wasn't young, but he wasn't doddering either. He was pretty damn good, as a matter of fact. Not one to throw a monumental curve like this unless the figures had been triple-checked.

'What's the time of impact?' Bradley asked.

Stewart's gaze was steady. 'Four or five hours. That's a crude estimate, Bradley. In another hour or so we might be able to do better. When are you firing Hercules?'

Bradley's smile was wry. He checked his watch. 'We're waiting for Houston to confirm. But, say, four hours approx.'

'Can you advance the firing?'

The room was suddenly very quiet. Every eye was rivetted on Bradley as each person did his own mental calculations.

It was only a matter of seconds before Bradley spoke. His voice was even, but unequivocal. 'No way.'

Manheim had come in to the circle, having promptly assessed Stewart's news. Adlon, Dubov, and Tatiana clearly understood also. Without realizing it, they had moved in supportively, close behind Bradley.

'Dr Stewart?' Bradley said.

'Yes?'

'How many on your end have this information?'

'Just Dr Berman and myself.'

'Could you keep it that way?'

'Of course. I understand. Talk to you later.'

'Thanks.'

California was off. Bill Hunter had poured himself a cup of black coffee and was now offering the stuff around. Taking a cup, Adlon said reflectively, 'If this Centre is hit . . . If we can't fire, that'll leave it up to Houston.'

'Our backup,' Manheim informed Dubov. 'But, Christ, I don't know. It's not their bag. The expertise is here.'

'Bag?' asked Dubov.

Hunter was about to explain, but cut it off. Sherwood, coat slung over his shoulders, had come down the stairs and was slouching towards them with an expression of weary cheerfulness.

'Greetings,' he said. 'From the President to all hands. And to you, Dr Dubov. The President congratulated Moscow right after the blastoff.'

Dubov nodded soberly.

Looking at them, Sherwood realized immediately that his good cheer was somehow out of place.

'What is it?' he asked.

Bradley told him. Splinter. Eastern Seaboard. Four to five hours.

'Jesus,' Sherwood said. He thought about it.

'I don't want to hand it over to Houston,' he said, confirming Manheim's appraisal. 'Too damn risky.' He swung around to face Bradley. 'But if we can't fire, Paul – if we go out of action – the Russian rockets aren't enough to do the job. You know that.'

As head of Hercules, Bradley had the final decision. But if Stewart's computations were correct, if they had four hours here in New York before the splinter hit, they could just get Hercules' rockets off. The timing would be close, too close for comfort.

They were all watching him, glad the decision was his.

Bradley made it. 'We wait.'

Sherwood accompanied him back to his office. 'Listen,' he said. 'Washington's going to have to be told about this.'

Bradley frowned. He could visualize the panic, the sheer pandemonium that would seize the nation's capital. 'The President,' he said. 'Only the President.'

'Okay,' Sherwood said. 'Just the President. Maybe he can keep the lid on. What about the authorities here in New York?'

'What authorities?'

'Well, for openers, the Mayor.'

Bradley could see Sherwood's point. It would be irresponsible to bottle up the news. He thought of the havoc the tidal wave had caused in Hong Kong. Mother of God!

'I'll call the Mayor,' he said.

'Better see him personally,' Sherwood advised. 'I wouldn't trust the phone.'

The Mayor was an energetic Brooklyn-New Yorker with a pragmatic approach to problems. Within minutes after hearing the grim news from Bradley, he'd put in calls to the fire and police commissioners and other key staff members, ordering them to City Hall. Top emergency alert!

He had a map of the northeastern section of the country brought in to his office. Bradley and Tatiana watched along with the city officials as it was set up on an easel in the middle of the room. A heavy circle had been drawn on the map, its circumference including Washington and Baltimore to the southwest, Pittsburgh to the west, Boston to the northeast, and Newark, Philadelphia and Annapolis to the south.

The Mayor made sure his door was closed and locked. He then asked Bradley if he could pinpoint any more accurately where the splinter might land.

Bradley's face was drawn as he walked over to the easel. 'We've had an update on our tracking data, Mr Mayor. The area of possible impact has been reduced considerably.' With a marking pencil, he drew a ring around Greater New York.

There was a hush, and then someone whistled.

The Mayor walked slowly back to his desk and sat down. He swivelled around in his chair, then looked towards Bradley again.

'Dr Bradley, any chance, the slightest, that you or your people have miscalculated?'

'Yes, of course,' Bradley said. 'But I wouldn't count on it.'

'I would'a bet you'd say that.'

'Even a near miss could be extremely serious,' Tatiana put in.

'I understand,' the Mayor said in a tired voice.

'When do you estimate this thing might fall?' asked the Police Commissioner.

'About three o'clock,' Bradley told him. 'We can be off a few minutes either way.'

The Fire Commissioner, a thin, compact man, spoke with a brogue. 'What's the size of the bloody thing?'

'Can't exactly tell yet,' Bradley answered. 'Figure, say, two hundred and fifty feet in diameter.'

'That doesn't seem so big.'

'It's not the size,' Bradley explained. 'It's the tremendous velocity – something like 36,000 miles an hour. A projectile this size would produce the same destruction as an atomic bomb. You'd have a crater perhaps two hundred feet deep and six hundred feet across. In terms of New York City, it would pretty much destroy the city itself and very possibly kill half the inhabitants.'

Bradley realized the effect of his words. He'd been living with this intimately; they hadn't. They stared back at him as if he were a doctor announcing a terminal illness.

The Mayor's intercom was flashing. 'Dammit,' he said into the box, 'I said, no one! Oh! Yeah, put him on.'

He leaned back in his chair and looked at Bradley. 'Yes, sir, he's right here now. No, sir, no plans yet. Right. Of course. Appreciate it, but we don't know yet what we'll need . . . will keep you posted. Thanks again for your concern. You too, sir.'

The Mayor put down the phone.

'The Man in Washington. In the time we've got, how can he help us? How can anybody help us? You tell me.'

No one told him.

The Mayor sat back again. 'As I see it,' he said, 'there's one decision we have to make right now. Do we try to evacuate the city or don't we?'

The question hung there, with no one willing to answer it.

The Police Commissioner half-raised his hand as if he were a schoolboy in class. 'It may sound hard-hearted, Mr Mayor, but I'm against it.'

'Why?'

'To begin with, everybody's looking up in the sky for that huge meteor coming in to smash us – so the big fear's been planted. Hell, it's over the whole country like a fog! Add to that what they've heard about Hong Kong! Now, you tell the people here they're going to get it in the neck with an earlier hunk, and you're going to have instant panic on your hands.'

The Commissioner turned to the uniformed Police Chief. 'John, what do you think?'

The Police Chief was a street-smart officer. 'We sometimes forget,' he said in a gravelly voice, 'that Manhattan is an island, just like Hong Kong. In a panic situation, there'd be very few get off it alive.'

'What about the other boroughs?' the Mayor asked. 'Have we got the right to restrict them?'

There was silence.

'I'm afraid they wouldn't get very far,' Bradley volunteered. 'The impact will affect the entire area.'

The Mayor turned to the Fire Chief. 'What about you, Tully?'

'I assume we'll have to anticipate a big risk of fire. Right, Dr Bradley?'

Bradley gave him a brief nod.

'Well, I wouldn't want to fight fires with millions of frightened, half-crazy people running through the streets. Then you've got the old and sick to get out of those buildings . . . you've got the hospitals, the rest homes. Thank God it's Sunday . . . at least not the schools.'

The Mayor came out from behind his desk and padded back and forth: 'Suppose,' he said, 'we tried to evacuate to Long Island, and suppose that's just where it hits. The same goes for any place we run to, doesn't it?'

He had answered his own question; he saw that. He smiled at them. 'Hope you guys have already been to church or synagogue, wherever the hell you go, because there won't be much time to pray now . . . just time to warn your top people, not the others, because then the news'll be spread.'

The Mayor paused as another thought struck him. 'In line with that, I want your sacred word that outside of your department heads, you'll tell no one, not even your own families. A final thing: I expect no one in this room to leave the city!'

Outside the Mayor's office, Bradley hung back, jumpy, irritable, giving a few more scientific details to the commissioners. Although Tatiana rarely had seen him with a cigarette, he was chainsmoking, bumming from everybody around. Suddenly, grabbing her hand, he headed for the elevators.

'Paul,' she said, pulling up.

'What is it?'

'Call her.'

'Call who?'

'Your wife.'

'Why in hell —?'

'Paul, tell her to take the children and drive somewhere, get away . . . You don't have to tell her why.'

'Would it be fair?'

'If my Nicolai were anywhere in the city, don't you think I'd try and get him away?'

His eyes met hers. He smiled a bit sheepishly. 'Yeah, okay.'

Downstairs, at a pay telephone, he called Helen. He waited while the ringing went on and on. No answer. Now where in God's name could she possibly be at this hour? Helen rarely went to church, and it wasn't likely she'd have spent the weekend somewhere without calling to tell him. On Sundays he usually called for a chat with the kids. Then there was Jamie's operation coming up . . . all the more reason for her to stick close to home.

He dialled again, in case he'd tried the wrong number. Still no answer.

He exited the booth sweating.

Tatiana desperately invented reasons to account for Helen and Nancy and Jamie being out. Just next door maybe. Or playing in the backyard – it was such a fine, clear morning. Or to the neighbourhood market – early, to beat the Sunday shoppers.

Bradley wasn't buying any of those excuses.

'Let's get back to the Centre,' he said.

'No,' Tatiana told him firmly. 'You need to stop thinking for a while. Get some fresh air. There's nothing you can do at the Centre, not till the Hercules firing.'

He managed a smile, trying to match hers.

'A cab up to Central Park? How's that?' He checked his watch. 'I guess we can afford an hour – would you buy a walk in the park?'

She put her hand into his, entwined their fingers. 'I would love it.'

'I'll call the Centre, tell them.'

He reached Sherwood, who had just come in. Sherwood agreed with Tatiana. 'Take an hour – no more.'

'Don't worry, Hal. And Hal – I tried to reach Helen . . . not there . . . in case you want to —'

'I know Helen isn't there,' Sherwood said in his New England drawl. 'Just sent her and the kids down to Houston on my jet. Oh, the plane had to go in any case, with some information on Hercules.'

Bradley could hardly talk for a moment. Relief flooded over him. Good old Uncle Hal!

Sherwood said, 'Told her I didn't want Olsen to do that surgery on Jamie till we got another opinion. Explained I had the real top ENT man down in Texas. She bought the whole package.'

'Thanks, Hal.'

'Sure. And Paul, that Russian tomato of yours – she's a beaut.'

Bradley hung up a little dazed, but Tatiana was enthusiastic. She had no scruples about it; she thought what Sherwood had done was only natural. And since the plane had to go to Houston in any case . . .

His eyes met hers, and they shared a slow, intimate smile of secret knowledge.

Central Park was at its best, the trees brushed with red and gold. In spite of the worldwide scare, skaters were out and there were a few Sunday strollers on the winding walks. Kids scampered around the benches, their watching parents determined that life must go on.

Bradley showed Tatiana the Children's Zoo and bought her roasted chestnuts. Munching as they walked, her arm in his, she seemed almost happy. Each of them tried to pretend it was any Sunday in any November.

Two young girls were feeding the squirrels, and Tatiana listened to them.

'They're going to let Harry know tomorrow,' one of the girls said. 'If he gets the job, we're going to be married right away!'

Tatiana pulled Bradley away, a look of pain on her face.

They left the park and made their way over to Madison Avenue. He wanted to show her the expensive boutiques, the art galleries.

They began to notice certain things happening. Men were hauling boxes of emergency rations and cans of water into a building with an Air Raid Shelter sign on it. Every now and then a city ambulance drove up the avenue, sirens off. Bradley knew from the briefing at City Hall that they were bound for predetermined destinations in different parts of the city. Large police vans were also in evidence, proceeding to the pressure points indicated by the Police Commissioner. Bradley wondered aloud what story the policeman inside the vans had been given, what excuse their superiors had concocted for summoning them to duty so abruptly on a Sunday morning.

Tatiana guessed that no one group would be told about the other, that no one group could know the call-up had been city-wide.

They watched a column of fire engines move silently into position on Fifth Avenue – pumpers, hook-and-ladders. Other fire department vehicles were moving uptown, towards Harlem. Occasionally a bright-red truck would peel off to take up a position on a side street. They seemed eerie and dreamlike without their sirens blaring.

An elderly man said to a woman at a stop-light, 'You don't understand. We've got nothing to worry about.'

'Nothing to worry about?'

'Listen, honey, they'll never let that happen. Look, will you relax? I'll have my pension and social security, too.'

Looking into the window of a maternity shop, a very pregnant young woman said, 'Tomorrow, we're going to have to decide on that bigger apartment. The baby'll be here in another month.'

Her husband tried to put his arm around her, but couldn't. They both tittered. 'I've already signed the lease,' he said, beaming.

Bradley and Tatiana exchanged glances. Tomorrow . . .

They kept walking, looking into faces now. Some people actually seemed relaxed, Bradley noted, as if Hong Kong were a million miles away, as if the meteor posed no threat at all. As if . . .

Tatiana scolded him. How else were ordinary people to react? They knew nothing of the splinter. Of course they were afraid of the meteor, but it was only normal to try not to think about that, to have faith in the people in charge. The Americans and the Russians together would pull it off!

'You're right,' he told her. 'I love you.'

'I love you,' she said, laughing.

Each wondered whether the other really meant it.

Bradley looked at his watch. 'Damn it!' He hailed a taxi. They went back to the Centre.

26

In the heavens, travelling at terrible velocity, the splinter made a frightening roar in its passage.

At the Hercules Communications Centre, they had a vague idea of what it looked like, and they now knew with certainty that it was headed for the New York area. All thoughts of the splinter had to be set aside however. The Centre's job was to stop the meteor itself – *before* the splinter hit!

The timing would be close, they all knew that.

The splinter, the tracking stations told them in a continuous stream of telemetry, could be expected to strike within minutes.

The firing of Hercules' rockets must be held off for another minute and forty-five seconds in order for Hercules to achieve rendezvous in space with the rockets of Peter the Great, so that they could send their rockets in concert against the invader. A fraction of a second earlier – or later – and the meeting in space would not result in a combined attack.

Unwashed, unshaven, Rolf Manheim was glued to his console, a virtuoso preparing himself to strike the first electrifying note.

TIME TO FIRING, the digital counter read, 1 MINUTE, 40 SECONDS.

Bradley, Dubov, Sherwood, Tatiana and Adlon were ranged behind Manheim, noting the readouts on the splinter's progress.

Sherwood spoke briefly to Houston over the telephone, put

the receiver down. Now the light on the special red telephone was flashing. Sherwood, his voice a weary whisper, spoke again. 'Yes, sir,' he said. 'We surely hope so, sir.' No one needed to be told who was calling now, who was pleading for reassurance.

Sherwood looked towards Manheim's counter. I MINUTE, 20 SECONDS. Grimly, he pulled a switch, cutting off the telephone extensions; they had no time for further interruptions.

Bradley was handed the latest readout. The splinter was in the outer fringes of the earth's atmosphere. And a big, mean-looking baby! Not a chance of the Pisa miracle. This one was coming in like an aimed missile!

'Time of impact?' someone asked.

It was Dubov. He had been solid as a rock ever since the emergency had begun. Now his smile told Bradley: So we live or we die; we do what we can.

Bradley, knowing that all present were hanging on his answer, smiled back.

'Who the hell knows?' he lied. 'Besides, she might get a flat, throw a tyre.'

They tried to laugh, but it was feeble.

Adlon was standing at attention, his eyes on Manheim's counter. The General was ready to salute the flag, Bradley thought.

Tatiana was glancing upward instinctively. She could imagine it coming in – a flaming torch, too big an object to burn off any substantial part of its bulk. It wasn't easy to stand here knowing that in less than a minute it would explode on top of your head.

Then she thought of the millions who didn't know, for whom it would be the end of the world.

On Manheim's counter the reading was 42 SECONDS.

Bradley waved off all new readouts proffered by the staff. Only two meaningful factors remained: time of arrival of the splinter versus blast-off time for the Hercules rockets. There was no way to save New York. But if they could activate Hercules before the splinter hit, they might save a hemisphere.

Bradley, Sherwood, and Adlon stood close behind Manheim. Dubov and Tatiana stood farther back. From here on, it was up to the Americans.

They were all visualizing the situation: Hercules in space, its rockets waiting for orders; the new splinter charging down, glowing, ringed with fire.

TIME TO FIRING, 22 SECONDS.

Manheim, the third finger of his right hand tapping the black surface of the console, threw a glance back of him, indicating that he was ready.

Bradley touched his shoulder lightly, signalling respect and confidence, then began to count in low tones. He was the only voice in the stillness of the Centre.

'Eleven, ten, nine . . .' Bradley stopped counting. In front of Manheim, the numbers were running down.

3, 2, 1 . . . ZERO!

Manheim bent over the console, hitting the switches one by one.

In space, Hercules, immobilized in orbit by man's decision, was now brought to cataclysmic life. Its rockets blasted, spitting sheets of fire.

In the Centre, all eyes were fixed on the computers.

Then it was all right! The firing data confirmed that all rockets were launched on schedule. There was cheering, shouting, hugging.

Then, as suddenly as it had begun, the celebration was aborted.

From far above the Centre, over the rumble of a distant subway train, over the hum of their own machines, came an ominous crackling thunder, as if a giant as tall as the skies was clapping his hands, calling for instant attention.

The clapping increased in tempo, became slightly muffled,

changed in character. And then a terrible thunderous roar shook the very foundation of the underground Centre.

White-hot, surrounded by a nimbus of glowing, jagged fire, as if the sun itself were descending, the splinter came hurtling downward.

The sound was deafening; to each of the city's millions of souls it seemed that life was coming immediately to an end. Options were few – to fall to one's knees and pray, to dive futilely under the nearest bed, to rush out into the unknown, into the inferno.

Even before impact, the air was squeezed, compressed. The heat was intolerable. The city rattled as if it were being shaken by an earthquake beyond imagination.

A second later the splinter struck.

There were two kinds of destructiveness: the intense heat, which set most of the buildings in lower Manhattan ablaze, and the physical damage inflicted by the incredible striking power.

Arriving over the Hudson River, the splinter swept past the Statue of Liberty, ironically severing only the head and the torch-holding arm. Then it tore its way up Manhattan, shearing the towers of the World Trade Centre, disintegrating the top thirty or forty stories of every building in its path.

The Empire State building trembled and fell.

At Rockefeller Centre, most of the structures were levelled as if by a scythe. The RCA building held together for a moment; then, slowly, like a pile of loose bricks, it cascaded down.

Onward, to the north, went the fiery fragment, to explode into the earth of Central Park.

Now the splinter detonated with a force equal to that of a nuclear device, sending tons of dirt and debris high into the air. Blasts of compressed air blew out every window in the buildings that surrounded the park. Where trees and grass and shrubbery had been, there was now only a smoking ugly crater five hundred feet across.

Hundreds of thousands of men, women, and children within miles of the park died at once, suffocated by the immense gaseous wave of heat that bellowed from the core of the crater.

The handful of structures in mid-Manhattan that had survived the passing of the splinter now trembled – and collapsed.

There were no places of absolute safety for the majority of inhabitants, even those lucky enough to have survived the initial blow. Almost every building in central New York was on fire. The firemen were helpless; the police and disaster crews were hopelessly inadequate.

New York was a pile of flaming rubble. Over half its people were, as predicted, dead or critically burned, wounded by falling stone and glass – or crazed with fear, like mice in a burning maze.

The AT&T Building had not survived any better than the structures around it. Its upper floors had been sliced away, and the rest had collapsed. The building looked, from the outside, like a huge mound of debris.

Below ground, during the moment of impact, the whole structure shook. The walls bowed and cracked, the computers, the rows of communication machines, swayed and jiggled, wildly pouring out unbidden readouts. The ceiling burst open. Pipes, cement, dirt, rained down on the Hercules personnel. The lights went out, plunging the complex into darkness, creating more confusion, more fear.

General Adlon, bleeding badly from a head wound, managed to make his way to a panel against the wall beyond the central console. He pulled a specially recessed switch that activated the emergency power system for the Centre. Unfortunately, with the ceiling half demolished, only a few of the Centre's light came on.

An enormously heavy illuminated panel beside the central

console had fallen on Rolf Manheim, pinning him down, half burying him.

On the floor nearby, Bradley was trying to shield Tatiana and himself against the continual rain of debris from above, which seemed to intensify as the huge building rumbled and shook and settled.

Bill Hunter, Bradley saw, was struggling under a spill of monitors, broken glass, and shattered electronic equipment. Sherwood was not in sight. Adlon was now trying to organize the uninjured into some sort of rescue and first aid squad.

Another rending noise interrupted the General's shouted commands. A huge section of wall had split and caved in. Screams rose from those it fell upon. Then more wall on the opposite side of the room came crashing down, bringing with it electric cables that hissed and writhed like snakes, sending out sparks and flames, creating psychological as well as physical havoc.

A deathly silence gradually took over the Centre, broken only by the low moans of the wounded. It seemed the worst was over, leaving the present to be dealt with.

In the dim light, Bradley couldn't begin to assess the damage. He was concerned about Tatiana; his fingers had found a deep cut on her forehead. But she stirred under his touch and sat up.

'Are you all right?' he asked.

'Yes. I think so. How are you?'

He was fine, he told her. Where in hell was Dubov?

As if magically illuminated by the question, Dubov could now be seen near the console. He was trying, with little success, to pull Rolf Manheim free. Manheim's legs were pinned below the panel.

Bradley struggled over to him, jumping a large cable.

'What about yourself?' Bradley asked gruffly.

Dubov touched his bleeding cheek and smiled wryly. 'Would you believe it? The broken bottle of vodka?'

Tatiana joined them. She tried to do something about Dubov's bleeding, using her scarf as a compress.

Hunter came over with several men, and then took on the job of removing the rubble around Manheim, who was either unconscious or dead.

Adlon, ignoring his own cuts, had put together a crew with fire extinguishers, and soon they had the burning cables under control. There wasn't much more anyone could do now, except hunt in the darkness for the wounded and cart them to the centre of the chamber where the ceiling seemed to be holding.

Sherwood was found near the staircase, working his way out from under a steel beam, miraculously unharmed.

As Bradley helped him to his feet, he asked, 'Did we do it, Paul? Did we kill it?'

My God! thought Bradley. The meteor!

'Sure as hell,' he said firmly. But had they? He must find out what was happening.

He started towards the corridor to his left, which led to the office wing of the Centre.

'Where are you going?' Tatiana asked.

'My office.'

'You can't get through – it's blocked.'

They reached the corridor entrance, and it appeared that Tatiana was right. The entrance was totally shut, a tangle of concrete and dangling pipes.

But yanking out a jagged piece of cement caused the heap to settle slightly, and then a rough, open triangle appeared at the upper right. Clearing away the loose rubble, Bradley slipped through into the darkness of the corridor beyond. Tatiana was close behind him.

About to remonstrate with her to go back, he saw she was carrying a small pencil flash, which now picked up the door to his office.

'Always carry one,' she said. She also had her bag slung over her shoulder. How had she managed that? Bradley marvelled.

'Come on,' he said.

One lamp in the office still worked. On Adlon's back-up battery system, he imagined.

They surveyed the damage. One wall caved in, litter everywhere, the world globe overturned, Africa a gaping hole where a pipe had landed. But, oddly, Bradley's own domain, his desk, was untouched, an immaculate island in the mess.

Bradley righted the globe, crossed to the desk and picked up the receiver of the red phone.

'It's working,' he told Tatiana, scarcely believing it.

He flashed the Houston digits and got an immediate response. There was great excitement on the other end.

'One moment, Dr Bradley. Mr Mason will be right with you. Are you all right? Are you —?' Mason came on. 'Mason here. My God, Bradley, it's good to hear your voice. What's happening. Can you tell us?'

No, he couldn't, he explained. They were underground, as Mason knew, and were cut off from the rest of the city. But they could imagine the tremendous damage if what had happened to them was indicative of destruction above ground.

'I'm afraid it is,' Mason said. 'Washington – the whole world – is holding its breath. We know you received a direct fragment hit. An Air France plane, coming in, was able to maintain altitude and respond. Other planes were literally burned up in the air. We're getting bulletins from the French pilot. All five boroughs are involved. In lower Manhattan very few structures remain intact. Casualty estimates are very high, but help is being flown in from all over.'

Mason paused to collect his thoughts. 'You'll be glad to hear this: all rockets are on course – both Russian and American. All functioning normally.'

A wave of relief swept over Bradley. At least they had done their job in time. The rockets were on their way.

Mason was expressing his congratulations, and then suddenly his voice was cut off.

The ground beneath Bradley seemed to slip. The structure above him settled with a noise like a groan, and a cable whiplashed across the room, almost felling him. As Tatiana screamed, Bradley ducked in time. His desk had a broad gash across its middle, where the cable still burned. The phone was dead.

'Let's get back,' he told Tatiana.

In the corridor, his eyes fell on a door marked 'Emergency Exit'. The door was jammed, but yielded after a moment of tugging.

Behind the door, Tatiana's flash revealed rubble piled high across steps, blocking any possibility of climbing up and out of the building. Then the flashlight picked up something else. Under the stairwell, they saw the duct of an air-conditioning unit, its metal housing twisted away from the wall. Bradley caught a glimmer of light through the wall.

At that moment, Tatiana's flash failed.

'Sorry,' she said. 'Battery's out.'

Bradley tried to put his eye to the point of light, but nicked his cheek against a jagged edge of aluminium.

'Okay, let's get back,' he said.

They found the door, the corridor, and felt their way back to the main chamber. As they were about to enter, Bradley paused.

'Tatiana . . .?'

'Yes, Paul.'

And she was in his arms.

They joined the others. Temporary lights had been rigged, they saw, and rescue operations were being carried out.

Sherwood, his hair white with powdered plaster, came forward.

'Bradley, what a time to disappear,' he said. 'Where the hell have you been?'

27

The city was aflame – from the Battery to the upper reaches of Central Park, as far east as the river, as far west as Riverside Drive.

In some cases the fire had jumped individual buildings, but the fire fighters, hopelessly inadequate to stem the ever-increasing conflagration, had abandoned the entire downtown section and retreated to a line running east and west across 110th Street.

Fire Chief Tully estimated that he had lost at least half of his men and equipment at meteor impact.

Ironically, the section of New York he could still save – or, at least, had a fighting chance of saving – included those areas which should really have been torn down and rebuilt: Harlem and huge stretches of Puerto Rican ghetto. On the plus side of the ledger was the wind, not by any means inactive, but only moderate.

The people of the city were out of control.

The survivors, instead of fleeing north, away from the blast centre, had turned to the rivers in a wild, desperate effort to escape the island. The problem was that few bridges remained usable. The George Washington, its Manhattan footings crumbled, was askew, that end of the span dangling like a broken watchband.

On the East River, though elements of the complex of bridges were intact, enough damage had been inflicted to make them impassable. In addition, they were clogged with vehicles that had been surrendered by their owners, who were trying the rest of the hazardous journey on foot. Many slipped from the slanting road bed; others fell from cables or girders and drowned in the turgid waters below.

The 59th Street Bridge was down, as was the Brooklyn Bridge. The Verrazano could still be considered a viable span, but it was inaccessible because of the raging fires in the district leading to it.

The great popular areas of the city – Times Square, Rockefeller Centre, Washington Square – were deserted. The north-south avenues running parallel to the Hudson were now bearing the brunt of the madness. They were overrun with people scampering like rats to gain access to the two tunnels, the Lincoln and the Holland.

Vehicles had long since been abandoned, but the numbers of pushing, shoving, savagely determined New Yorkers trying to fight their way to safety in New Jersey made survival in the tunnel problematical. The police had given up, overwhelmed by the impossibility of stemming the tide. The human snakes in the tunnels were able to move no more than inches at a time. Many older or weaker people had already expired, yet were held upright by the press on all sides.

In the Holland Tunnel, with power supplied from the Jersey end, the lights were still functioning. But there was no fresh air. The blowers, New York powered, had been out of commission from the beginning.

But to the thousands in the tunnel, the greatest threat lay elsewhere. The impact of the meteor had seriously damaged the outer casings of the tube itself. Now water began to seep through. It was hardly noticed by the frightened people inside, who could think only of keeping their heads high enough to breathe, of staying on their feet so as not to be trampled by those behind them.

Now the great weight of the earth and river above began to increase the size of the crack in the tunnel. It expanded suddenly, and the entire tunnel lurched violently.

A scream, a blend of thousands of individual screams, rose like a primal wail. There was no place to go, neither back nor ahead. The tunnel had become a terrifying trap.

Suddenly, somewhere in the middle of the river, it ruptured completely. The inside pressure spewed people out, even as river water rushed in to drown those still inside.

A little more than a minute and it was over. Only the bodies slowly surfacing in the black tidal waters gave evidence of the tragedy below.

At last a peace of sorts came to New York. There were many fires still burning, but most of the buildings had burnt themselves out. The city lay in a quiet, crackling stupor as the big helicopters loaded with National Guard, army troops, the mobile hospitals, the food, the other essential supplies, began to arrive. The sky became full of them; it was as if New York was occupied by a flock of enormous birds, their chatter deafening as they landed on the scorched earth. The nation had finally been mobilized to help.

From Houston, they flashed word to Washington: Most of the Hercules people in New York had survived the initial impact, but they were apparently buried in the Centre under thousands of tons of debris. What could be done to get them out?

Nothing, Washington replied – at least not right away. The armed forces were moving into New York in a gigantic rescue operation, but it would be days before specific areas could be dug out. First must come the task of getting food and medical aid to the thousands alive above ground – and the removal of the countless dead to prevent an epidemic.

Abe Holland spoke with General Easton in Houston.

'Your baby now, Tom,' the Secretary of Defence said. 'I mean that meteor up there. New York has scared the shit out of the world. If a small splinter can annihilate New York City, what can that monster of a thing five miles wide do to the rest of us?'

'We're monitoring it, Mr Secretary.'

'What are our chances?'

'At the moment, sir, all rockets are on course.'

'Keep me informed,' Abe Holland said, and hung up.

Easton repeated the conversation to Sam Mason.

Mason, worried stiff about Sherwood and Bradley and other friends buried under that pile of masonry in Manhattan, had no response. He thought of the red-tipped rockets of Peter the Great, surging this minute through the twilight of outer space. And in a converging pattern the blue-tipped rockets of the U.S.

Mason prayed that the two sets of stars would find each other and move towards a common goal, that the telemetry that had set their course would be correct.

He went to join his colleagues in his own Communications Centre.

Sherwood and Adlon had organized the survivors into three details – one to search the rubble for possible survivors, one to care for the wounded, the third to hunt for an escape from their underground prison.

Dubov, a man of miracles, had actually found an unbroken bottle of vodka half buried under the console. His own face a mass of coagulated blood, he doled out sips to the dazed and battered around him.

Bill Hunter, an assistant to Adlon, found a dripping water pipe. Not sewer water as at first he imagined, but good clean drinking water. Thank God for small favours! Somebody remembered seeing a maintenance closet, apparently untouched. Pails were procured, rinsed, filled with water, and sent to the first aid group in the centre. At least wounds could be washed. The same closet yielded three flashlights and a spare fire extinguisher. All came immediately to use; a fire that had broken out in the corner formerly occupied by Hunter's communications and monitoring equipment was extinguished.

The few remaining lights in the big room had begun to dim; the emergency system itself had evidently been damaged.

Adlon, carrying his own flashlight, joined the escape crew, directing them to the staircase leading to the elevators. It had been cleared somewhat, but the blockage looked solid higher up, effectively ruling out passage to the elevators. Enough concrete had fallen over the security doors and the stairwell to give a bulldozer trouble.

Then Adlon saw something else. The security guard, probably trying to join them below, had been trapped in the fall from above. His lifeless face grimaced at them from a corner of the pile.

Adlon led the way slowly back down to the others.

Tatiana had forced Dubov to sit while she cleaned his cheeks with gauze – a box of first aid supplies had been salvaged.

Dubov was concerned with only one thing: Were the Peter the Great rockets on course?

So far, Tatiana reassured him, the Russian rockets were A-okay – as the Americans put it. Bradley had been able to speak to Houston before communications were cut.

Dubov grinned at her. 'That's good, little one. And don't you worry, Tatya . . . I'm fine. Really.'

'You're made of Siberian iron,' she told him dryly.

The men working to free Rolf Manheim finally succeeded. Levering the enormous weight of the central console up several feet, improvising wedges to hold it stable, they pulled him free. Obviously in enormous pain, he was placed gingerly in a space close to Dubov and given a shot of morphine.

Manheim looked down at his legs, mashed and bloody. Then

his gaze moved up to find Tatiana and Dubov and Bradley.

'Anyone for tennis?' Manheim asked with a faint smile. Then he fainted.

'Mr Sherwood . . . will you come here, please.' It was Alan Marshal with one of Adlon's search crews, calling from a far corner of the room.

Sherwood and Bradley made their way over together, threading their way through a jungle of smashed computers, monitors, broken concrete, and twisted cables.

Marshal looked odd to Bradley; he was standing erect, his eyes not directed at them. Then, with a trembling nod of his head, he indicated something behind him.

Bill Hunter stood by a large accumulation of broken equipment and rubble, the first place the ceiling had fallen. In his hand, Hunter held a long piece of pipe, which he had been using as a combination pick and probe. Now he moved slightly away, revealing what his labour had produced – a woman's hand sticking out of a pile of rubble.

The men stared down at it.

'It's Jan . . .' Marshal said behind them.

Turning, Sherwood said, 'We'll attend to it. You go help the first-aid crew.'

'But it's Jan,' Marshal repeated, his eyes staring blankly, his voice lifeless.

Adlon appeared to make his report. 'The stairs are completely out of the question. Even if we could escape that way, there must be tons of buildings on top of us —'

His glance went past Hunter and the others, caught a flash of what they had seen. Hunter was poking carefully now, beaming his searchlight below the hand.

'Oh my God,' Alan Marshal said, starting forward.

'No,' Sherwood said. He placed himself between the young man and the white face of the woman that stared at them from the rubble. 'Alan, I'm sorry. Now will you go help the others?'

'Yes,' Alan said finally, all expression drained away.

They watched him as he obeyed, and then Sherwood turned to Hunter. 'I'm afraid she'll have to stay where she is for the time being.' To Adlon, he said, 'General, any other possible exits?'

Adlon shook his head. 'Doors from the canteen, the support rooms are blocked. Some chance of getting through to the computer room . . . possibly crawl space above it where the cables feed in. We're trying.'

'Keep at it. Anybody got any other ideas?'

Bradley said, 'That damn subway I heard rumbling half the day yesterday. Any way into it?'

Adlon's big square face wore a curious smile. 'Follow me.'

He lighted their way past obstacles, leading them into the recess under the stairwell, past the maintenance closet. They were now directly under the security doors. The ceiling had collapsed into the elevator shafts, forming a concrete barrier yards thick.

'Beyond the elevator shafts,' Adlon said, 'there's a small corridor that leads to an old, barred wooden door. That door leads to your subway, Bradley.'

They were silent.

Adlon went on grimly, 'With the proper tools and a full crew working night and day, how long would it take us to break through to it? A week?'

At first aid, where they were splinting Manheim's legs, it was now possible to assess the human damage. Sixteen able-bodied had survived and were mobile; this number excluded Manheim and a technician named Riley who had a broken leg and possible internal injuries. There were four others with wounds from worrisome to serious. At least eight were dead, including Jan Watkins.

Adlon and his men were working now to clear a way into the computer room, and the desultory sound of their efforts could be heard in the quiet of the main room. They must be working with their fingernails, Bradley thought despairingly.

He caught Tatiana's look and managed a smile. 'By tomorrow they'll be coming down for us,' he said, loudly enough for everyone to hear.

Bullshit, he thought. Tomorrow the authorities would just be beginning the impossible job of extricating the millions entombed throughout the city. Here, with thousands of tons over their heads, what chance did they have?

Hunter, who had been doing his own exploring, came into the area of light and dropped wearily next to Bradley.

'Lights will be going soon,' he whispered. 'Emergency generator's just about had it.'

The fault lay partially with him, Bradley reflected, partially with Sherwood and Adlon. But in the planning of Hercules, who could have foreseen the possibility of a direct hit on the Centre itself? What had been the odds? How many millions to one?

'Water's down to a drip,' Hunter told him grimly. 'What we were getting was the residue in the pipes.'

Bradley said nothing. They could do without food for a long period and survive. Water was something else, especially with the wounded. Crossing to Tatiana, he kissed her lightly, not caring who witnessed it.

They smiled at each other, smiles of knowing. Whatever happened, they had this – the knowing.

Dubov was asleep, snoring.

Manheim was awake and in great pain. Tatiana bent over him, and he tried to grin at her.

The young technician who was in charge of the first-aid supplies came over and gave Manheim another shot. Then his eye caught Bradley's. 'That's it, sir,' he said. 'The last of it.'

'What have you got left?' Bradley asked.

The young man shook his head. 'Bandage, a couple of bottles of physic, half a bottle of iodine.'

'Anybody got a cigarette?' Bradley asked.

Hunter produced one from a crumpled pack. 'Coffin nails. If we get out, I'm going off,' he said.

'I'll join you,' Bradley told him. 'Meanwhile, let me borrow your flash.'

He moved off into the darkness, not wanting to use the flash until he had to.

The slit leading to his office corridor wasn't too hard to find, and he slipped through it. Now he was in total darkness, and it was necessary to use the flash to find the exit door that he and Tatiana had explored previously.

He wanted to look again at that air-conditioning duct.

Nearing the earth, though still hundreds of thousands of miles away, it looked, if possible, even more menacing. Every telescope in the world was glued to it; every observatory tracked its approach.

It had not lost any of its bulk, its capacity for destruction. The splinters that had preceded it, wreaking such terrible damage, were merely tiny scavenger fish compared to this leviathan of the sea, this whale.

And the whale was coming not simply to swallow the earth, but to hammer it, to lash it, to beat its brains out.

Counterattack!

The powerful flock of twenty-foot-long rockets bearing the insignia of the United States seemed to be holding perfect formation as they headed towards rendezvous – or at least Houston's telemetry said so. The Red Star rockets were also on target; at Yaroslavi, their telemetry agreed.

Yaroslavi was now in direct telephonic communication with Houston – an open line. There was no need for translators. Cosmonauts of both nations, who had flown in space together some years before and had become bilingual, manned the phones, chatting back and forth, confident as such men of space tend to be. Their laughter was full of tension and excitement.

Ditroff, who had been flown into bitter-cold Yaroslavi the night before and hated every moment of it, listened to the easy talk in the monitoring room and smiled sourly to himself. The younger generation! What was his world coming to?

Bradley came back from his reconnaissance to find the main chamber lighted now by flashlights. All other illumination was out.

Sherwood, Adlon and Hunter were holding a melancholy council of war in the narrow circle that included the wounded. The dampness from the burst pipes, the running sewer water beyond the broken walls, had permeated everything, and the stench was growing. The absence of normal lighting made the scene seem ever colder, more desperate.

It was hopeless, Sherwood told Bradley in an aside, unless help could get to them. And from where could they expect help? The city above them, undoubtedly buried in rubble, had its own problems.

Bradley shamelessly bummed one of Hunter's last cigarettes, managed to give Tatiana a reassuring smile, and tapped Adlon's hand.

'General, you have any explosives stashed away?'

Adlon, his heavy face stained with dirt and sweat, growled back ill-humouredly, 'We're not an engineer outfit. Why in hell would we have explosives? And what good would it do if we had?'

'General – and you, too, Hunter – maybe you ought to come with me.'

Bradley saw Sherwood's questioning glance. But Sherwood kept silent, figuring Bradley would elaborate when the time came – if it was to come at all.

'Can you manage with just one flash?' Bradley asked.

Sherwood looked around at the wounded; light didn't appear to be their main requirement at this point. Nodding, he said, 'Try not to be too long.' He watched Bradley lead Adlon and Hunter towards the corridor. Looking exhausted, but moving well enough. Dubov caught up with them; he had had enough of sitting on the sidelines.

Guiding the other men through the slit in the door and into the debris-filled corridor. Bradley led them on to the emergency door, which he had propped open with a fallen timber.

And then he showed them his jewel – the point of light he had discovered with Tatiana. But the point had been widened – it was now a couple of inches in diameter – by dint of Bradley's labour.

One by one, at Bradley's bidding, the men bent to look. They saw a stretch of subway platform and tracks, dimly lit by distant emergency lighting.

'Christ,' whispered Adlon. 'The old subway system . . . I'll bet it hasn't been used for years!'

'But leading into the regular system?' Bradley asked.

Adlon couldn't say for sure, but he imagined so.

Dubov's eye was to the light. Straightening, he said, 'What good? Too much stone, earth, between us and subway?'

Bradley was still facing Adlon. 'General,' he said, 'in the original plans for Hercules, I recall the file room was in this corridor.'

'Near my – the Commander's office, your office. Yes.'

'Back then, we discussed all sorts of security for those files – all sorts of fireproof precautions, right? And something else, I remember, an additional safety factor. After I left . . . was that extra safety factor actually built in?'

General Adlon was staring at him. 'Hell and damnation,' the General said.

Adlon ran out into the corridor, and they followed him to the door of the file room. No problem there; the door had been sprung half open.

The General was aiming his flash into the room; now he

turned, smiling at Bradley. When Adlon smiled, Bradley decided, he looked almost human.

'It's there,' the General said. 'Goddammit, of course it's there!'

'What's there?' asked Hunter.

'Explosives behind each cabinet,' Adlon said. 'In case of tampering or attempted removal these files were designed to self-destruct!'

Their problem wasn't solved, they agreed, but they had a worthwhile shot at it.

The trick would be to remove the explosives without blowing themselves out of the ballpark, burying the entire Hercules complex – or what was left of it – under the tons of stuff above them.

A particular problem, they discovered immediately, was that of the Americans only Hunter had any experience with explosives, and he had damn little.

It was Dubov who stepped into the breach. Grabbing a flash from Bradley, he disappeared into the file room. When he came out, he was grinning.

He patted Bradley on the shoulder. 'I used to be pretty good at this – construction work when I was a kid. I can do it.' To Hunter, he said, 'You my assistant. You help.'

Adlon sent Bradley an agonized glance. For once, Bradley shared the General's concern. Was the Russian merely bragging, or could he do it? And what choice did they have?

The survivors in the big room were given the news: escape was at least possible. But there were ominous rumblings from overhead, a reminder to one and all that their situation could deteriorate, that the whole damn AT&T complex could collapse on them at any moment.

Bradley outlined the possibilities, his audience listening intently. *If* Dubov succeeded in freeing enough explosives without blowing himself up, and *if* the explosives could blast a big-enough hole, they had a chance of reaching the old subway line. The possibility that the new line itself was destroyed or blocked off from the surface was not mentioned; Bradley tried to keep that thought even from himself.

Leaving Sherwood to organize the move-out, which included improvising stretchers for the wounded, Bradley went back into the corridor.

Adlon's posture outside the file room told him that the delicate project was underway. At least Dubov hadn't yet blown himself and their chances to smithereens.

Bill Hunter, providing Dubov with light, began a running commentary for the benefit of Bradley and Adlon.

'The stuff is in boxes fixed to the rear of the file cases – explosive charge and detonator all in one pretty package. Dubov's got to remove each box – five in all. Fumble one, drop it, and goodbye Charlie!'

'What kind of detonators?' asked Adlon.

'Chemical, Dubov thinks. Same as some land mines. Designed to trigger the charge if someone tries to cut into the files or move 'em. Detonators would yell '*Tilt*,' acid inside the box reacts – and BAM!'

'The file clerks knew about those detonators,' Adlon explained. 'They had a strict safety procedure they had to follow.'

Dubov had carefully edged the first file back another inch. He could work his hand in now. They could all see the sweat collecting on his brow.

He called for Hunter to hand him their only tools – a small screwdriver and a chisel.

Working with infinite patience, Dubov exclaimed suddenly in Russian. Then, carefully but triumphantly, he held a small black box in the air. It looked, Bradley thought, like a slimmed-down shoe box. All the onlookers were smiling now, even though there were four more files to go, four more boxes to be moved. And even that much explosive, Dubov had warned, might not be enough to do the job.

Dubov got a second box out. Hunter placed the two boxes carefully in a corner, taking care to hold them in their original position.

Dubov paused in his labours to give Bradley a thumbs-up sign. He seemed in excellent spirits even though he was soaking wet. It was the vodka coming out of him, he joked to Bradley. He went back to work, and suddenly his hand slipped, jamming the screwdriver into a corner of the box he was trying to loosen.

For a long moment, no one moved. Then Dubov laughed and continued his efforts. The problem now was light; the flashlight batteries were running down.

The third and fourth boxes were removed . . . then the fifth.

Bradley went back to collect the main party.

Dubov and Hunter, carrying the five boxes, with Adlon holding the light for them, proceeded carefully to the place under the stairs where they would attempt to blow an access hole into the subway.

The five detonator boxes, five tidy little bombs, were placed side by side against the wall just under the air-conditioning duct. Hunter tied them all together with a ball of twine he had found in one of the files. He unwound the ball out into the corridor, a good thirty or forty feet from the demolition site. Then Dubov and he went back and piled pieces of broken concrete on top of the boxes to tamp the charges, direct them inward.

By now the entire group was crowded into the corridor, far enough back for safety but close enough to take advantage of the opening if the explosion was successful.

Bradley feared that the explosion, instead of creating an exit into the subway, might loosen the precariously balanced tonnage above them, burying everyone – or even creating a final barrier to the exit.

Dubov returned from an inspection of his work. 'Ready any time you are,' he said.

Bradley turned to Sherwood.

'Ready here,' Sherwood said.

The two stretcher cases, Manheim and Riley, were behind him. The stretchers had been improvised from pipe and blankets, but they would do. Everybody else was ambulatory, though exhausted and scared; Bradley wasn't the only one who feared the roof might fall in.

Bradley held Tatiana's hand in his. 'Let 'er ride,' he told Dubov.

Dubov nodded to Hunter, who gave a yank at his length of twine.

There was only silence.

'Shit,' said Hunter. He went back to investigate.

The boxes were supposed to have been upset, so that the chemical inside them would set off the charges.

Returning, Hunter reported that the twine had caught on a protruding piece of ductwork. It should work this time.

They waited again, a single flashlight illuminating their tight, weary faces. Hunter bent, yanked the twine.

They were all staggered by the force of the explosion that reverberated through the corridor. It was world's end; it seemed that the walls were shaking, would certainly cave in, that they would be buried forever in this darkened tunnel. Covered with the dirt and silt that had rained down, they waited for the final, awful smothering that was sure to come.

But it didn't happen, and then Hunter and Bradley and Dubov were sprinting for the explosion site.

The door of the stairwell had been blown off completely, and part of the stairs themselves. And before them was light!

Several feet below the level of the corridor were the tracks and a little farther on the ancient platform they had seen before through the tiny crack.

The jagged opening was wide; they'd have no trouble getting through, even with the stretchers.

'Get them out. Everybody!' Bradley said. 'Hurry!'

Already he could hear an ominous cracking and shuddering, as if workmen with levers were trying to pry everything loose above them.

Hunter and Dubov jumped down to the tracks, ready to help the others down. In a moment they were all there, the able-bodied leaping to the tracks, the injured being lowered by Bradley and Sherwood from above. There were two women besides Tatiana, Kelly and Berg, both from the computer room. They scorned help, managing by themselves.

Sherwood took charge of the two stretcher cases as they were eased down to the men below. 'Watch it . . . careful! . . . careful! . . . careful!' he kept yelling, worried about Manheim and Riley.

Bradley was suddenly aware that Tatiana was missing. Grabbing a flash from Adlon, he ran back into the gloom of the corridor. At the end of it, he found Tatiana with Alan Marshal. Marshal was sitting on the floor, his arms folded, his eyes glazed.

'He won't come,' Tatiana said.

'Come on, boy,' Bradley wheedled. 'You're holding up the show.'

There was a sudden shaking from above and part of the corridor cascaded down between them and the subway.

Alan Marshal did not move.

'She's in there,' he said, pointing to the main room. 'And I'm going to stay with her.'

He got slowly to his feet. Bradley caught his arm, pulled him around and hit him on the chin as hard as he could, feeling his hand go limp with the pain of the blow.

Marshal slumped and Bradley caught him, slung him over his shoulder, and staggered forward towards the light.

There was another crashing sound, and then the corridor was sealed off behind them. Project Hercules, Bradley suspected as he and Tatiana reached the tracks, had ceased to exist.

At Houston, in the Communications Centre, they were monitoring a three-way race: the Hercules rockets, the Peter the Great rockets, and the meteor.

Sam Mason never left the floor, checking and re-checking readouts as if, should things go wrong, it would be possible for him to personally destroy the monstrous thing heading for Earth.

But at this point, along with all the others stationed at the computers, he was a spectator, a mechanical reader of events. Not a damn thing more.

Easton was on the phone to Washington, reporting to the Secretary of Defence, Abe Holland.

'The situation,' Easton told the Secretary, 'is A-1 functional. Sixty-six minutes to impact. We'll keep relaying information until conclusion.'

'Thank you.'

Abe Holland, surrounded by generals and civilian aides, had turned up the conference speaker – they had all heard Easton's words. There were no comments now, not even any of the usual optimistic appraisals.

'Have you heard from Hercules?' Holland asked.

'No,' said Easton. 'I'm afraid they've got to be considered lost. The rest of the city's a shambles.'

There was no answering comment from the Secretary.

They walked the short distance to the old platform and established themselves there – a ragged, wounded force, the tag-end of a retreating army.

They hauled the stretchers up to the platform. Torn and faded advertising posters, scribbled with illegible graffiti going back twenty years, were still visible on the tiled walls. Somewhere beyond, it stood to reason, must be the new line – and, they hoped, access to the living world above.

A few lights still glowed in the old tunnel. A happy accident of the electrical system. Bradley suggested, or the old tunnel had been deliberately supplied with minimum illumination for safety reasons.

Adlon thought otherwise. 'They might even use this line for equipment storage,' he said. 'I'll bet anything you like we can hike straight through to Brooklyn.'

He got a laugh.

They could still hear the earth moving above them. Then, abruptly, there was a deeper rumbling noise, and cracks appeared in the rounded retaining walls between the platform and the tunnel. As they watched, fearing the worst, the earth burst through, great chunks of it mixed with dust and rubble.

But when it was finally over, when the earth above stopped heaving, the tunnel was not completely blocked. There was a gap of about six feet at the top.

And, except for dirt that continued to filter down over the platform, the people on it were unhurt.

But for how long? Bradley asked himself. How long until the next upheaval? They were actually little better off than they'd been in the Centre.

He took Sherwood's flashlight. 'Be right back.'

Jumping from the platform, he climbed the mound of dirt to the gap on top, conscious that they were all watching him as if he were a damned hero who could get them out alive.

He had hurt his right knee somehow. His side was bruised, and he felt anything but heroic. But they were, after all, his responsibility.

He was through the gap now and into the tunnel, trying to avoid slashing himself on the twisted wires and knifelike edges of broken pipe that stuck out everywhere from the rubble.

He looked up the tunnel. The old tracks *did* join the new! He could see the joining, a hundred feet away!

At the angle where the old rails met the functioning subway, gloomily lit by several low-wattage bulbs in the tunnel roof, was a subway car, its sides caved in, its windows broken.

They would have to pass through this obstacle to reach what lay beyond.

About to turn back, Bradley became aware of the sound of trickling water. Training the flashlight on the tunnel wall, he saw that it had begun to give way – mud and water were oozing through.

Christ!

Running, scrambling up the mound below the gap, Bradley pushed himself through.

Waving the flash, keeping his voice calm, he called to the people waiting on the platform. 'All right, come on now! You have to climb over – be careful! Stretchers first.'

Dubov was lead man on Manheim's stretcher. He grinned at Bradley as he came scrambling through the gap on all fours, then turned to help his partner keep Manheim from sliding off into the tangle of debris on all sides.

Tatiana came through with the next stretcher. For a moment her eyes met Bradley's. Then she went on.

When he was satisfied that the entire column had entered the tunnel without incident, Bradley took the lead again, making for the caved-in subway car. There was a gaping hole in the front end, probably the result of a rockfall from above. He climbed through the hole.

He felt suddenly as if he had been punched in the stomach.

Massed in the entry, where they had obviously run seeking escape, but which had apparently been the place of greatest impact, were at least a dozen dead men, women, and children. They were all tumbled together, a few still half-erect, butchered by the flying glass and by the force of the collision.

Bradley could only assume that the other cars belonging to the train had been luckier, had been able to disengage and reverse to a station.

He pushed forward along the half-blocked aisle towards the far end of the car. A door here had been partially sprung. With his foot against the jamb, he was able to edge it open a little more until, with a hiss, it obediently recessed completely.

Now he could see, some thirty feet up the track, a real 'in use' station, its platform empty. And towards the rear of the station – never mind that it was stationary – was an escalator!

Bradley went back and helped the first of the group, the stretcher people, into the car, warning them of the grisly tableau which would greet them.

Sherwood, helping Adlon lift his stretcher into the car, looked up to find the vaulted ceiling of the tunnel cracking open. Through the crack, mud and silt and water poured down in a torrent.

Nevertheless, the car, damaged as it was, gave them a sense of security – of having achieved a reasonably safe plateau.

Then, without warning, there was a new shuddering above, shaking the entire subway car. One of the dead men fell over on his face; others slid into more crookedly grotesque positions.

Anxiously, Bradley scanned the station. The platform itself seemed intact. Then he saw that it wasn't – not any more. The wall behind the escalator had ruptured, as had the wall in the tunnel behind them. Mud and water sluiced out of it, tumbling in waterfall fashion down the escalator steps.

28

They were bunched together, the Hercules rockets – shiny, splendid, superbly crafted, aesthetically satisfying, the secret of their holy mission buried deep within them.

Far away, on a course designed to bring them together with their American counterparts, the sleek rockets of Peter the Great continued their epic journey through the heavens.

But within the group of Peter the Great rockets something went wrong. Gradually – so gradually that at first it seemed an illusion – two of the Russian rockets edged away from the others.

In time the diversion became more apparent, the drift of the two aberrant rockets unmistakable. Though the main body was proceeding as ordered, the rebels were on a track of their own, angling away into the vastness of space.

At Houston and at Yaroslavi, of course, it was noted even as it was happening.

Yaroslavi, unwilling to admit fault, began to re-check its telemetry, and the Russian scientists were forbidden to pass the word on to the Americans.

By the time the matter of the lost rockets was perceived to be a fact, and Yaroslavi in good conscience could no longer keep quiet about it, it was already too late – the Americans were calling, asking for confirmation of the bad news.

At Houston, General Easton had just been put through to Abe Holland, who was having a stiff drink with an aide in his office at the Pentagon.

'Goldstone Tracking Station reports Peter the Great has lost two,' Easton told the Secretary.

The pause on the other end was long and meaningful. Easton could not know that Holland had just taken a long slurp of his whisky.

'How bad is that?' Holland asked presently.

Easton was reassuring. 'There's a safety factor of five.'

'But if two go wrong, what assurance do we have that the others . . .?'

'None.'

'I see.'

Easton said, 'The trajectory of the rest is holding true, sir. I don't think there's any cause to worry.'

You're a goddamn liar, thought Abe Holland, and he swigged at his whisky again.

'Time of impact?' he asked.

'Thirty-five minutes, forty-two seconds.'

'Thank you, General. I'll inform the President.'

Bradley had made a reconnaissance to the subway platform, had stared a long moment at the water gushing down the escalator, and then made his way back to the subway car.

Sherwood, Adlon and Dubov were waiting for him at the open door. Dubov gave him a hand up from the tracks. 'How does it look?' he asked.

'Lousy,' Bradley said. 'But better than in here.'

People were huddled at the back of the car, as far as they could get from the dead at the other end. The stretcher cases looked reasonably good. Manheim waved. Tatiana was holding his other hand. The man must be in tremendous pain, Bradley thought.

They would all be leaving, he announced. Better to take their chances than to stay here – did they agree?

They did.

'All right,' he told them. 'There are stairs leading from the tracks to the platform ahead. Walking wounded first. Others immediately after. Stretchers last.'

Adlon started out as point man, but he had hardly hit the tracks when they heard a familiar frightening roar behind them.

Sprinting back to the rear end of the car, Bradley saw that the old tunnel had burst – a cascade of mud was vomiting through the huge crack. And this mud, perhaps because of a slight grade on the tunnel floor, was heading down towards the car.

He worked his way back. Almost everyone was now out of the car. Hunter and a man named Crocker were struggling with Manheim's stretcher. Tatiana was with them.

There's time, Bradley thought. That mud can't fly here!

He was wrong.

From overhead came a rending noise, a great hammering on the roof. Then a boulder crashed through. More rocks, water and mud shot down into the car. In an instant the mud seemed to have covered the corpses at the far end; now it was flooding towards Manheim's stretcher.

'Get down! Hurry!' Bradley yelled to Tatiana. Damn it, what was she waiting for?

Tatiana took off, reached the door and jumped down. Hunter and Crocker, knee-deep in the mud, pushed after her. Bradley helped pass the stretcher down to them.

'The stairs!' he yelled.

But then he saw that they couldn't reach the stairs. Nor could the larger group. Mud was flowing from the side wall ahead of them, trapping them between the car and the platform.

Bradley reached Sherwood's side.

Spitting mud, Sherwood asked mildly, 'Where do we go from here?'

'We'll go through. It's only a shower. Get a move on, everybody!'

They obeyed. Bradley brought up the rear.

Adlon had reached the stairs with a few others and was

helping the newcomers up to the platform. Mud poured from a half dozen gaps in the roof and siding.

Adlon shouted, 'Where's Sherwood? Where's Bradley?' He watched the mud filling the tunnel, like a flood crest moving higher and higher, overrunning everything before it.

Sherwood had gone back to help Bradley. The problem was the stretchers, difficult to manoeuvre in the slippery, treacherous footing. Also, having been improvised with piping, the stretchers were inordinately heavy.

Tatiana bent over Riley. Caught in a downfall at the Centre, he had been haemorrhaging from internal injuries. She shook her head. Riley had no pulse; he was gone.

The men carrying his stretcher still struggled to keep his body from the mud. Dubov yelled at them to let go, to make for the platform – no time now to worry about the dead.

Reluctantly, they lowered the stretcher. Riley's body floated briefly on the brown surface, then was engulfed.

Bradley and Sherwood helped Hunter to carry Manheim, the mud lapping at their hips.

It was clear to all of them that sooner or later a new tremor would bring the tunnel roof crashing down over them. But the more pressing danger was the sea of mud which was rapidly cutting off their escape.

They plodded slowly on, keeping Manheim's body well above the dark soup.

New freshets of mud were coming at them from the side walls now. The entire structure was beginning to crumble, the loosening earth accelerating its deterioration.

They could see the platform only dimly, twenty feet beyond. The river of mud had reached their chests now, was lapping over Manheim's face. Fortunately, he had long since lapsed into unconsciousness.

On the platform, Adlon, having sent all but a few men to relative safety at the foot of the escalator, was delighted when he saw them struggling towards him with the stretcher. He and the others reached eagerly for it, and in a moment Bradley, Sherwood and Hunter were relieved of their burden.

Bradley and Hunter were climbing the steps when a cry from Adlon made them turn.

Sherwood had held back to guide Tatiana and Dubov to the steps. They had reached the safety of the stairway when mud and water broke through a new crack in the tunnel wall, battering Sherwood down and under, sweeping him back towards the now inundated subway car.

'Sherwood!' Adlon yelled.

Bradley hurled himself into the mud again. Catching hold of Sherwood's jacket, he jerked his head clear of the mud.

In the next moment, Adlon was at his side. The two men battled back towards the steps with Sherwood and dragged him up.

Sherwood seemed none the worse for the incident. Somewhere in his clothes he found a packet of Kleenex, and began delicately to clean the dripping mud from his face.

'Thank you,' he said to Adlon and Bradley. Then he wiped the face of his watch and glanced at it. 'How long?'

For the life of him, Bradley couldn't figure out the question.

Patiently, Sherwood said, 'The meteor.'

Then Bradley remembered. He took a Kleenex from Sherwood, cleaned his own watch, and checked it. 'About fourteen minutes.'

'Thank you,' Sherwood said. 'My watch seems to be broken.'

They moved past where Manheim lay on his stretcher, getting emergency first aid. Conscious now, he flashed them a weak but indomitable smile, his shiny gold tooth gleaming.

Bradley and Sherwood made their way over to the escalator, where Adlon was directing people up the wet but passable stairway.

They were approaching each other on steadily converging trajectories, the red-tipped rockets from Peter the Great still in advance, the rockets from Hercules speeding in from three o'clock.

At a point determined by the men below at Houston and Yaroslavi, the rockets would meet and continue together for the remaining distance to target.

But now another unforeseen event was reported. The report was picked up at once at Houston; no effort had been made to conceal it from the world.

General Easton was immediately on the open line to Washington. 'We're losing one from Hercules,' he informed the Secretary of Defence.

'What happened?' Abe Holland asked.

'We don't know, sir. Possibly a fuel line break. It's falling behind the others. Most certainly a power loss.'

'That critical? Losing one?'

'No, sir. But let's hope we don't lose any more.'

'Very good. Time to impact?'

'Thirteen minutes, twenty-nine seconds.'

They struggled up the motionless escalator, away from the rushing brown river, the wrecked tunnel, the drowned, the dead.

In the ticket-and-turnstile area above, about a hundred people regarded them with astonishment. These were the fortunates who had either escaped from below earlier or, having entered the station when the splinter hit, had been trapped by the detritus of the shattered buildings. The steps to the entrance from the street were still filled with bricks, glass, pieces of plumbing, whatever could possibly rain down from the city above. Groups of men laboured in relays at the rubble, trying to clear it away by hand.

For the moment, the Hercules crew were too exhausted to join them.

Bradley had been able to cadge some cigarettes. He brought

them back to the wall where Dubov and Tatiana were slumped shoulder to shoulder.

As Dubov and Bradley lit up, Dubov murmured something in Russian.

'What did he say?' Bradley asked Tatiana.

' "One day you will come to Moscow, and you will see real subways," ' she translated, smiling.

Dubov mentioned towards the people toiling at the entrance. 'I go . . . give 'em a hand,' he said. 'We get the hell out of this damned place!'

'He's all right,' Bradley commented as the Russian moved off.

Tatiana was very solemn. There were no clean places on Bradley's face to kiss, so she tapped him lightly on the head. 'So are you.'

Sherwood and Adlon, standing nearby, were looking upward. 'Three minutes,' Adlon announced, glancing at his watch.

The meteor was an enormous, inanimate chunk of rock, nothing more, so perhaps no anthropomorphic allusions were in order. But one could assume a growing excitement within its core, a realization that it was nearing its target, that its great, ugly, craggy mass would soon be smashing into the soft surface of the planet Earth.

On the other hand, among some cultists, there is the belief that flowers can suffer pain, that carrots can weep when cut, that even stones can cry.

So perhaps the meteor could sense the ultimate triumph, the pure ecstasy it was about to experience. The time of impact was, given the meteor's dazzling speed, only a breath away.

At Houston, on the floor of the Centre, they were all business. Readouts were being passed to Mason in a rapidly increasing stream; he would decipher them and pass them on to Easton, who sat at a desk with an open line to Washington.

Scanning what Mason had just handed him, Easton was now giving a quick report to Abe Holland in the Oval Office. The President was there with Holland.

'Two minutes, fifty seconds,' Easton said.

'Any further rocket losses?' Holland asked. The President, pacing behind him, paused as he awaited the response.

'None,' Easton said.

'None,' Holland told the President.

The President raised his hand, fingers crossed.

The people trapped in the subway station were grouped around a handful of transistor radios.

'Medical teams are moving into New York from all directions,' the radio voice said. 'Helicopters over the city are trying to pinpoint the areas of greatest damage and greatest need. These rescue operations are being supervised by the army.

'We have a bulletin from Washington: The rockets launched to deflect the meteor are speeding towards their targets. If all goes well, contact is expected shortly. The President is confident the meteor will be diverted. Here at KCNB in New Jersey, we'll keep you informed. WE WILL NOT GO OFF THE AIR! WE WILL REPORT CONTINUOUSLY!'

The rockets streaming together through space were now within sight of their target. It loomed far in the distance like a small black spot, a cinder in the eye of space. Slowly, it became something more, something approaching at unimaginable speed, growing in size and menace.

At Houston, they had begun the final countdown. The tension in the vast room was like a rubber band stretched towards breaking. Small sounds were startling – sudden breaths, a man clearing his throat.

The big digital clock overhead registered the seconds for all to see, but Mason's voice – soft, sepulchral – intoned the numbers aloud '. . . six, five, four, three . . .'

The Russian and American rockets, as if savouring the attack, homed in on the great mass of the meteor with the precision of monster artillery shells. They were not mere artillery shells, of course; their explosive power was almost cataclysmic. Never before had man created such a devastating accumulation of force.

The rockets arrived on target.

The impact of the explosions, following each other so closely as to constitute one gigantic blast, sent a sheet of fire across the surface of the meteor. There was a thunderous, rolling wave of sound that could actually be monitored by the instruments on Earth below.

Streams of metallurgical fragments spewed out from the meteor, fiery geysers blackening the atmosphere, polluting space with billowing, charred waste.

For a moment the meteor was like another sun – smaller, but no less sulphurous.

And then, as if it were indeed an exploding star, the light was extinguished. Like an enormous wounded animal, the meteor appeared to turn on its side and drift away.

The combined nuclear blast had achieved its aim. Its orbit significantly altered, the meteor slid away from Earth, began to recede into the distant reaches of space.

At Houston, in the Communications Room, they were cheering.

In the White House, the exultant President was repeating to everyone, 'God damn! God damn!'

In the Kremlin, the Premier was receiving congratulations from his colleagues. Vodka flowed freely, and the Premier was amused to see his generals and marshals accepting the plaudits with him. He thought briefly of telephoning Ditroff up at the Yaroslavi station, but never got around to it.

He did put in a call to the American President.

At last the news reached the people gathered in the subway station in New York.

'We interrupt our coverage of the New York disaster to bring you an official announcement just received from Houston. Two minutes ago, at ten thirty-eight, the combined rockets of the United States and the U.S.S.R. struck the meteor which had been coming towards us. It has been deflected from its course and is now in a harmless orbit away from Earth. The danger is past!'

People cheered, shouted, applauded, wept.

The Hercules personnel, as if drawn by a need to share, gathered together.

Bradley looked to Sherwood, who was smiling.

'We did it,' Sherwood said quietly.

From behind him came a crashing noise. At the clogged entrance, men were backing away. Something big and steely, a huge blade, was thrusting through the rubble, knifing towards them.

The blade belonged to a bulldozer. It pulled back; there was a rumbling noise, stones and boulders fell. Now came a sudden beam of dust-filled daylight.

People rushed towards the light.

29

Walking hand in hand in the dusk, silent and preoccupied, Bradley and Tatiana found themselves drawn back to the park.

The crater made by the splinter – long and narrow and ugly – extended as far as the eye could see.

The reservoir was gone, most of its water forced out by the impact, the rest evaporated by the intense heat.

Makeshift camps for the homeless had been set up in the park around the perimeter of the crater, the only area clear of debris in the lower portion of the city. Thousands of people waited more or less patiently to be moved to more permanent camps in New Jersey and on Long Island.

Finding themselves with so much to say, Bradley and Tatiana were nevertheless hesitant. The future was clouded, uncertain. Bradley couldn't believe it was over between them; that seemed too unfair, too unreal. Tatiana was quiet; he couldn't know what she was thinking.

Afraid to say what was in her heart, Tatiana talked about other things. She wondered if New York would be rebuilt simply as a replica of the old – or would the builders embody new concepts as well as new technology. What a marvellous opportunity, she thought, to build an exciting new city.

They walked past a grove of trees – leafless, stark, trunks burned to charcoal. Suddenly Tatiana let go of Bradley's hand and strode eagerly to a couple reclining on the grass.

'It's you,' Tatiana said.

The woman looked up, not understanding. She was big with child.

'You were going to rent an apartment,' Tatiana said. 'We saw you on the street yesterday.'

The husband looked at her. 'The building's burned down,' he said.

'But you're alive . . . and the baby . . . !'

'Yes,' the woman said, smiling.

Tatiana glanced back at Bradley. 'You remember?'

'I remember,' said Bradley, and they smiled at each other.

30

The band played the Russian National Anthem; the American and Russian officials stood at attention. The President, who could never manage a military posture, nevertheless did his best, knowing that the photographers were grinding away.

The Soviet plane had been flown in with a military escort to transport the Russian heroes Dubov and Donskaya home in proper fashion.

Tatiana looked very chic in the wardrobe Madame Luchec had supplied on short notice. She was separated from Bradley now, standing with her own people, but she kept her eyes on him. He was with Sherwood and Adlon, close to the President of the United States.

There was a final speech from the President. He spoke of the spirit of cooperation that had turned aside the terrible threat of the meteor. He hoped that this spirit would provide an enduring example to both great powers and to the entire world. The President thanked the men and women of Hercules, whose skill and dedication had saved them all; he thanked the scientists in Yaroslavi, in distant Siberia . . .

Now the Russians were ready to board their plane. Dubov shook hands with each member of the Hercules group.

Reaching Bradley, Dubov disdained the handshake and gave the American a tight embrace. 'Goodbye, friend,' he said. 'In the future, may all our rockets point in the right direction.'

Grinning, he slapped Bradley's shoulder and was gone.

Tatiana came up to Bradley. She hesitated.

'Do not forget,' she said at last.

'No,' he said.

The military band segued into Auld Lang Syne, but in swinging tempo. The crowd was laughing, happy.

At the top of the steps that led into the plane, Dubov paused with Tatiana, looking down.

'I think you'll return one day, eh?' he said.

'Who knows?' Tatiana said.

They entered the plane, and moments later it took off, lifting into the skies above Washington, the band below still playing Auld Lang Syne.

Prices and postage and packing rates shown below were correct at the time of going to press.

FICTION

All prices shown are exclusive of postage and packing

GENERAL FICTION

☐ THE CAIN CONSPIRACY	J. M. Simmel	£1.20
☐ THE AFFAIR OF NINA B	J. M. Simmel	£1.20
☐ HMS BOUNTY	John Maxwell	£1.00
☐ A REAL KILLING	William Keegan	80p
☐ SEARCHING FOR CALEB	Anne Tyler	95p
☐ CELESTIAL NAVIGATION	Anne Tyler	95p
☐ THE ENTREPRENEUR	I. G. Broat	£1.00
☐ THE SOUNDS OF SILENCE	Judith Richards	£1.00
☐ THE BOTTOM LINE	Fletcher Knebel	£1.25
☐ ON THE BRINK	Benjamin Stein with Herbert Stein	95p
☐ CHAINS	Justin Adams	£1.20
☐ RUNNING SCARED	Gregory Mcdonald	85p
☐ V. J. DAY	Alan Fields	95p
☐ THE HEIR	Christopher Keane	£1.00
☐ THE LAREDO ASSIGNMENT (Western)	Matt Chisholm	75p
☐ TY-SHAN BAY	Raoul Templeton Aundrews	95p
☐ A SEA-CHANGE	Lois Gould	80p
☐ THE PLAYERS	Gary Brandner	95p
☐ RIDDLE	Dan Sherman	90p

CRIME/THRILLER

☐ THE TWO FACES OF JANUARY	Patricia Highsmith	95p
☐ THOSE WHO WALK AWAY	Patricia Highsmith	95p
☐ A GAME FOR THE LIVING	Patricia Highsmith	95p
☐ THE BLUNDERER	Patricia Highsmith	95p
☐ THE TREMOR OF FORGERY	Patricia Highsmith	80p
☐ STRAIGHT	Steve Knickmeyer	80p
☐ FIVE PIECES OF JADE	John Ball	85p
☐ IN THE HEAT OF THE NIGHT	John Ball	85p
☐ THE EYES OF BUDDHA	John Ball	85p
☐ THE COOL COTTONTAIL	John Ball	80p
☐ JOHNNY GET YOUR GUN	John Ball	85p
☐ THE PEKING PAY-OFF	Ian Stewart	90p
☐ THE TEN-TOLA BARS	Burton Wohl	90p
☐ FLETCH	Gregory Mcdonald	90p
☐ CONFESS, FLETCH	Gregory Mcdonald	90p
☐ THE TRIPOLI DOCUMENTS	Henry Kane	95p
☐ DEADLY HARVEST	Peter Mallory	85p
☐ THE EXECUTION	Oliver Crawford	90p
☐ FROGS AT THE BOTTOM OF THE WELL	Ken Edgar	90p
☐ TIME BOMB	James D. Atwater	90p

(H13A:4-6:79)

NON-FICTION

☐ KILLING TIME	Sandy Fawkes	90p
☐ THE HAMLYN BOOK OF CROSSWORDS 1		60p
☐ THE HAMLYN BOOK OF CROSSWORDS 2		60p
☐ THE HAMLYN FAMILY GAMES BOOK	Gyles Brandreth	75p
☐ STAR-FILE ANNUAL (Ref)	Dafydd Rees	£1.50
☐ THE OSCAR MOVIES FROM A-Z (Ref)	Roy Pickard	£1.25
☐ THE HAMLYN FAMILY MEDICAL DICTIONARY (Ref)		£2.50
☐ LONELY WARRIOR (War)	Victor Houart	85p
☐ BLACK ANGELS (War)	Rupert Butler	£1.00
☐ THE BEST OF DIAL-A-RECIPE	Audrey Ellis	80p
☐ THE SUNDAY TELEGRAPH PATIO GARDENING BOOK	Robert Pearson	80p
☐ THE COMPLETE TRAVELLER	Joan Bakewell	£1.50
☐ RESTORING OLD JUNK	Michèle Brown	75p
☐ WINE MAKING AT HOME	Francis Pinnegar	80p
☐ FAT IS A FEMINIST ISSUE	Susie Orbach	85p
☐ AMAZING MAZES 1	Michael Lye	75p
☐ GUIDE TO THE CHANNEL ISLANDS	Janice Anderson and Edmund Swinglehurst	90p
☐ THE STRESS FACTOR	Donald Norfolk	90p
☐ WOMAN × TWO	Mary Kenny	90p
☐ THE HAMLYN BOOK OF CROSSWORDS 3		60p

KITCHEN LIBRARY

☐ MIXER AND BLENDER COOKBOOK	Myra Street	80p
☐ HOME BAKED BREADS AND CAKES	Mary Norwak	75p
☐ MARGUERITE PATTEN'S FAMILY COOKBOOK		95p
☐ EASY ICING	Marguerite Patten	85p
☐ HOME MADE COUNTRY WINES		40p
☐ COMPREHENSIVE GUIDE TO DEEP FREEZING		40p
☐ COUNTRY FARE	Doreen Fulleylove	80p

All these books are available at your local bookshop or newsagent, or can be ordered direct from the publisher. Just tick the titles you want and fill in the form below.

NAME...

ADDRESS..

....

Write to Hamlyn Paperbacks Cash Sales, PO Box 11, Falmouth, Cornwall TR10 9EN

Please enclose remittance to the value of the cover price plus:

UK: 22p for the first book plus 10p per copy for each additional book ordered to a maximum charge of 92p.

BFPO and EIRE: 22p for the first book plus 10p per copy for the next 6 books, thereafter 4p per book.

OVERSEAS: 30p for the first book and 10p for each additional book.

Whilst every effort is made to keep prices low it is sometimes necessary to increase cover prices and also postage and packing rates at short notice. Hamlyn Paperbacks reserve the right to show new retail prices on covers which may differ from those previously advertised in the text or elsewhere.